PROJECT ARMA

WYATT

NYSSA KATHRYN

WYATT

Copyright © 2021 Nyssa Kathryn Sitarenos

All rights reserved.

Cover by Dar Albert at Wicked Smart Designs
Edited by Kelli Collins
Proofread by Marla Esposito

❀ Created with Vellum

A story that could cost her everything...

Investigative journalist Quinn Ross isn't a woman who can just let major news pass her by. So, when she stumbles across a story like no other, she makes it her mission to report it to the masses.

She doesn't count on the lengths to which some may go to keep her story from seeing the light of day. When Quinn suddenly finds herself in need of escape, she heads straight for tiny Marble Falls and her brother, Mason.

When he's not running his company's IT department, Wyatt Gray—former SEAL and co-owner of Marble Protection—spends every spare minute searching for those who betrayed him. The ones who turned him and his teammates into something beyond mere mortals. He doesn't have time for distractions—but that's exactly what he gets, in the form of his best friend's sassy, spunky, sexy sister...who's moved in right across the hall.

From the moment they meet, Quinn and Wyatt's chemistry is combustible. But they both have big secrets. Then there's Mason, who may consider Wyatt a brother, but he might still kill him for lusting after his baby sister.

But soon, none of that matters. When a killer sets his sights on Quinn, any chance at happiness with Wyatt may end before it's had a chance to begin.

ACKNOWLEDGMENTS

Kelli Collins, thank you for being a superstar editor. You always manage to take my work to the next level.

Thank you to my readers. You guys are amazing. Without you, Wyatt and Quinn would not have gotten their story.

CHAPTER 1

*I*t took a lot to shock Quinn Ross. Her years as a *New York Times* journalist had exposed her to everything, from the good and the bad to the downright ugly.

You name it, Quinn had written about it.

But the words in the email shocked the heck out of her.

Most people would disregard them as lies. A fabricated story created to get attention, perhaps.

Quinn wasn't so sure.

The woman who had written the email was a scientist. Hell, she was one of the best in her field. She worked at Novac, one of the most reputable pharmaceutical companies in the country.

The woman was smart. Educated. Her words had to hold some merit, right?

Men so fast, they're a blur of movement. So strong, they can bend metal with their hands.

No. No, no and no. It wasn't possible. It didn't even begin to fit into her preconceived notions of reality.

Quinn scrubbed a hand over her face before leaning back in her chair.

She was a realist. Human behavior didn't surprise her because she'd learned that humans were capable of anything. Keyword being *human*. What Maya Harper described were super-villains. Fictional character who belonged in movies.

But why would the woman claim that she'd witnessed a man's neck being snapped with minimal effort if it wasn't true? That she'd seen a colleague get thrown twenty feet across the room and die on impact?

This was simply too much information for her sleep-deprived brain to absorb.

Pushing away from the table, Quinn moved to the kitchen. It was six-thirty in the morning. Far too early to be reading about supermen breaking into pharmaceutical labs. Killing technicians with their super strength.

It was even more amazing the lone witness to the robbery had been the one to respond to Quinn's email. No, it was a damn miracle.

Quinn had emailed all employees on the pharmaceutical company's website, even though she'd been almost *certain* no one would respond. Yet, here she was, weeks later, reading an email from Maya.

Maya hadn't responded from her company email. Not that it was a surprise. The woman had disappeared shortly after the event.

Quinn wanted to know how she'd survived when no one else had, and what was taken.

Only now she was concerned the trauma of the experience had effected the woman's mental health.

Quinn needed coffee. Stat. It was what she'd been beelining toward before the ding of an email had stopped her.

Opening the pantry door, she scanned the contents of the shelves. Rather, Mason's shelves. Because it was her brother's apartment, not hers. And she thanked her lucky stars every day that it was vacant for her to stay in, otherwise there was the distinct possibility she would have been homeless.

After a few seconds of scanning, Quinn stopped and groaned out loud. There was no coffee. None.

Of course there wasn't. Because she was supposed to grab some from the store yesterday. She hadn't.

Quinn dropped her chin on her chest. "It's official. The world hates me."

Was she such a terrible person that the world needed to *keep* spiting her?

The last four weeks had been the month from hell. All stemming from her being fired from a job she excelled at. Fired! She could *still* barely believe it.

She'd lived and breathed that job. It had been her entire life.

And the worst part was, she'd been fired for something so trivial that most people would just get a slap on the wrist.

It was like one giant nightmare.

To make matters worse, she'd stayed in New York, hoping she could convince her boss to take her back. Hell, his wife was one of her best friends, it shouldn't have been hard.

But he hadn't taken her back, and no one else had seemed interested in employing her. Because rent in New York was so expensive, all she'd done was eat into her savings.

Now, here she was, broke, jobless, living in Marble Falls, and out of coffee. Oh, and her one lead on the story that had cost Quinn her job was a lady talking to her about men with powers.

You're screwed, Quinn. Screwed and coffee-less.

Quinn eyed the door. She could run to the store, but this wasn't New York. Not even close. Did the stores even open this early in Marble Falls? Maybe a cafe or diner?

Lifting her phone, Quinn began to search what was open. Then a thought came to her. The day she'd moved into the apartment, she'd met a neighbor from across the hall. An incredibly sexy neighbor whose voice alone had made her stomach do somersaults.

It was highly likely *he* had coffee. Most adults had some kind of caffeine dependence, didn't they?

And if he didn't have coffee, well, at least she'd get an eyeful of those beefy biceps and that powerful chest again.

Smiling to herself, Quinn touched her fingers to her lips. The lips that had been kissed by that god of a creature. Leaving her door open that day had been a stroke of genius. So too had the choice to give the man a kiss on the lips instead of her name.

The kiss was supposed to be a peck. Boy, had it been more than that. He'd leaned right into her. Touched her. *Tasted* her.

Goose bumps rose on Quinn's arms just thinking about it. Her entire body tingled. It had been the best damn kiss of her life.

She moved toward the door. Maybe it was time to learn her neighbor's name.

WYATT HEARD the footsteps before the knock. He didn't know who stood at his door, but he did know they were female. The light, graceful steps had given them away.

Most people wouldn't be able to hear what Wyatt could. He wasn't most people. He could hear better, move faster, and lift far more than most. But then, that's what happens when your genetics get permanently altered.

Moving away from the coffee machine, Wyatt headed toward the door. He had no idea who it could be. Maybe the elderly lady from down the hall?

When he looked through the peephole, he couldn't stop the heat that slammed into his gut.

Quinn Ross. Little sister to Wyatt's good friend and business partner, Mason Ross. And Wyatt's new neighbor.

Not that she realized he knew who she was.

Pulling the door open, Wyatt gave the woman a smile. Just like the previous time he'd lain eyes on her, awareness tore through his body. Her long black hair cascaded over her shoulders like a waterfall, and her piercing blue eyes warmed at the sight of him.

"Why hello there, handsome. I have a problem that I'm *praying* you can help me with. A gigantic, might-be-life-threatening-if-nothing-is-done problem."

Wyatt's body immediately tensed. Was there a threat close by?

He listened to any and everything in the building. There were many heartbeats. None of them seemed to be coming from inside Quinn's apartment.

"Are you okay?" He was a millisecond away from grabbing the woman and pulling her inside his apartment.

"No. I'm out of coffee."

Wyatt's brows pulled together. "Your life-threatening problem is that you're out of coffee?"

She stepped back, feigning shock. "You think it's *not* life-threatening? Buddy, if that liquid gold is not hitting my bloodstream in the next hour, I'll be a puddle of human remains on the ground. Either that, or turn into a homicidal maniac, attacking anyone I see. Do you really want either to come to fruition?"

Wyatt's body relaxed. "I have coffee. Would you like to come—"

Before he had a chance to finish the sentence, Quinn was brushing past him. "Thank the lord! I mean, I hoped you would, but there are some rare human species who don't seem to need the stuff. I don't get it myself. Lucky for us both, you're not one of them. You have now entered friendship status."

Wyatt had to focus to keep up with what she was saying. For a woman who had only met him the one time, she sure wasn't shy.

"You're aware it's not even seven in the morning, right? How desperate could you be?"

"I am very aware of the time, and my desperation for coffee knows no bounds. I should have had coffee at least half an hour ago." Quinn stopped when she reached the counter before turning to look at him. Her face was a mixture of relief and gratitude. "And you have a coffee maker. You truly are the man of my dreams."

Well, that was fitting, seeing as he hadn't been able to get the sassy woman out of his mind. "I'll tell you what. If you give me that name of yours, you can have as much coffee as you like. Seeing as I didn't get it last time."

Even though Wyatt knew her name, for some reason, he didn't want her to know that yet. Maybe because he was enjoying the anonymity. Maybe because he didn't want her view of or actions toward him to be swayed by his relationship with her brother.

A small smile tugged at her lips. "You don't play fair. Lucky for you, there's not much I wouldn't do for caffeine." Taking a step toward him, she extended her hand. "Quinn Ross. Lover of words. Workaholic. Coffee addict."

Seeing as his lips had been on hers the last time they'd been together, they were probably past the handshake stage. But he'd take any excuse to touch the woman.

Stepping forward, he took her hand in his.

"Wyatt Gray. Business owner. Also workaholic. Computer nerd."

At the first touch of her skin, he wanted more. He wanted to pull her body into his and see if she tasted as good as last time.

Quinn smiled. "Hm, I see we're both keeping our cards close to our chests. I like it."

When she pulled her hand from his, he turned and headed for the coffee machine. He'd like to think it was to make the coffee but, in reality, it was more to stop from touching her again. She was too damn enticing.

"How do you take your coffee?"

"Milk and two sugars."

That was a surprise. Wyatt tossed a look at her over his shoulder. "I pegged you for a black coffee woman."

She shrugged as she took a seat at his kitchen island. "People have pegged me as many things in my life. They rarely get it right."

That was likely because she was a woman who couldn't be categorized. She sure seemed like a puzzle so far.

Quinn tilted her head to the side. "What about you? How do you take your coffee?"

"Milk with a heap of sugar." Because one teaspoon was never enough. "Like you, I like my beverages sweet."

He gave her a wink before turning back to the machine. Wyatt was the only one out of his friends who took his coffee sweet. He couldn't stand the stuff without sugar. It was far too bitter.

"Something we have in common."

That it was.

Once both coffees were ready, he placed them on the kitchen counter. Quinn all but jumped on hers. She reminded him of a starved chipmunk. Cute, but if you got in the way of her and her treat, you would lose a limb.

When she swallowed her first sip, her eyes rolled up into her head, and she moaned. A sweet moan that had him hardening to an uncomfortable degree.

She was going to be the death of him.

When she opened her eyes, she looked straight at him. "Okay. I'm going to be honest with you. My plan was to buy a bag of instant coffee today, but I don't think I can do that anymore. I can't drink that crap when I know you have *this* right across the hall." She leaned forward. "I'm probably going to be back. And when I say probably, I mean I *will* be back. Every morning."

If a good coffee is what it took to get this woman into his home, then he'd be making damn sure nothing happened to his coffee machine.

"You're welcome back anytime, Quinn."

A slow smile tipped her lips. It made his heart thump.

She took another sip of her coffee. Again, her eyes rolled

back. "Today you found out my name and that I'm a hopeless coffee addict. I wonder what you'll learn tomorrow."

Wyatt had actually learned more than that.

He'd learned that she had a sensual moan that set his blood pumping. That even though this was only his second conversation with her, he couldn't see himself getting bored in her company. That he didn't need to be kissing the woman to feel the electricity of her touch.

"And what did you learn about me?" Wyatt asked, keeping his thoughts to himself.

Quinn ran the tip of her tongue over her lips. "That you tap your fingers when you think."

Wyatt's hand stilled. Damn, he hadn't realized he'd been doing it.

"That you scan every room and hallway before entering, like you expect something to be there. Which is interesting, seeing as Marble Falls feels so safe. And of course, I learned that you make coffee that is *almost* better than an orgasm. But then, that might be more due to the machine than you."

Wyatt leaned across the counter. "I like to think the man behind the machine can make or break the coffee *and* the orgasm."

One side of her mouth twitched. "I think you might be right."

Oh, Wyatt was definitely right.

He watched her as she sipped more coffee. He felt like he could watch her all day. There was something incredibly enticing about the woman. Something so much deeper than appearance.

Wyatt took a sip of his own drink. "So, seeing as we're friends now, tell me what you're doing in Marble Falls."

Something flashed across her face. It was slight. So slight, most would have missed it. Wyatt didn't. "I'm trying to figure some stuff out, and Marble Falls is as good a town as any to do that."

Cryptic. There was more to that story. A lot more. "Anything I can help you with?"

He hoped she'd say yes. Give him another reason to spend time with her.

"Nope. I like to work alone." Quinn finished the last of her coffee before pushing her cup across the island. "Thank you, Wyatt. For turning my not-so-great morning around and convincing me that maybe the world doesn't hate me quite as much as I thought."

"Anytime, Quinn Ross."

She stood and left. And Wyatt was already looking forward to the next morning, when he would receive the next piece of the Quinn Ross puzzle.

CHAPTER 2

*Q*uinn shot a glance at the sign that welcomed her to Tyler, Texas. She'd been driving for over four hours and oh lordy, did her butt know it.

She'd lost track of the number of times she'd considered pulling over and stretching her legs. *Not* stopping had been a mental battle. But she'd won. Not one stop.

Because even though her butt would have thanked her, she didn't have the time. And that was entirely her fault.

She should have left earlier. A lot earlier. That was easier said than done. Tearing herself away from the witty and oh-so-beautiful Wyatt was no easy feat.

Hell, she could stay and talk to the man all day. Not just talk—stare at, laugh with, swoon over.

Every morning for the last week, she'd joined him for coffee. And each day their time together grew longer. At this rate, they'd be spending entire days together. Maybe then she'd be able to find a flaw in the guy.

So far, she'd found he had a hot bod—check. He was easy to talk to—check. And whenever he smiled, there were these lines around his eyes that crinkled and turned her insides to mush—check, check.

God. She was losing it. Obsessing over her new neighbor. How cliché was that? They barely even knew each other. Their topics of conversation were as far from the important stuff as it got.

Not that she was complaining. Wyatt was an escape from her real life. The last thing she wanted to talk about was her job loss, the story she couldn't finish, or her quickly depleting bank account.

Shaking her head, she darted her eyes to the GPS. She was damn glad Mason had a car he'd let her use. Otherwise, this trip wouldn't be possible. She was a street away from The Diner. The place was actually called "The Diner." Maya had chosen the meeting location.

Over the last week, Quinn and Maya had been emailing back and forth. It was only a few days ago that Quinn had discovered Maya's location. And she could not believe her luck. Tyler, Texas!

Not only was that the same state as Quinn, it was also within driving distance. Yes, the travel there and back would take all day, but she wouldn't have been able to afford a flight anywhere, and she always preferred to speak to a witness in person.

The fact that the other woman had disclosed her location could be good or bad. Good, because it meant she trusted Quinn. Or bad, because she was drawing her to Tyler for a reason.

It was a chance Quinn was willing to take to acquire the information she needed.

Quinn had discovered early on in her career that there were two ways to learn more about a person's story. The first was over the phone. Some people enjoyed the anonymity and could open up more without the added pressure of meeting.

The other way, and Quinn's personal preference, was hearing a person's story face-to-face. Mostly because she could read their body language. Catch the micro expressions that crossed the other persons' face before they had a chance to hide them.

Turning onto Broadway Avenue, Quinn spotted the eatery. Her gaze flicked to the clock. Five minutes early. It wasn't the twenty minutes she'd planned for, but early was early. And it was a whole lot better than late.

Being late wasn't an option. From their email exchanges, Maya seemed flighty. Scared. Who the heck wouldn't be after what she'd seen? That meant if Maya arrived at the diner first, and didn't spot Quinn, there was a chance the other woman might just turn around and walk back out. And that was something Quinn didn't want to risk.

Pulling into a parking lot beside the diner, Quinn grabbed her bag. There was a notepad inside but she wouldn't be using it. People were a lot more open when there was no pen and paper. They were more relaxed when they felt like they were just having a conversation with a friend.

Climbing out of the car, Quinn headed to the entrance. She knew what the other woman looked like because she'd looked her up. Her picture had been connected to an academic paper she'd written.

Late twenties, soft features, light brown hair and eyes.

The moment she stepped inside, her eyes scanned the place. Booths and tables sat to the left, with a long counter to the right.

No sign of Maya.

Choosing a booth in the corner, Quinn sat so that she had a good view of the entrance.

As she waited, Quinn tried to stop the nervous tapping of her foot. She hated to admit it, but she was tense. This story was important. She needed to know why pursuing it had cost her a job.

Maya was her only lead. Every other witness was dead. The only other people who had any information were law enforcement, and they wouldn't tell her diddly-squat.

When a young woman with light brown colored hair and intelligent eyes stepped inside the diner, Quinn straightened. It was her. She could feel it.

Maya's gaze immediately went to Quinn, but the other woman didn't move. She looked anxious. For a moment, Quinn thought she might turn and leave again.

Quinn's hand went to her bag, ready to jump up and chase.

Just before Quinn stood, Maya began walking forward, her eyes constantly scanning her surroundings.

Taking the seat opposite Quinn, Maya's chest rose and fell in quick succession. Like she was trying to calm herself. Dark circles shadowed her eyes and her skin was pale.

Quinn smiled, wanting to appear as friendly as possible. "Hi, Maya, I'm Quinn Ross. Thank you for agreeing to meet with me."

Maya studied Quinn's face. It almost seemed like she was searching for something. What, exactly, Quinn wasn't sure.

"I can't stay long. I'm trying to remain off the grid. I only came because you said you may be able to publish my story. I want everyone to know what happened. I don't want more lab technicians dying."

She sure *hoped* she could publish the story. She wasn't an employee for *The New York Times* anymore, but there were other newspapers that may publish it.

"Is that why you left New York? Because you felt like you needed to hide from someone?"

"I couldn't stay there. I didn't feel safe. I *needed* to leave. Disappear."

She could understand why Maya would feel that way. She'd seen multiple murders. Was the only living witness. Quinn was surprised she hadn't been placed in some kind of government protection facility.

"Will you tell me about what you saw?"

Before Maya could respond, the waitress came to the table. "What can I get you ladies today?"

Maya shrank back, remaining silent.

"Two coffees and an order of fries, please." Quinn looked across at Maya. "Did you want anything else?"

Maya shook her head, avoiding eye contact.

Jeez. Maya was in worse condition than Quinn had thought she'd be.

The waitress nodded. It wasn't until they were alone again that Maya spoke softly. "How did you find out about all this?"

Sheer luck. At first, Quinn thought stumbling across the story had been *good* luck. So far, it had brought nothing but problems.

Quinn wouldn't turn back time, though. There was a reason she'd discovered this story. And she needed to work out what that reason was.

"I lived in an apartment in New York. On my walk to work, I used to pass the pharmaceutical company you worked for, Novac. I'm an early riser, so it became a habit to get to work early." Quinn leaned forward. "Like, before-the-sun-comes-up kind of early, because I'm a bit of a nutter."

Maya didn't even crack a smile.

"Just over a month ago, I noticed the building was cordoned off. Police and paramedics were out front. There were also bodies being rolled out with sheets over them. I tried speaking to the police, but no one would give me any information about what was going on. So, the moment I got to my office, I began researching the company. I couldn't find anything that would raise an alarm."

That hadn't stopped Quinn. She'd felt in her gut that this was something she should be looking into.

"I widened my search. Looked at pharmaceutical companies across the country. Employees of pharmaceutical companies. That's when I found a lab technician in Alabama who'd died less than two months earlier. When I dug deeper, I found three more had died that same day, in the exact same town. And do you know where they all worked? Briar's Pharmaceuticals."

Maya was now watching Quinn closely.

"You wrote to me and told me that your colleagues, the other lab technicians, were killed right in front of you. That excipient and active pharmaceutical ingredients were stolen. I don't think it was the first time. And the thing is, it *should* be newsworthy. Heck, it deserves at least a small online article. But there's nothing. Absolutely no story anywhere. No one has reported on what happened in Alabama, just like no one reported on what happened in New York."

And Quinn wanted to know why. No, she *needed* to know why.

Maya's chest expanded as she took a deep breath. "Now you want to be the one to write the story and publish it in *The New York Times?*"

She *had*. Quinn hadn't told Maya about losing her job.

"That's what I *wanted* to do," Quinn corrected. "My boss told me to drop the story. When I didn't, when I kept digging, he fired me."

Which told Quinn that there was something going on here. Something bigger than a few petty thugs, stealing materials to sell on the streets.

Maya frowned. "You lost your job over the story and you're still researching it?"

Yes. Absolutely, yes. "Maya, I write about the news because I believe in freedom of information. I believe that everyone should have access to all the facts. If, for example, you had known about the break-in in Alabama, that a workplace very similar to yours was raided and lab technicians were murdered, you would have been able to make an informed decision about whether to keep working for a pharmaceutical company. And so, too, would your colleagues who didn't survive."

Tears gathered in Maya's eyes. "That's true. They were good people. Smart. They had lives. Families. And they were murdered right in front of me. Like their lives meant nothing."

Quinn reached her hand across the table and placed it on top of hers. "Tell me."

Maya hung her head but didn't pull her hand away. "There were six of us on shift. These men just walked in. Huge men. The doors were locked, so they shouldn't have been able to access us." She looked up with so much anguish in her eyes it almost caused Quinn pain. "Steve was closest to them. They walked up to him and snapped his neck like it was a twig. Josie turned to run. She'd only taken one step when one of the men appeared in front of her. He ran so fast, no one saw him move."

Goose bumps rose on Quinn's arms. "Are you sure that's what you saw?"

"I know it sounds crazy, but I saw it. I thought I was in a nightmare. But it happened right in front of me. The man lifted Josie by the neck like she weighed nothing and choked the life out of her. This man was strong. Inhumanly strong."

Maya paused as the coffees were placed in front of them.

When the waitress moved away from the table, a tear slid down Maya's cheek. "I just stood there as the life left Josie's eyes. Too terrified to move."

Quinn was already shaking her head. "You wouldn't have been able to stop him if you did move. You would have just gotten yourself killed."

"One of the men moved around the lab and filled sacks with materials, and the other two killed my team one by one. At one point, a man commented on being able to *hear* a person's heart. He was laughing about the fact that he could hear when it stopped beating."

Maya moved her hands to the coffee. Her fingers were visibly shaking.

"Why are you still alive, Maya?" Because it sounded like the criminals had wanted every person in the room dead and were more than capable of achieving it.

"I was the farthest from the door, so I was last. The man

grabbed my arm and threw me against the far wall. When I hit the ground, I was barely conscious. I was waiting for him to come and finish me off...but he didn't. They seemed to get distracted by the sound of police coming. Of an ambulance siren."

"I don't understand. Why would they leave you alive?" If the man was as fast and strong as Maya described, it would have taken two seconds for him to snap her neck like he had her colleagues'.

"I think it's because of my congenital heart condition. It's called atrial septal defect. Basically, I have a hole in my heart. One of the side effects is that my heart can skip a beat. The only thing I can think is that, after they threw me, my heart skipped a beat right before they left in a hurry." Maya gave a sad smile. "I know the odds of my heart skipping a beat at exactly the right moment are a million to one. I've gone over it so many times in my head, and that's the only thing I can think of that may have saved me."

Quinn didn't know what to say. That was one hell of a story.

"I know you probably won't believe any of this," Maya continued. "Even I struggle with it, and I was there."

Quinn couldn't believe what she was about to say. "I believe you. And I'm going to try and help you."

"I don't want anyone's help." There was desperation to Maya's words. "I just want to disappear. I only agreed to come today because I don't want anyone else to experience what I went through. I'm leaving it with you so you can get this story out there."

"I'm going to get to the bottom of this. I'm going to find out what's going on, and I'm going to warn people. But, I also want to help you."

The other woman didn't look convinced. If anything, Quinn seemed to upset her further. "You didn't see these guys. They weren't men. They were something else. Unstoppable. Killers without a conscience. The only thing I can do to save myself is vanish." Maya shook her head. "Maybe I shouldn't have come today."

She stood abruptly. Throwing money on the table, she began walking toward the door.

Quinn scrambled to do the same and follow. "Maya, wait!"

Maya was halfway across the parking lot when Quinn grabbed her arm. The other woman turned but didn't make eye contact.

"I know you're scared. I'm sorry that you had to go through that. I'm being honest when I say that I'm going to try to help you. I don't know how yet, but I will. Just please, don't drop off the face of the Earth. Email me. Call me. You have my number. I know you must need a friend. I want to *be* that friend. Anything you need."

She felt a level of responsibility for Maya's safety. Maybe because she'd trusted Quinn enough to meet. Or maybe because it looked like she had no one else.

"If you care about your safety, you'll leave this alone."

Quinn shrugged. "I can't. I'm too invested." She had to follow through. There was no way she was walking away now. "Please. Promise me you'll stay in contact."

Another beat of silence passed before Maya nodded. "Okay."

Yes. At least the guilt of not helping and not knowing if Maya survived wouldn't suffocate her.

"Thank you. And thank you for meeting me today and telling me your story."

"Just don't say I didn't warn you."

CHAPTER 3

*M*rs. Potter's Bakehouse was the most loved bakery in Marble Falls. Wyatt doubted there was a single local who *didn't* rave about the place. Everything Mrs. Potter baked turned to gold.

Today was no different. He'd devoured his apple crumble, while Luca and Bodie had finished their slices in record time.

Heck, even the coffee was amazing. His second coffee of the day. He hadn't finished the first. It had gone cold. All because he'd spent too damn long staring into those deep blue eyes of Quinn's.

Keeping his eyes off her was a problem.

He hadn't told his brothers about his mornings with Quinn. He hadn't told anyone. Mason had even called a week ago, letting him know his sister had moved into his old apartment. Wyatt hadn't mentioned a thing about meeting her. Had yet to mention he'd *been* meeting her each and every morning.

He needed to figure out where their friendship was going first. He had an idea but needed to be sure before he broached the topic with his friend and business partner.

"I'm going to propose to Evie."

Wyatt's gaze flew to Luca.

Bodie threw his head back and his arms in the air. "Hallelujah! It's about damn time."

Hell yeah, it was. The couple was the epitome of the perfect pair.

Leaning forward, Wyatt clamped a hand on his friend's shoulder. "Congratulations. That's awesome news."

Luca smiled ear to ear. "I would have done it sooner, but with everything that's happened..."

Luca didn't need to explain. Wyatt got it. "Everything" was the constant threat of their enemies.

Before they were business owners, Wyatt and his friends were Navy SEALs. That's when their commander signed them up for Project Arma. A program that was supposed to make them better soldiers.

It did a lot more than that. The people running the project had their own agenda. The drugs administered to Wyatt's team had permanently altered their DNA. When the true purpose of the project was uncovered, the government tried to shut them down, but the people behind the program went underground. Wyatt's team had been hunting them for years.

Bodie's expression hardened. "At least now that the commander has had his main facility raided, it should be a hell of a lot safer. He's lost the majority of his guards, his scientists...the guy's even lost his lab materials."

Less than a month ago, they'd finally had a breakthrough. They'd found the location Hylar was working from and raided it, killing dozens of genetically altered guards in the process, as well as freeing prisoners and ensuring lab technicians were arrested.

Luca shrugged. "I can't hold off forever. It could be years before we locate Hylar. I'm not willing to wait that long."

Their old commander, Hylar, was the final piece of the puzzle. Well, Hylar and his few surviving guards and scientists.

Wyatt crossed his arms. "Got a proposal plan?"

"I'm still working out the finer details. Happy to accept ideas."

Bodie leaned forward. "Go big. Women love that extravagant stuff. Maybe a hot-air balloon. When you get high enough, she looks down to see 'Will you marry me' written in the sand below with a thousand roses."

As ideas went, Bodie's didn't sound terrible. Although, Luca didn't look so convinced. "I was thinking something more intimate. Evie's not really into the big public displays of affection."

Bodie was already shaking his head. "Women say that, but they rarely mean it. In high school, I was dating this girl, and she told me not to plan anything for our anniversary. She said it more than once. So I didn't. And you know what happened? Huge fight. It was like I'd gone out of my way to end us."

Wyatt chuckled. "I think some women are more open and upfront than others. In this case, I'm with Rocket. I can see Evie preferring something private."

The woman was quiet by nature. She'd been through a lot. When she'd arrived in Marble Falls, she'd been running from a dangerous ex. Luca managed to kill the asshole, but internal scars were hard to heal.

"I do like the roses part of your idea, Red," Luca said. "It might be hard to get a thousand."

Bodie pointed to Wyatt. "We call this guy Jobs for a reason. What can't be achieved with the click of a button these days?"

Wyatt shrugged. "I'm sure it can be done. Just say the word." With technology today, just about anything could be acquired. Wyatt knew that because he had a knack for IT. His whole life, anything to do with coding and technology had come easy to him.

He couldn't imagine that locating a thousand roses to be delivered would be hard.

Luca smiled. "Thanks. I'll let you know."

Bodie frowned. "Well, if you're not going to use the hot-air balloon idea, keep it to yourselves. I don't want Hunter, Striker, or Eagle stealing it."

Wyatt fixed his gaze on his friend. "You need a woman to propose to first."

Eden, or Hunter to the team, was dating Shylah Kemp. A nurse at Marble Falls Hospital. While Asher, also known as Striker, had just had a baby with Lexie.

Mason, Quinn's brother—and referred to as Eagle by the team—was dating Sage, the team doctor.

Bodie shrugged. "Eagle said his sister has just moved into his old apartment. Maybe I'll go introduce myself."

Wyatt stiffened at the mention of Quinn.

Luca laughed. "If that happens, I want to be there when you tell Eagle you're making moves on his little sister."

"You're right. There's a strong chance I wouldn't live long enough to propose. Okay, scratch that. Maybe someone will come to town and fall all over themselves for me."

Women already fell all over themselves for Bodie. Not that he would be saying that to the guy. His ego was inflated enough.

"Hey, if a woman can come and take you off our hands for a bit, that would be great," Wyatt joked, dodging a whack on the shoulder from his friend.

Luca chuckled and looked at his watch. "Okay, time for us to get back to work."

The three men pushed up from the table. Not only had Wyatt remained good friends with his seven Navy SEAL brothers after serving, they also ran a business together. A successful security and self-defense business they'd built from the ground up called Marble Protection.

Not that it felt like work.

The government had paid each of them a large chunk of money as compensation for what had happened after Project Arma. That's what had allowed them to finance the business.

Wyatt trailed the other two, only to stop once he'd stepped outside.

Walking his way was none other than the woman who occupied way too much of his thoughts.

Quinn.

Her eyes were on her phone, so she hadn't seen him yet. It gave Wyatt a moment to take her in.

God, she was beautiful. The sun bounced off her tall, curvy figure. And the concentration on her face made her look damn cute.

Wyatt turned back to his friends. "I'm just going to do something. I won't be long."

Though he wouldn't be complaining if he took all day.

QUINN STRUGGLED to figure out how to respond to Tanya. They'd been friends for years. Good friends. But her husband was Quinn's ex-boss. The man who'd fired her for very little reason.

Was it immature for Quinn to let that get in the way of their friendship?

Probably.

Tanya had apologized profusely. Told Quinn she'd begged Darren to reconsider.

It wasn't Tanya's fault. Of course it wasn't. She didn't control her husband's actions. At the same time, Quinn couldn't be quite the friend she used to be. Mostly because of Tanya's close connection to the man who'd cost Quinn her life in New York.

Tanya had made sure to maintain contact. She'd called and messaged just about every day, checking in.

"Better watch where you're going, pretty lady, or you might walk right into something."

Wyatt's silky-smooth voice pulled Quinn's attention from the latest message on her phone. He stood a few feet in front of her, wearing the same gray shirt he'd had on that morning. And boy, but it looked just as good now as it had then. It stretched across his huge chest and biceps.

Holy heck, the man was hot. She wouldn't be surprised if she just melted into a pool of liquid on the ground.

She came to a stop in front of him. "If that something was you, I don't think it would be so bad."

"I don't know, you might find my chest a pretty hard hit."

Well, if that wasn't an invitation to touch the man, she didn't know what was.

Raising her arm, Quinn glided a hand across his firm chest. Muscles rippled beneath his shirt.

Yep. He was right. There wasn't a single thing that was soft about him.

"Might not be a soft hit, but I can't imagine I'd be complaining."

Not. One. Bit.

For a moment, his eyes heated before they quickly cleared. "You here to try some of Mrs. Potter's cakes?"

Quinn looked up to see she was standing in front of the very place she'd been heading. It was probably lucky Wyatt had stopped her, otherwise there was a good chance she would have walked straight past it.

"I'm here to do *something.*" Quinn gave him a wink before stepping up to the door. She couldn't help the smile that touched her lips at Wyatt's confused expression.

Confusion looked cute on the guy.

When she stepped inside, she was surprised that Wyatt followed her. Not that she minded. The man could follow her around all day if he liked.

The bakery had a small eating area with maybe a dozen tables. There was a display case with a ton of baked treats behind glass. Behind the counter was a small work bench and oven space. The door at the back was open and seemed to lead into a kitchen.

An older lady smiled at her from behind the till. "Hello, dear, what can I do for you today?"

Quinn gave the other woman her best smile. "You must be Mrs. Potter. We spoke on the phone. I'm Quinn."

"Ah, yes. You're the young girl looking for the job. Thank you for coming in. I always think it's better to discuss these things in person. Phone conversations can be so impersonal."

"I couldn't agree more."

"Do you have any experience in this type of work?"

She felt Wyatt's gaze burning holes into her.

"None. I've never baked a cake or used a coffee machine in my life. But what I lack in experience, I more than make up for in hard work and perseverance. I'm also a fast learner. Plus, I happen to love baked treats and coffee. Coffee in particular."

A look of apprehension crossed Mrs. Potter's face. "Thank you for your honesty. But if *I'm* being honest, you being new in town, with no bakery experience, is a bit concerning. I like to know who I'm hiring. Do you have someone to vouch for you, maybe?"

Quinn opened her mouth to respond when Wyatt jumped in first. "I can vouch for her. Quinn's my neighbor, and we've spent a lot of time together since she arrived in Marble Falls."

Quinn wasn't quite sure their time together would qualify as *a lot*, but hell, whatever got her a job. She needed money, and she needed it fast. Every day her funds diminished that much further. Even though she didn't have to pay rent at the moment, she still needed to feed herself and pay for utilities. Soon she'd be on a bread and water diet.

Mrs. Potter's face cleared. "Well, then, if Wyatt says you're a trustworthy person, I'll take his word."

Quinn beamed at the other woman. Wyatt was coming in handy more and more every day.

"How does a trial run sound?" Mrs. Potter continued. "I pay a competitive hourly rate, and you're welcome to help yourself to coffee and food on your breaks. You're also welcome to take any leftover food home at the end of the day."

"Mrs. Potter, you had me at free coffee." And the word "pay," but she wouldn't be admitting that out loud. "I won't let you down." Besides working at the local bookstore while she was in college, Quinn had never done anything outside of journalism. But there was nothing she enjoyed more than a challenge.

Mrs. Potter dipped her head. "You're welcome, dear. We've become a bit busier of late, and I'm afraid I can't run the place on my own any longer. It will be nice to have someone to shoulder some of the hours. Does an eight a.m. start tomorrow sound okay?"

It sounded perfect. That would leave just enough time for a coffee with her hunky neighbor first. "Sounds great. I'll see you tomorrow morning."

"See you then."

When Quinn was back on the street, she wanted to punch her fist into the air. The only thing that stopped her was the tower of muscle beside her.

She didn't need the guy knowing that she could barely afford a weeks' worth of groceries.

"I thought you were taking a break from working."

"A break from *writing*," Quinn corrected. "Not working."

"And Mrs. Potter's Bakehouse is the place to work?"

"I don't see why not. Free food. Free coffee. A boss who seems absolutely lovely. Correct me if I'm wrong, but I've yet to find a negative."

Apart from the fact she had no idea how to do the job, but how hard could it be?

"That's very true." Wyatt glanced down the street, then back at Quinn. "What are your plans now?"

"Well, when I'm not having coffee with you, I spend every other minute of the daydreaming about our next coffee date."

She expected a laugh from Wyatt. Or at least a chuckle. Instead, his brows lifted. "They're dates, are they?"

Stepping forward, Quinn rose up to her toes. Wrapping her fingers around his neck, she pulled his head down until his ear was by her lips.

"They're whatever you want them to be, sexy."

Then she pressed a kiss to his cheek before turning and walking back the way she'd come.

CHAPTER 4

*Q*uinn studied the stairs in front of her. She couldn't for the life of her understand why there was no elevator in the apartment building. It wasn't an old building. Would it have been so hard for them to install one?

Damn her brother and his beyond-fit body. He probably didn't think twice about the stairs when choosing the place.

Most days she didn't mind the stairs herself. Far from it. She loved incidental exercise. But not today. Today, she was carrying two large bags of groceries, which she'd already lugged all the way from the store. And the reason she'd lugged them from the store was because the car was low on gas.

Like, will-barely-make-it-to-the-gas-station low.

And her broke ass needed to be as money savvy as possible. At least until she got her first paycheck from the bakery.

Four floors of stairs. That's how far she had to lug her groceries. Damn, she hoped her tired arms and legs held out.

Blowing out a long breath, Quinn began the first flight of stairs.

Where was Wyatt when she needed him? That man looked strong enough to carry both her *and* the groceries without breaking a sweat. Not only would that save her from sweating like a pig, but having his powerful arms around her body sounded pretty damn good.

Better than good, actually. It was the stuff dreams were made of.

For a moment, she wondered what the man would do if she laid another kiss on his lips. She wanted to progress their relationship. Boy, but did she want to. She hadn't been with a guy in a long time. *Too* long. She'd let her work utterly consume her life. And it was only now, when she was finally taking a step back from it all, that she was able to recognize that.

Wyatt was the perfect person to break the dry spell. Perfect with a capital *P*. And from the heated looks he threw her way, it seemed he might just be interested in her, too.

The question was, did she wait for him to make a move, or did she take the initiative?

She didn't know a whole lot about him, but she spent half an hour with the guy every single morning. He wasn't a stranger anymore. He made her the best cup of coffee on Earth, then proceeded to make her laugh and smile for the next twenty-five minutes.

Stopping on the second floor, Quinn dropped the bags onto the floor and stretched her tired arms. Studying the next flight of stairs, she cringed.

Jeepers, if she was going to continue walking to the grocery store, she would need to do smaller, more frequent shopping trips. Either that or stop eating altogether.

Quinn almost laughed out loud at the thought. Yeah, right. She loved food. It was probably the third most important thing to her, right behind sleep and journalism. No way would she give that up.

Quinn had just lifted the groceries when her cell started ringing from her back pocket. Switching the bags to one arm, she fished it out.

Tanya.

Quinn was tempted to let it go to voicemail. But she'd already done that...about half a dozen times. The woman had been calling and messaging nonstop.

Reluctantly, Quinn answered the call. She kept moving up the stairs, trying to ignore the bags straining her arm.

"Hey, Tan. How are you?"

"Quinn! I'm so glad I caught you. I'm good. Are you okay? I mean, I know you're not okay. What with having to move and everything. What I mean is, are you okay right now? You sound out of breath."

Quinn smiled at her friend's babbling. That was Tanya. It's something she'd always loved about her.

"I *am* out of breath. I'm just walking up a bunch of stairs. The smart thing to do would be to stop. But when have I ever been smart?"

Not recently, that was for damn sure.

Moving the phone to sit between her head and shoulders, she switched the bags so that there was once again a bag in each hand.

"Oh, gosh. Okay. Sorry! I'll be quick, I promise. I just wanted to ask you something."

Quick sounded good. "Shoot."

"Have you seen Darren?"

Darren? As in, Tanya's-asshole-husband-who-had-fired-her Darren? Why the heck would she have seen him? The man lived in New York.

"No. I'm in Marble Falls, Tanya. You know that. Why would you think I'd seen him?"

There was a brief pause down the line. "Don't get mad. But Darren's in Marble Falls. He flew over this morning."

As Quinn stepped onto the fourth floor, she almost fell over her own feet in surprise. "What? Why is he in Marble Falls?"

Before Tanya had a chance to respond, Quinn looked up to

see the man himself, down the hall, standing in front of her apartment.

What the heck?

"He's at my door." Quinn said the words more to herself than to her friend.

Tanya breathed out a relieved sigh. "Oh, good. He wasn't answering his phone, and I was worried. Sorry I didn't warn you. He just wants to talk to you."

Confusion swirled through her mind. What on Earth would be so important that it needed to be said in person, rather than over the phone?

"Let me know how it goes, okay?"

Quinn had a million questions she could ask her friend, but seeing as all those questions could be answered by the man standing a few feet away, she didn't voice them.

"Thanks for the heads-up." The two-second heads-up. "Bye, Tan."

Quinn walked the few steps down the hall to meet Darren. As she did, she studied him. Most women would describe the man as good-looking. Once upon a time, Quinn would have too.

He stood just over six feet and had shaggy brown hair that he had to push out of his eyes numerous times a day. He had a bit of a prince charming look to him.

Shame he had the personality of a snake.

"Hi, Quinn."

Stopping in front of him, she dropped a bag to fish the key out of her pocket. "I would like to say this is a pleasant surprise, Darren, but you *did* fire me."

After pushing the door open, she wasn't surprised when he didn't so much as offer to take one of the bags that she was clearly struggling with.

Heading straight for the kitchen, she lifted both bags onto the counter. When her arms were finally free, she stretched them.

God, it was good to put them down.

Darren closed the door after himself, immediately scanning the apartment. "Nice place."

Nope. She was not going to stand here and have small talk with the guy. "How did you find me?"

Not that she was surprised he had. Before Darren was the executive editor for *The New York Times*, he was a damn good investigative journalist. She doubted the information would have been hard to source.

"I went to your old apartment. The building manager told me where your mail was being forwarded."

If that wasn't an invasion of her privacy, she wasn't sure what was.

"And why exactly are you here? If I remember correctly, the last time we spoke you told me there were absolutely no circumstances under which I would be getting my job back. You also said that I may as well leave town." She waved a hand around the apartment. "As you can see, I left town."

Darren took two large steps forward, shrinking the space between them. "I know. I feel terrible about how things ended, particularly because you and Tanya are such good friends. My hands were tied. That's why I'm here, to check that you're okay."

He was here to check that she was okay? Yeah, right.

Quinn scoffed. "You fired me for doing my job. The only thing I'm struggling with is the why behind it all."

"You know why you were fired, Quinn. I told you to drop the story. I told you we weren't publishing it. You kept digging. You went against a direct order and forced my hand."

"And tell me again why I couldn't write the story."

Darren's eyes turned sympathetic. "I know losing your job was hard."

Quinn didn't miss that he'd dodged the question. She also didn't want the man's sympathy. She highly doubted any of it was genuine. "Are you here to offer me my job back or to tell me the real reason I was fired?"

He looked at her as if she were a child. "I've told you why you were fired. I wish I could offer you your job back. You're a damn good journalist. But I can't."

"That's bull. You're the executive editor."

"If you'd just done what I'd asked, you'd still have your job. You've only got yourself to blame."

Quinn shook her head. "I'd like you to leave." Because the guy clearly wasn't going to tell her what she needed to know.

Darren reached his hand out, placing it on her arm. "Is this really about losing your job, or is this about us?"

Quinn took a hurried step back. Even that small touch made her skin crawl. "Us?"

He tilted his head to the side. "Don't pretend you don't remember that night, Quinn."

Quinn wanted to gag at the memory. "First of all, we were both drunk. Second, you plastered your lips onto mine before I could pull away. Thirdly, you're married! The only reason I didn't tell Tanya was because you begged me not to. Said it had never happened before and would never happen again."

Walking around him, she pulled the door open. "If you have nothing constructive to add to this conversation, then please leave."

Darren frowned. "I flew all the way over here to see you. I thought maybe I could sleep on your couch for the night."

Quinn laughed out loud. "Maybe you should have called, and I would have saved you the trip. The answer is no." Yes, she was good friends with his wife, but that in no way made her responsible for giving the guy a place to sleep. "There's an inn and a motel both within a few minutes' drive. I'm sure one of them has a vacancy."

Darren moved to the door, but instead of walking out, he stopped in front of her. "Okay, I'll leave. But before I do, I need to know something. Have you dropped the story?"

The story? As in, the one that got her fired?

Ah. So that's why he was here. Finally, it was making sense. Darren hadn't flown two thousand miles to check that she was okay. He'd flown all this way to ask her in person if she'd dropped the story. Because, just like her, he liked to get his information in person.

"I know how you get when you find a story," Darren continued. "You don't let it go until you've acquired all the facts and it's published. I need you to tell me you're dropping this one."

There was an urgency in his voice that hadn't been there before. It intrigued the hell out of Quinn.

First, the man fired her for looking into the break-in. Now, he'd flown across the country, spending both money and time, to *check* that she'd let it go.

Why? What was it about this story that was so important to warrant both actions?

"Why is it so important I let this one go?"

His eyes lifted and he looked around the room. There was a nervousness about his expression. "I just don't want you to get hurt. Some drugged-up street thugs are probably responsible for the whole thing, and I doubt they're people you want to mess with."

Except drugged-up street thugs weren't organized enough to pull off what happened at Novac. Quinn knew that. And she sure as hell knew that *Darren* knew that.

All of his actions and words just confirmed for Quinn that this was a story that needed to be investigated. Not that she was about to tell Darren that.

"My safety is not your concern."

A wave of frustration passed over his features. "So you're still researching it?"

Quinn didn't answer. It wasn't any of his business either way. He wasn't her employer anymore. He wasn't her anything.

The frustration fell from Darren's face, to be replaced by...desperation?

Reaching out, he grabbed her arm in a tight grip. His fingers digging into her skin, causing pain to shoot up to her shoulder.

Immediately, Quinn tried to pull away, but his grip was unyielding. "Let go. You're hurting me."

He didn't let go. Instead, he stepped closer, his fingers tightening. "I'm not messing around, Quinn. You need to drop it."

She firmed her voice. "Unless you want a knee to your balls, get your hand off me right the hell now."

CHAPTER 5

Wyatt stepped out of his car. It had been a long day at work. A large chunk of it had been spent searching for Commander Hylar. The man shouldn't be so hard to find, but he was.

The search was both exhausting and frustrating.

Pushing through the entrance of the apartment building, Wyatt headed up the stairs. If all went to plan, his night would entail a cold beer followed by a night of doing nothing.

No computers. No searching. No work.

When Wyatt reached his floor, he did what he always did—attempted to block out the hum of people from the surrounding apartments. This evening, one of those voices caught his attention.

Quinn.

"Let go. You're hurting me."

Wyatt stopped as a male voice followed. "I'm not messing around, Quinn. You need to drop it."

Wyatt was moving again before the man had finished speaking.

He arrived at Quinn's apartment in time to hear her threat.

"Unless you want a knee to your balls, get your hand off me right the hell now."

Wyatt took in the scene in front of him. A man had his hand on Quinn. Was *threatening* Quinn.

Big mistake.

Moving to stand beside her, Wyatt towered over the man. "You have one second to remove your hand, otherwise I'll be adding a broken arm to the bruised balls."

The guy turned his head and studied Wyatt. He didn't remove his hand.

Another mistake.

Grabbing the arm that was holding Quinn, Wyatt squeezed in what he knew was a painful grip. The asshole let out a yelp, immediately releasing Quinn, and Wyatt shoved him against the wall.

Fear crossed the stranger's face. "Who the hell are you?"

Wyatt moved a step closer so that only a few inches separated their faces. "I'm someone you don't want to mess with. I suggest you leave this building immediately. And if I catch so much of a glimpse of you again, you'll regret it."

Wyatt listened as the man's heart begin to gallop. "This is none of your business."

Oh, but it was.

The guy attempted to pull his arm from Wyatt's grip. That wasn't going to happen. "The second you put your hand on her, it became my business."

After another few seconds, Wyatt released the man but positioned himself in front of Quinn. He was giving the guy the chance to leave on his own but wouldn't hesitate to provide "assistance" if required.

Quinn stepped beside Wyatt. "Darren, just leave."

The man looked angry. But he clearly knew he had no choice in the matter. "Fine. I'll leave. But I meant what I said."

Wyatt watched the guy leave before turning to Quinn. He

studied her face, expecting to see fear. Maybe some uncertainty or dread.

He saw none of those things. The woman glared at the closed door with nothing but rage.

Touching her elbow, Wyatt didn't take his eyes off her. "Are you okay?"

She nodded. "I'm okay. I didn't expect him to grab me like that. Lesson learned. Don't underestimate a jerk and always keep pepper spray in the back pocket."

Something stronger than pepper spray would be Wyatt's preference.

He lifted her elbow to study her upper arm. Angry red marks discolored her skin. There was no doubt they would bruise.

A spark of anger shot through him. Why the hell had he just let the guy leave? He should go out there and chase him down. Teach him some manners.

"We should get some ice on this. I have some at my place…"

"It's okay." Quinn shook her head, pulling out of his hold. She crossed her arms, clearly frustrated about what had happened.

Lifting his other hand, Wyatt trailed his finger down her cheek. "I'm sorry I didn't get here sooner. Before he touched you."

Her eyes softened, and she pressed her hands to his chest. He felt the heat from her skin through the material of his shirt.

"My brother taught me self-defense, so I'm pretty good at saving myself. He was a second away from being on his knees, howling in pain. But it was nice to have you here."

Wyatt had no doubt the woman was badass when she had to be. But if he could save her from having to fight a man, any man, he would.

"Who was he?"

At Wyatt's words, Quinn dropped her hands and took a step back. He felt the loss of her touch immediately.

"He's my…ah…my boss."

Wyatt frowned. Quinn lived and worked in New York. That was a long way for her boss to travel.

There was also the fact that her voice had hitched at the end. Meaning there was something that wasn't quite true in her statement.

"What did he want?"

Quinn turned and walked behind the kitchen counter. "Don't worry about it, Wyatt. My problems are my own. I can handle them."

Only, he *was* worried. People didn't fly across the country for nothing. They also didn't assault people over nothing.

Wyatt wanted to push it. Hell, he wanted to sit the woman down and not let her back up until he got every little life detail.

He didn't. Because her body language screamed that the conversation was done. Over.

But there was definitely something going on. Something to do with her work. And there was a strong possibly that something was dangerous.

For a moment, he wondered if Mason knew. But he quickly dashed that idea. If Mason knew his sister was in trouble, he would either be here to help her, or he'd have asked one of them to look out for her.

"Wyatt, stop."

Quinn had placed her hands on her hips and was now watching him. Damn, had he made his thoughts too obvious?

"Stop what?"

"You're trying to figure things out. Your mind is moving a thousand miles an hour, I can see it on your face and read it from your silence. There's nothing to figure out."

He smiled. Not because there was anything remotely good about his suspicions, but because he wanted Quinn to be at ease. "If I can't think about you, what can I think about?"

Her body visibly relaxed at his comment. "Okay, you can think about me a little. But only about how awesome I am."

Oh, he already spent a great deal of time doing that. "It's hard for me not to."

If the woman knew how often she was on his mind, she would probably be more than a little freaked out.

"Don't worry, it's completely normal and very common."

Wyatt chuckled. "That's good to hear because I *was* starting to worry."

"Nothing to worry about."

Shoving his hands into his pockets, he glanced at the door. "Okay, well, if you're sure you're okay, I'll leave."

He looked back at her in time to see her eyes roll. "I'm sure."

He'd almost made it out the door when her voice stopped him.

"And Wyatt…thanks again."

He dipped his head. "Anytime. And I mean that, Quinn, I'm just across the hall. The door is always open for you."

He gave her a final smile before stepping out and into his own apartment. The moment the door closed, he beelined for his laptop.

The technology-free night was no longer an option. Quinn was supposedly taking a "break" from her job at *The New York Times*. Wyatt was almost certain that was a lie.

Quinn wouldn't appreciate him researching her. But she was Mason's sister. Mason was more than a friend, he was family. No blood connection needed.

If there was something going on with Quinn, Mason would want to know.

There were questions that needed answering. Questions that he would love Quinn to answer herself once their relationship grew, but if danger lurked, then he needed to know now.

∼

QUINN HAD JUST CLIMBED into bed when her phone began to ring.

No! She was not going to answer that. She had a date with her laptop. She planned to fall asleep watching mindless sitcoms and drinking hot cocoa.

The whole "Darren" situation had frustrated her to no end. He had answers. Answers that he wasn't sharing.

Quinn listened to the ringing without so much as looking at the cell.

When the room went silent, she clicked on Netflix. It had saved her overactive mind many a time, and not once had it failed to de-stress her.

She'd just clicked into a show and snuggled under the sheets when her phone rang again.

God dang it. Could this person not take a hint?

Reaching across to her nightstand, Quinn intended to switch the thing off, but stopped when she saw whose name flashed across the screen.

Mason.

Crap. If she didn't answer, he would just keep calling. Either that or send in the whole damn police force to check that she was okay.

Reluctantly, Quinn lifted the phone to her ear. "Hey, big brother. How's Lockhart treating you?"

"Why didn't you tell me you were fired?"

Quinn shot up into a sitting position at her brother's words. "How the heck do you know I was fired?"

"Answer the question, Quinn."

At Mason's authoritative tone, Quinn's spine straightened. "How about you answer mine first?"

"Wyatt told me."

For a moment, Quinn thought she'd heard wrong. "Wyatt? As in Wyatt…"

"Who lives across the hall from you? Who was a member of my SEAL team and now runs Marble Protection with me? Yes, him."

Holy jam on a cracker. Wyatt knew her brother.

No, not just *knew*—served with him, ran a business with him. Christ, the guy was basically family to Mason.

Suddenly, things began making sense. The muscular body. The intelligence.

How had she not fit those pieces together?

"You've talked about your team plenty of times and I've never heard you mention a Wyatt. And why didn't you tell me one of your team members lived across the hall from me?"

"The team calls him Jobs, and I just didn't think to mention it."

He didn't think to mention it? It seemed like pretty important information to Quinn.

"So, this whole time he's known that I'm your sister?"

"Of course. I told him you were moving into my apartment."

That sneaky bastard.

On one hand, she hadn't shared much information about herself with Wyatt, either. On the other, he'd lied by omission. He'd probably known her name before the words had left her mouth.

"Quinn!"

"Not that it's any of your business, but I was fired because my boss told me to drop a story and I didn't. I kept researching it. I kept digging and asking questions. And he fired me."

"What was the story?"

"Oh, did Wyatt not discover that part?"

Her brother sighed. "Q. Please. Tell me."

She shook her head. "There's really nothing to tell. It was a story about a burglary where some innocent people got killed. You don't need to worry, I'm done looking into it." She crossed her fingers and toes as she lied through her teeth. She couldn't very well tell her overprotective brother that she was still researching a story that involved super-human killers.

Not only would he think she was insane, but he would probably cut his trip short, come home and lock her away until he made sure there was no danger.

She didn't need him to do that. She was capable of protecting herself just fine. As far as she was concerned, there would always be danger in the world. And there was no way Quinn would lock herself away to stay safe.

"Are you okay?"

Quinn paused at Mason's question. She knew what he was asking. He knew how much she loved her job. She lived and breathed it. That was just one of the reason she couldn't drop this story. Quinn needed to know why it had cost her everything.

"I'm okay, Mason. Just figuring out my next step."

"Wyatt told me you're going to be working at Mrs. Potter's Bakehouse."

Quinn was going to kill that guy.

"I was hoping my boss would reconsider and take me back. He didn't. And while I waited in New York, rent chewed up my minimal savings."

If you could even call what she'd had in the bank "savings."

"Do you need money?"

"No!" Hell no. It was bad enough she had to ask to live in his apartment rent-free. No way was she taking cash handouts, too. "Mrs. Potter was good enough to give me a job. That will keep me going."

"Okay. What about this boss? Wyatt said he paid you a visit?" There was an edge of danger to Mason's voice. An edge she was all too familiar with.

"Darren's harmless. Mason, I really appreciate that you care. I love that you're always looking out for me. But I'm okay. If I need your help, I'll call."

She could just imagine Mason rolling his eyes. "You swear?"

"I swear."

Quinn was damn glad she wasn't speaking to her brother in person. He had a weird knack for being able to spot a lie.

Not that what she'd said was a *complete* lie. It just wasn't the complete truth.

"I'm due back in a couple of weeks, but I can—"

"Don't even think about coming home early. It sounds like Sage needs this time with her brother."

Mason sighed. "Fine. Just…keep out of danger. At least until I get back."

Quinn smiled. "No problem. I hate danger. Thanks for calling. I love you."

"I love you too, Q. Night."

When the line went dead, Quinn sat there considering her options. She could march across the hall right now and confront the no-good ratbag. But if she did that, she might lose her head. She might even cause some bodily harm.

She needed to sleep on it. Figure out a plan that didn't involve exploding on the guy.

But if she woke up and the plan still involved killing him… well then, that's just what she would do.

CHAPTER 6

Q uinn watched as Mrs. Potter sipped the coffee. A lot was riding on that coffee. Not just because Quinn had made it. But because it was her *third* try. Third! Who knew making a good cup of coffee was so hard!

The first two attempts had been disastrous. The milk had burned and the coffee itself had been too weak.

Mrs. Potter had told her the drink was a disaster in the nicest possible way. But if Quinn failed again, surely the older woman's kindness would run out.

This time, Mrs. Potter had not only talked Quinn through the entire process, she'd also watched each and every step, right down to the chocolate sprinkle on top.

Quinn bit her bottom lip as Mrs. Potter lowered the cup. When she didn't immediately grimace, Quinn's optimism went up a notch. Maybe there was hope after all.

"This is a lot better, dear."

Better. Still not the bees-knees of coffees, but not spit-it-out-and-demand-a-refund bad. Quinn could work with that.

"Good. That's good. It's progress, right?"

"That it is. Try the next one on your own. See if you can remember all the steps."

"Sure." Quinn could do that. She'd investigated some of the biggest stories in the country. She could use a coffee machine without Mrs. Potter watching over her shoulder and directing the ship.

"While you do that, I need to run out and grab some flour from the store. Unfortunately, the delivery doesn't come in until tomorrow and we've run out."

Almost without thinking, Quinn took a step toward the other woman. "Really? Leave me and the coffee machine by ourselves? Someone could come in and order a coffee. Multiple people could come in and order coffees. I could go to the shop?"

Please, oh please, let me go to the shop.

Mrs. Potter shook her head. "You'll be okay, dear. No need to worry. Besides, I need to go because I like to butter up Ed, the store owner, so that he gives me a discount." She laughed. "I won't be long."

"Okay."

It didn't actually feel okay, but what else could she say?

Quinn watched as Mrs. Potter grabbed her bag and waved goodbye. It was like waving goodbye to the person holding the last raft of a sinking ship.

Okay. Maybe she was being a tad dramatic. That didn't mean she wasn't tempted to walk over and put the closed sign on the door.

Ha. Yeah, right. That would be a sure way to get herself fired.

Turning back to the machine, she got started on the next one. She was halfway through heating the milk when the dinging of the door sounded.

Ah, crap. *Please be a kid wanting chocolate milk.*

When she glanced over her shoulder, she noticed it wasn't a kid. Far from it. Four fully grown men stood inside the bakery.

They were huge. Huge and good-looking as heck. Particularly one of them.

Wyatt.

Double crap. She hadn't gone over to his place for their regular coffee that morning. She'd planned to, but when she'd woken up, she'd still had might-kill-him mentality. Going straight to work had seemed the safest option for everyone.

Putting down the half-heated milk, Quinn walked over to the counter.

Holy heck, if these guys were all Mason's SEAL brothers, she had to question whether there was some Navy SEAL requirement that you needed to be a foot taller than the regular citizen.

When they stopped at the counter, Quinn gave a sweet smile, avoiding Wyatt. "Hi, what can I get for you guys today?"

A man with short brown hair and dimples on his cheeks smiled back. "Well, hello there. Mrs. Potter didn't mention she'd hired a new employee. I'm Bodie. This is Kye, Oliver, and Wyatt."

She looked at Kye, whose dark, intense eyes were softened by his smile. When her attention swung to Oliver, she had to smile at the wink he gave her. Both men had military written all over them. They all did.

She left Wyatt for last. When her gaze fell on his, she noticed he was studying her. Probably trying to assess just how annoyed she was.

Very, buddy. Very annoyed.

"Nice to meet you, guys. I'm Quinn Ross."

Recognition hit all three of Wyatt's friends at the same time.

"Eagle's sister?" Kye asked.

"The one and only. I've heard a lot about you guys. I hope you haven't heard a lot about me. Mason seems to only remember when I get into trouble."

"We've only heard good things," Oliver commented.

Yeah, right. Quinn would pretend like she believed him. "What can I get you?"

Bodie, Kye, and Oliver ordered lattes, while Wyatt ordered a cappuccino with sugar.

Quinn glanced over at the coffee machine, then back at the guys. "Mrs. Potter should be back in a moment if you'd like to wait for her?"

It was Wyatt who responded. "We're actually running late for a team meeting at work."

Of course they were.

"Okay. I'll have them right up." Or, at least, she hoped she would.

Once the men paid, they sat at a table by the window.

Quinn eyed the door.

Come on, Mrs. Potter. Walk through the door. Save me.

She didn't. The door remained firmly closed, dammit.

Heading back to the machine, Quinn tried to think positive thoughts. Lifting the jug of milk, she studied the contents. It should be enough for four coffees.

"Need some help?"

Jumping at the sound of Wyatt's voice near her ear, she spun around. "Holy cow, make a noise or something next time."

He straightened beside her. "I'm sorry."

She frowned. Was he saying sorry for scaring the crap out of her just now, or was he saying sorry for the other stuff?

"I should have told you that I knew your brother, and therefore knew who you were," he continued.

So, the other stuff. "Why didn't you?"

He lifted a shoulder. "Because I enjoyed it just being you and me, and I had a feeling it would change if I brought up Eagle."

Quinn had liked that too. But dishonesty by omission was still dishonesty.

"You still should have told me you knew who I was. But I get that. Kind of. There's still the other part, though. The part where you went back to your apartment yesterday, researched me, then called my brother."

Gosh, even saying it out loud made her feel like a kid getting told on by her teacher.

He took a small step closer. Even though she was mad, it didn't take away from the fact that the man smelled good. Smelled good, looked good. The whole shebang.

"I was worried. Your brother said you were taking a break from work, but things weren't adding up."

Quinn turned back to the machine and poured more milk into the pitcher. "I get it. He's your friend. You guys are close. Of course you did what you did. You and I just met."

"You and I are friends, Quinn. Well, I consider *you* a friend."

She shook her head. "Then I guess you have some making up to do. You know, to get back into my good graces." She began frothing the milk. At the same time, she noticed Wyatt fiddling with the machine. "What are you doing?"

Rather than stopping, he started the process of bean grinding. "Working my way back into your good graces by helping."

"Maybe I don't need your help?"

She definitely did. Not that she would be admitting that to him.

"Your milk is about to overheat."

Her eyes flew back to the thermometer.

Dang it! Quinn quickly pulled the pitcher away.

Cursing under her breath, she moved to throw out the milk, only to stop at Wyatt's hand on her arm. Wyatt's tanned, muscular hand that sent jolts of electricity up her arm.

"It was *about* to overheat. It didn't. It's good to use."

"It will be too hot."

He shrugged. "We're a tough bunch. We can handle it." He placed four cups, which now contained coffee, in front of her. "You might find it easiest to do the cappuccino last."

Quinn began to fill the cups as Wyatt placed a large teaspoon of sugar in his.

"Will the guys complain if these taste like dirt?"

"Nah. They'll just get their coffees from Joan's Diner when-ever they spot you in here."

Great!

One side of Wyatt's mouth pulled up. Okay, the man was messing with her.

"Yeah, okay. Don't forget to tell them you helped." Popping the lids on the cups, Quinn placed them in a cup holder. "Even though I could have done it myself, I appreciate your help."

She placed the tray of coffees into his waiting hands. Rather than walking back to the table, his gaze remained fixed on her. "I missed you this morning."

She'd missed him, too. It had been one lonely, instant-coffee kind of morning.

"I was a tad grumpy. I wouldn't have made good company." *And you may have ended up injured.*

Placing the coffees on the counter, he lifted his hand and pushed a lock of stray hair behind her ear. And oh lordy, did she enjoy the way his skin brushed against hers.

"Good. I was worried you were avoiding me."

"I was. But now you've apologized and we've decided you have some major making up to do. I won't be missing that." Plus, avoiding the guy for any long period of time would probably be impossible.

"That I do."

"But don't do it again. The lying by omission *or* the researching me and telling my brother. Got it?"

"Got it."

She blew out a breath. "You are one lucky man that I'm so forgiving."

Wyatt chuckled before dipping his head and placing his lips by his ear. "I am *very* lucky. I'll see you tomorrow morning, sunshine."

His breath brushed her skin. And just for a moment, she thought she felt the slightest touch of his lips.

Then he straightened and walked back to his friends. A moment later, they were waving and exiting the bakery.

Christ, she was in trouble. She was catching feelings, and she was catching them fast.

Shaking her head, she walked back over to check her phone. She needed a distraction. Maybe Maya had finally responded to her. A few days ago, the woman had stopped replying to her emails and texts. Quinn had no idea why, and she was getting worried.

Maya had already been able to provide Quinn with brief descriptions of all the men. It was actually quite impressive. For a woman who must have been scared out of her mind, she had been able to take in a lot of detail.

Quinn believed every word the woman said about what she saw. It was crazy. She was the last person to believe that people with such abilities existed.

The thing was, she hadn't detected an ounce of insincerity in the scientist. She seemed like a normal, sane, educated woman— who had witnessed something impossible.

And that scared the crap out of Quinn. Because she knew how much bad existed in the world. She knew that people could commit inherently terrible acts. The only thing that helped her sleep at night was the fact that the bad guys were *human*. And humans could be stopped.

She wasn't so sure about the men Maya had described.

When she clicked into her emails, she noticed there was no message from Maya. Before she could put down her phone, a message popped up from Tanya.

Quinn had told her friend the bare minimum about Darren's visit. Tanya knew nothing about the story she was researching. Her friend didn't get involved in her husband's work. And the last thing Quinn wanted to do was tell Tanya about the story and land her in the middle of danger.

So, Quinn had told Tanya that her husband had stopped by,

checked on her, then gone to stay at a hotel. Not the whole truth. But not a complete lie.

She read Tanya's message, thanking her for the update on her husband's visit. Quinn wished she could be honest with the other woman. Tell her what had really happened yesterday.

But there wasn't much she could say. She didn't know why Darren was so dead set on her staying away from the story. She could only hope she'd find out.

CHAPTER 7

*W*yatt cracked an egg into the pan. Eggs and bacon. If that didn't win his way back into Quinn's good graces, he wasn't sure what would.

When she hadn't come around for coffee yesterday, he'd been disappointed, but not surprised. Mornings with Quinn had fast become the highlight of his day.

That's why he'd convinced the guys to grab coffee from Mrs. Potter's Bakehouse. They had a perfectly good coffee machine at Marble Protection, which his friends had been quick to point out. But he'd wanted to see her. Talk to her. Assess just how mad she was and whether he had a chance at redemption.

The moment her gaze had brushed over him, annoyance tinging her delicate features, he'd thought for sure he was screwed.

Then he'd helped her prepare their order. And little by little the ice had thawed.

There was hope.

His friends had listened to every word he'd said to her. Wyatt knew it would have been impossible for them not to. They'd given him crap about it for the rest of the afternoon. Questions were asked—about their coffee dates, their relationship...

Wyatt had been honest. They were friends. Possibly building toward something more.

Thank God, the guys had agreed not to mention anything to Mason. Wyatt needed time to talk to her brother himself. Preferably in person.

Flipping the bacon in the pan, Wyatt was about to move on to the coffee when a knock on the door sounded.

Right on time.

Turning the heat down, he went to open the door. Quinn stood there, arms crossed, looking absolutely breathtaking as per usual.

"I haven't forgiven you. Not yet. But—" Quinn paused, a small frown creasing her brow. "Is that bacon I smell?"

Wyatt was almost a hundred percent certain that was *not* what she'd been about to say. "It is. I've also got eggs and coffee."

Her eyes widened before tilting her head to peer around him. "And how much of this bacon, eggs, and coffee do you have?"

"Enough for you, me, and leftovers." Wyatt took a step back. "Have breakfast with me."

She bit her lip. Wyatt had to clench his fists to stop from reaching out for her.

"Is this part of your ploy to get me to forgive you?"

"Is it working?"

"Heck, yeah." She brushed passed him and headed to the kitchen. "Oh my goodness, the closer I get, the better it smells."

Closing the door after her, he went to retake his position at the stove. "Take a seat while I finish." Wyatt made a start on the coffees. At the same time, Quinn slid onto a stool at the island.

"So, tell me, how did you find out I was fired? It's not like it was public information."

Wyatt filled a coffee mug and added milk. "A bit of digging."

"Legal digging?"

He lifted a shoulder. "I tend to be able to find things that others can't."

"Didn't answer my question. Which is an answer right there. What exactly did you find?"

Not nearly as much as he'd hoped. "That you were fired for not following orders."

As he turned his head, he caught her eye roll. "Darren's an asshat."

Wyatt could think of a lot worse names for the man. "What did you do that got you fired?"

"My job." She shook her head. "I was researching a story about a break-in. He told me I wasn't allowed to. That the story was 'off-limits,'" Quinn used her fingers to do air quotes, "so naturally, I kept digging. Next minute, he fires me."

Wyatt placed her coffee in front of her but remained quiet, knowing she had more to say.

"At first I thought it was some kind of joke. I mean, what kind of investigative journalist gets fired for investigating a story? I stayed in New York hoping for the call that I could come back. All I did was waste my time and money."

Sounded frustrating as hell. "I'm sorry."

Even though she tried to mask it, he could see the entire situation caused her a lot of stress. The woman clearly loved her job.

"Thank you. Who knows, maybe the break from journalism will actually do me some good. I wasn't lying when I told you I was a workaholic."

Wyatt didn't doubt it. When people were passionate about what they did, they didn't tend to need a break.

"But you're still working on the story?"

Quinn remained silent for a moment. "I'm not really *working* on the story, seeing as I don't have a job as a journalist. I'm researching it. Do not tell my brother that, though. It's some harmless online searches I'm doing, nothing that will put me in danger."

"Quinn, the guys and I don't keep secrets—"

"It's not a secret," she interrupted. "I'll tell Mason all about it when he gets home. If I tell him earlier, he'll rush back here like a madman for no reason. Please, Wyatt. It's completely safe."

Wyatt leaned over the counter. "I'll keep your secret on one condition. You come straight to me if Darren returns or you feel you're in danger."

"Done."

That was quick. Almost too quick.

Narrowing his eyes, he studied her face. She didn't so much as blink. He couldn't tell whether he believed her or not. And it frustrated the hell out of him. "Okay."

It was better Quinn trust him than no one.

"Good. Because if you'd said no, I don't know how we could have maintained this friendship."

"Lucky I'm a smart man and was gifted with a large supply of brain cells."

Quinn threw her head back and laughed. His gaze was drawn to her neck, and he suddenly got the urge to run kisses over her exposed skin.

"You were gifted with a large supply of something."

He chuckled. Ten minutes later they began eating. Well, Wyatt was eating. Quinn was talking his ear off. God, he would never get tired of conversations with this woman.

She groaned out loud as she took a mouthful. "Bacon has got to be my all-time favorite food. Just the right amount of salt and grease. Did you know bacon was another addiction of mine?"

"I didn't ask your brother, if that's what you're asking. You just look like a bacon lover."

A sexy bacon lover.

"Hm, and how does someone 'look' like a bacon lover?"

"When they have the perfect combination of beauty and brains."

The hand that was reaching for her coffee paused partway. A smile curved her lips. "Did you just call me smart *and* beautiful?"

"I believe the word perfect was in there too. Although, I should admit, I've already said it a hundred times in my head."

Her smile widened. "You're pretty sweet when you want to be."

He leaned closer. "You've barely scratched the surface of who I am."

But he had a feeling his "sweetness" knew no bounds when it came to Quinn.

QUINN LIFTED ANOTHER NAPKIN. Folding napkins should be a boring, mundane task. Not today. Not when her mind kept flicking back to Wyatt.

She'd thought he was going to kiss her that morning. Heck, her skin had tingled in preparation for the touch of his lips. The way he'd looked at her after she'd laughed…she was sure she'd seen heat in his eyes.

But he hadn't kissed her. Probably a good thing. She might have latched onto the guy and never let him go.

"You look happy, dear. What has you smiling so wide?"

A god-like creature sent from heaven.

Instead of saying that, Quinn glanced up to find Mrs. Potter watching her with a knowing smile. "I didn't hear you come in."

There was a twinkle in Mrs. Potter's eyes. "It's because you were distracted. It's a man, isn't it. A woman only gets that look in her eye from a man."

The lady was onto her. "It is."

Mrs. Potter put down her tray of rolls and stepped beside her. "Do I know him?"

Quinn was pretty sure everyone in Marble Falls either knew

him, or at least knew *of* him. He and his friends stood out from the average person like a sore thumb.

When Quinn remained silent a beat too long, Mrs. Potter began to look excited. "I do! It's one of the boys from Marble Protection, isn't it?"

Quinn's brows pulled together. "How did you know?"

"Dear, those boys are the heartthrobs of Marble Falls. And you waltz into town, pretty and smart...it was only a matter of time. Which one? Bodie? That boy has charm in spades."

She laughed. "I only met Bodie yesterday. He does have charm, but he's not the guy I've been getting to know."

Getting to know, swooning over, same thing, right?

A thoughtful expression came over Mrs. Potter's face. "It's Wyatt. He's smart, like you. Plus, he could use some of your spunk."

Quinn laughed. She wasn't sure what Mrs. Potter meant by "spunk" but she would take it as a compliment. "His apartment is across the hall from mine. Makes not falling for the guy that much harder."

Mrs. Potter nodded. "Yes, any of those boys would be easy to fall for. That's wonderful to hear. What does your family think?"

Family? Gosh, they weren't even at the holding hands stage yet. "We're not dating. I hope we *end up* dating. But we aren't yet." Quinn hesitated before mentioning the next part. "And I haven't told my parents because my parents aren't around anymore. My mother passed away from breast cancer, my dad suffered a heart attack."

Even though it had happened quite a few years ago, it was still difficult to say out loud. Losing her parents had been the hardest periods of her life.

"Oh. I'm sorry to hear that."

"Thank you. It was a few years ago..." Not that time took away the pain. It dulled it somewhat. But didn't eliminate it completely.

"Do you have siblings?"

"Actually, Mason is my brother."

Mrs. Potter's brows lifted. "Mason from Marble Protection?"

"The one and only."

The other woman nodded, like she'd just worked out a piece of a puzzle. "I see it. It's in the eyes. Not just the color, the look. Like you really see the world and want to do your part to make it a bit better."

Quinn was pretty sure that described her brother more than it did her. "Mason's the do-gooder. I'm the handful. Where Mason always did what he was supposed to do, I've always been a bit more impulsive. A loose cannon, as some would describe."

"Some" being just about every teacher she'd ever had growing up.

Mrs. Potter didn't look so convinced. "I've only known you a short amount of time, but I wouldn't describe you as a 'loose cannon.' I would say that you seem confident. Hardworking. Not afraid of a challenge."

Quinn liked that description a heck of a lot better than what she'd said. "Thank you."

The other woman was really growing on Quinn. In a way, she reminded her of her mother. Kind. Easy to talk to. And she had a way of making people feel comfortable without even trying.

"I only speak the truth. Now, why don't you head off early."

Quinn glanced over at the clock. "My shift isn't supposed to finish for an hour."

"I won't tell if you don't."

Quinn laughed.

"We aren't busy, and I can close up on my own."

"Okay. If you're sure…"

"Go."

Quinn didn't need to be told a third time. Thanking Mrs. Potter, she grabbed her bag and headed out. She didn't actually have any plans this evening, so she didn't know what she would do with an extra hour. Would it be too much if she knocked on Wyatt's door to see if he wanted to hang out?

Smiling at the idea, she turned a corner. Her apartment wasn't far. Plus, the breeze was warm. It was a perfect afternoon to walk.

She'd almost made it home when a crackling noise sounded behind her. Like footsteps over leaves.

Turning her head, she frowned when she was greeted by an empty sidewalk.

Strange. Maybe it had been some kind of animal. A bird, perhaps? Or maybe she was losing her mind.

Shaking her head, she turned back—only to jump when she saw a figure standing in front of her.

"Holy crap! What the heck, Darren?"

The man stood there with his hands shoved in his pockets, not looking the least bit apologetic. "I thought you heard me, and that's why you stopped."

Placing her hand on her chest, she waited for her heart rate to slow. "I stopped because I heard *something*. I didn't expect to turn around to find you less than a foot away."

He lifted a shoulder. "Sorry."

She almost scoffed. The man was far from sorry. "What are you doing here? Shouldn't you be on your way to the airport? Tanya said you were leaving tonight."

"I am. My flight leaves in a couple of hours."

And he'd decided to spend his last hours in Marble Falls stalking her?

Stepping around him, she continued walking home. If he wanted to talk to her, let her in on some of those secrets he was keeping, he could follow.

"Are you here to tell me the real reason it's so important to you that I don't research the story?" Not that it mattered. One way or another, she was going to find out.

"Yes."

Quinn's feet stopped. Yes? As in, Darren was finally going to tell her the truth?

"Okay. Tell me."

"The truth is, the people responsible for the break-in are dangerous. That's why you need to stop."

Quinn almost rolled her eyes. That was a no-brainer. "I know that already."

"Do you?" Darren took a step forward and for a moment, fear flashed across his face before he cleared it. "Do you know they're so dangerous they could tear your arm off in under a second? So fast, you could never even dream of outrunning them? These aren't people you want to mess with, Quinn. They're barely people. I'm trying to help you."

So it *was* true. Darren had just confirmed what Maya had told her. That men who posed irrevocable, unstoppable danger on society existed.

"How do you know that?"

He shook his head. "Does it matter?"

Absolutely. "Yes. It does."

"Are you even listening to what I'm saying? They'll kill you!"

Quinn was listening. The man was saying he *still* wouldn't tell her the role he played in all this. "Does Tanya know what you know?"

"No. This has nothing to do with her."

At the aggression in his voice, a spark of anger shot through Quinn. Tanya was his wife, yet he'd never treated her well. Like she was too stupid to understand anything important.

"Thank you for your warning. If that's all the information you have for me, I need to go."

She took a step toward her apartment but stopped when Darren yanked her back by the arm. "Are you going to stop researching this or not?"

"Get your arrogant, egotistical hand off me."

"Quinn—"

"I don't have to tell you anything. You're not my boss anymore. But you want to know my opinion on the whole matter? If men like that exist, people have a right to know. So make your own deductions about whether I'm researching the story."

Anger washed over his face. When his hand tightened, pain ricocheted up her arm.

Shooting a knee up, she kicked him between the legs.

Darren released her arm before keeling over and grunting in pain.

"You touch me again, and I'll do worse. Go back to New York and don't even think about contacting me again."

Turning, Quinn continued to her apartment. She heard Darren's voice calling her from behind, but she ignored him. The man was the biggest ass she'd ever met in her life.

Why couldn't he just tell her how he knew about these men?

She was tempted to call Tanya right there and then and tell her exactly what had happened. The only problem was, she'd have to tell her friend why Darren had acted the way he did. And she did not want to drag her friend into the middle of this story.

If Tanya didn't know anything about these men, the last thing Quinn wanted to do was inform her. It could potentially put her life in danger.

Quinn was still huffing and puffing when she reached her apartment. She'd taken a step inside her place when the door behind her opened.

"Something bothering you?"

Something? Try someone.

Breathing out a frustrated breath, Quinn spun around and attempted a smile. She was sure it looked completely wrong. "Just contemplating the stupidity of men."

"Surely not all of us? I'm a man. I like to think I teeter closer to intelligence than stupidity."

Quinn would agree with that. The man in front of her seemed

different from the one she'd just left in many ways. "The only way I'll work out if that's true is if I spend more time with you. Want to come over for a movie night tonight?"

The moment the question left her mouth, she knew it was a good decision. She needed something to take her mind off Darren and the story that was going nowhere fast.

One side of Wyatt's mouth lifted. "I'd love to."

"Great. Oh, and by movie night, I meant movie and dinner." Anything to prolong her time with him.

Wyatt nodded. "Of course."

"I'm a terrible cook, but we could order in?"

"It's the company that makes the night."

God, the guy was a charmer. "How about you pick the movie and I choose dinner?"

"Done. I'll just finish up what I'm doing and come back."

"Great." She was about to close her door when she stopped. "Oh, and one more thing. No sappy, overly fake romantic comedies."

His brows lifted. "Not a fan...?"

"Of cliché story lines, predictable endings, and pathetic male leads? Not even a bit."

CHAPTER 8

Quinn flicked her gaze from the TV to Wyatt, then back again.

The man wasn't touching her. Not even close. In fact, an entire person could fit between them on the couch.

She'd sat down first, expecting him to sit close. He hadn't. He'd sat down on the *other* end. At least a shoulder-to-shoulder touch would be better than the ridiculous distance between them.

She could always move closer to him, but now it would just seem weird. And it didn't explain why he hadn't sat next to her.

Was it possible she smelled bad? She'd jumped in the shower as soon as she'd gotten home, but it had been quick. Plus, she probably hadn't spent as much time washing as usual because she'd spent the entire time thinking of different ways to maim Darren if he ever got close to her again.

"Did I choose the wrong movie?"

No. You chose the wrong seat.

Quinn drew her attention back to Wyatt. If she was honest, she had no idea what was going on with the movie. Not a single clue. "Sorry, I'm a bit distracted."

"A bit" was one big fat understatement.

"What's got you distracted?"

The story. Her old boss. Why the heck Wyatt was still so damn far away from her. "It's nothing."

Wyatt's expression didn't change. He just sat there looking perfect, waiting for her to spill her guts. Wasn't going to happen.

"Okay."

When his attention flicked back to the screen, a moment of irritation swirled through her. The man didn't even attempt to scoot closer. There was no sneaky arm around the back of the couch. No subtle shuffle. Nothing.

"So, tell me, why no romance movies?" he asked.

Quinn scoffed. "They fill women's heads with lies, giving them unrealistic expectations of dating in the real world."

Wyatt chuckled. "That's a bold statement. Give me an example."

Had the man never watched a romance movie?

"Okay, how about the grand gestures of love, which are painted as normal. Flying the woman to Europe at a moment's notice, organizing flash mobs, filling rooms with a thousand roses. That's not real. Men don't do that."

His attention remained on the TV. "Some guys probably do that. Maybe you haven't been spending time with the right men."

Well, that was a given. "Come on, do you know anyone who's done any of those things?"

Wyatt's silence gave her the answer she was looking for.

"Romance today is a card and a kiss on Valentine's Day. A bouquet of flowers on an anniversary. And that's if you're lucky."

Wyatt lifted his shoulder. "Women could always go the extra mile for the man."

"Oh, I'm sure they do. However, when the reciprocation stops, so do the gestures."

His brows pulled together. "I didn't know you were such a pessimist."

"I prefer the term realist." She gave Wyatt an innocent smile. It did kind of sound like she hated men. And romance. And love. Which wasn't true at all. She just preferred the real and the raw. It saved her from disappointment. "Take us, for example," Quinn continued. "In any romance movie, the guy would not be sitting so far from the girl."

And close proximity on a movie night wasn't even a large expectation. Not in Quinn's mind, at least.

"You'd like me to sit closer?"

"Yes." She'd prefer the man to be a *lot* closer. "I'd also like to know if I smell bad."

Wyatt wrinkled his nose in confusion. "You don't smell bad. You smell good. Really good. It's actually a large reason for the distance."

Smelling good didn't sound like a reason for distance to her. "Why would me smelling good make you want to sit over there?"

"Because the closer I am, the more I want to touch you. And if I start touching you, I probably won't be able to stop."

A warmth heated in Quinn's chest. "And why is that a bad thing?" It only sounded good to Quinn. Really good.

Wyatt ran a hand through his hair. It was the first time she'd seen him look uncomfortable. Like he didn't want to tell her the reason.

Then it hit Quinn. "It's because of my brother, isn't it?"

When Wyatt's silence continued, Quinn knew she'd hit the nail on the head.

Blowing out a frustrated breath, she began to stand, but stopped at Wyatt's hand on hers.

"I like you. A lot. But your brother is like family to me. I feel like I should speak to him first, preferably in person, before anything happens between us."

Quinn loved her brother. But he had no place in this relationship. He had no place in this *room*. "If you like me, kiss me."

A muscle ticked in Wyatt's jaw. "Quinn..." His voice was strained.

She leaned forward and snaked her fingers through his hair. A smile flirted across her lips. "I like you, you like me, and I'd like you to kiss me."

He watched her for another beat. She could almost see the internal battle raging inside him. Then his head lowered...

And when his lips touched hers, desire whipped through her body. Her limbs grew heavy.

The touch was tentative. Light. She wanted more. She wanted all of Wyatt.

Climbing onto his lap, Quinn straddled his thighs, his hardness immediately pushing against her core.

It did nothing to still her racing heart.

Quinn explored his mouth. Nipping and teasing. Her hands ran through his hair, pulling his head closer.

When his tongue snaked its way through her lips, she couldn't help the soft groan that escaped her throat. Need rippled through her fast and hard.

Their tongues danced while her breasts pressed to his chest. It was a tantalizing combination.

Wyatt's lips began their slow exploration down her cheek and jaw, before landing on her neck. She tilted her head back to give him better access.

Holy heck, his lips were magic. She almost had to remind herself to breathe.

At the feel of his warm hands touching the bare skin of her stomach, a quiver shot through her body. Her skin was overly sensitized to his touch. And she wanted to feel him against every inch of her.

At the tug of her sweater, Quinn lifted her arms. When she sat there in just a bra covering her top half, Quinn leaned in again... but was stopped by Wyatt's hands.

Forcing her eyes to focus, she noticed he was staring at something. Something on her upper arm. The lust seemed to fade from his face.

Glancing down to where he was looking, she saw it. Blue and black bruising marred her skin. It was in the shape of a hand.

Ah, hell.

"Who did this?"

She attempted to push off his lap, but the hands on her hips held her firm.

"It's from the other day, when Darren was here."

Wyatt's eyes narrowed. Crap. He knew that wasn't true. "Don't lie to me, Quinn. These bruises are fresh. Someone had their hands on you today. Who?"

He knew that just from looking at the marks? And what was with the guy demanding information from her?

"Wyatt, I'd like to get up now."

His hold on her hips released, and when she stood, he stood too. Grabbing her sweater, Quinn quickly tugged it over her head.

"Was it him?"

Her gaze shot up to Wyatt's. She was trying to remain calm, but the guy's demanding tone was beginning to grate on her. "It's none of your business, Wyatt."

She took a step toward the door—and suddenly Wyatt stood in front of her.

What the...the man was damn quick for someone so big.

"Okay, it was Darren. Happy?"

"Not even close. So he's still in town. Why?"

She didn't like the way the guy was talking to her one bit, but clearly he wasn't going to let it lie until she told him. "He should be on a plane right now, flying back to New York. And yes, he was asking me if I'd dropped the story. When I wouldn't confirm that I had, he grabbed me."

Fury flashed over Wyatt's face.

Quinn held up her hands. "Before you get ahead of yourself, I kicked him in the balls and walked away. I'm safe. I took care of myself. And now he's gone."

Wyatt ran a hand through his hair. He looked like he had the weight of the world on his shoulders. "You said you'd tell me if he came back."

That was true. "I took care of it. So I didn't see the point in stressing you out."

Because the guy was clearly stressed and agitated by the whole thing.

Quinn crossed her arms over her chest. A moment ago, she'd been wrapped around Wyatt's big, heated body. Now she just felt cold. "Maybe you should go."

Her words seemed to snap him out of his anger. Clearing his features, he lifted a hand and touched her cheek. Even though she was frustrated at how the evening had ended, she couldn't help but lean into him.

"I could stay for a bit."

If he'd said those words a few moments ago, in the midst of their kissing, she would have been ecstatic. But the only reason he was saying them now was because he was worried about her safety.

"I'll be okay. Darren will be back in New York by morning, and even if he isn't, I'm not worried. We both know this apartment has a very good security system if I was in danger."

Which she didn't think she was.

Wyatt didn't look so convinced, but still he conceded. "Okay."

She expected him to turn and leave. He didn't. Instead, he dropped his head and pressed his lips to hers. The kiss was sweet. And over way too quickly.

"Lock the door behind me."

Then he left. She had no doubt that in a few seconds, Wyatt would be in his apartment, researching Darren. Making sure he got on the plane.

Walking to the door, Quinn locked it before resting her head against the wood.

Tonight, while he'd been kissing her, she'd felt something. Something new and real. And she wished that none of the drama in her life had interrupted.

CHAPTER 9

*D*arren never got on the plane. The asshole was still here. The question was, where? So far, Wyatt had searched all the accommodations in Marble Falls, including inns, motels, and short-term rentals. He'd found nothing booked in the guy's name.

Next, he'd looked into all car rental services. Again, absolutely nothing. Wyatt had even recruited Evie's help to track the guy's credit card and phone. He wasn't using any of them.

Leaning back in his seat, Wyatt ran his hands through his hair as he glanced around the Marble Protection office. The guy had put his hands on Quinn twice. Wyatt wanted eyes on him. He wanted to know why he hadn't gotten on the plane.

Wyatt had spoken to Mason this morning, expressing his concerns about her ex-boss. They'd both agreed that, until their questions were answered, it was best to have someone from the team keep eyes on her.

Even though Wyatt hadn't spoken to his friend about his deepening relationship with Quinn, he was almost certain Mason suspected something was going on. Hell, he might have even expected something to happen.

Mason hadn't questioned Wyatt on how he knew about the bruises. Just like he hadn't asked how Wyatt knew Darren was still in town.

Either way, Wyatt would need to tell the man everything soon enough. In the meantime, his focus needed to be on ensuring Quinn's safety.

She didn't know it, but today, Kye was watching her apartment. He would also be trailing her to work.

Glancing at the time, Wyatt cursed under his breath. He'd spent the entire morning researching Darren and had made no progress.

About to switch off the laptop, Wyatt stopped when an email popped up. An email from Sinclair. The agent from the CIA who Wyatt and his team had been working with to shut down Project Arma.

Clicking into it, he scanned the contents, a heavy weight of guilt settling in his gut.

He opened the attached image. And not only did the guilt intensify, but a strong urge to get up and punch something consumed him.

Pushing back from the desk, he scrubbed his hands over his face. There was the small possibility this *wasn't* his fault. He hoped like hell that was the case. Chances were slim.

Lifting his phone, Wyatt sent a quick message to his team. Not everyone was at Marble Protection, but whoever was would join him in the office. Everyone else would be updated later.

While he waited, Wyatt printed off the image. It wasn't until Luca, Eden, Oliver, and Bodie took seats at the table that he dragged his eyes away from the picture in his hand.

Kye was the first to speak. "What's happening?"

Wyatt pushed the image to the center of the table. All four men leaned forward to look at it. A mixture of horror and anger flashing across their faces.

"Who is it?" Luca asked.

"And who the hell did it?" Eden added.

Wyatt shut the laptop in front of him. He didn't need to see the email any longer. He knew how it read. The picture of the decapitated man in the middle of the table was a big enough reminder.

"Jack Nettle." Wyatt wasn't surprised by the blank stares he received. Even though this man had helped them numerous times, it was only Wyatt who'd been in contact with him. "I sent him Striker's blood sample after he was drugged with Toved. He analyzed it and sent us a list of the ingredients."

Toved was a drug designed by Project Arma. Asher had been the first to be drugged with it. It had sent him into a murderous rage.

Luckily, the guys had been able to subdue him. They'd also been able to take a blood sample. Jack had studied that sample.

"Not only that, but when we wanted another set of eyes on Fletcher's blood, he was the man we sent the sample to."

Kye leaned forward. "You must have known him well to trust him with the samples."

"We've been friends since high school. He's a good guy. The only guy I trusted to get us the results we needed." And now Wyatt couldn't help but feel he might be responsible for his friend's death.

The smile Bodie usually wore was gone. "How did you get this picture of him?"

By not taking no for an answer.

"Jack and I keep in regular contact. I hadn't heard from him in over a week, so I reached out to his family. Said I was an old friend." His sister had been distraught on the phone. It had torn Wyatt up. "They told me he'd died."

"Do they know how?" Luca asked.

That was where it got prickly. "The family was told car accident."

The men scoffed, almost in unison.

"I wanted proof he was dead. So I contacted Sinclair." The man had access to a lot of information. If anyone could confirm his death, it was him. "I demanded evidence. He emailed me that. When I demanded the real cause of death, he told me it was a workplace break-in. Some drugs were also stolen."

The drug theft could easily have been a ruse to cover the real reason they were there—to kill Jack.

"Jack worked at the Salina Pharmaceutical Drug Lab," Wyatt continued. "While I was waiting for word from Sinclair, I looked into some of his coworkers. Two others died on the same night."

Kye's eyes narrowed. "So, why wasn't his family told the truth?"

"My guess? Because Sinclair connected it to us and didn't want the story to become public knowledge."

Eden swore under his breath. "Would it be possible for Hylar to link Jack to you?"

"It would be damn hard. I've installed the highest security on my devices. Hylar wouldn't be able to hack my phone or email. Jack's email or phone could have been hacked, but Hylar would have needed to suspect him to begin with. He would have needed to know about the connection between me and Jack first."

What was the other alternative? That Hylar had hacked every single scientist in the country—in the *world* even—before randomly coming across Jack's connection to Wyatt? That wasn't logical.

Oliver's eyes remained on the image as he spoke. "You said Jack was a friend from high school. Maybe Hylar has people rifling through our lives, right back to school years. They could be trying to cut our ties with people who could help us."

That was a possibility, but again, it would be damn time consuming. Unless he had an army of people working for him. Which Wyatt didn't think he had. Not after they'd raided his facility.

"The guys who killed him clearly didn't care about raising suspicion," Bodie added. "Maybe it wasn't Hylar's men."

Wyatt preferred that scenario. Because that would mean none of the blame lay on him. The way he had died though…it raised a lot of suspicion.

Blowing out a long breath, Wyatt rubbed his eyes. "Jack was a good guy. He didn't deserve this shit."

"Jobs. This is not your fault, so get that out of your head right now. Do you even know for sure that he's dead because of his connection to us?"

Wyatt looked over at Luca. He *didn't* know that. "The way Jack died, in combination with his connection to us…"

"Still not your fault." Oliver shook his head. "Just like it's not our fault that we're caught in the middle of a war with an underground organization that altered our DNA. A hundred percent of the blame for all of it lies with *them*."

The other three guys nodded in agreement.

Wyatt appreciated their support but still felt like hell, guilt almost suffocating him.

~

QUINN WAS JUST GETTING ready for work when her phone rang from the kitchen. Her brows lifted in surprise when she saw it was Maya.

Yes. This was the call she'd been waiting for. Quinn had been trying to reach the woman for days with no success.

"Maya?"

"They did it again." Maya's words were rushed, her underlying panic and fear thick through the line.

"Who did what, Maya?"

"Them! I have a friend in Salina. She said she could help me. I was going to go stay with her for a bit. I told her about what I saw, but she didn't believe me!"

Maya spoke so quickly, her words were running into each other. Quinn could barely understand the woman.

"Calm down. Take some deep breaths and tell me what happened."

"She's dead!" A sob sounded through the line. "Her mother told me when I reached out to the family."

Oh, crap. Crap crap crap. Not again.

"And I can feel eyes on me," she continued. "It might be in my head. I don't know. I don't know anything anymore, other than I don't think I'm safe here. I have to leave town again. Disappear for good this time!"

Quinn scrambled to think of a solution. She wanted to help the other woman. She *needed* to. Not just because of the story, and not just because she'd said she would, but because no one else was helping her.

"Wait. Give me your address and I'll come get you. I've got work today, but I'll come tomorrow."

There was a pause across the line. That was okay, a pause was good. It meant Maya was considering Quinn's offer instead of instantly dismissing it.

"Please, Maya. Let me help you."

Maya's voice was shaky when she spoke again. "Okay."

Relief hit Quinn hard. She was too late to help the last wave of victims, but maybe, just maybe, she could help Maya.

As Maya rattled off her address. Quinn grabbed a piece of paper and a pen from the kitchen drawer and wrote it down. It would be a long drive, but as long as she got to the other woman, helped her, that was what mattered.

Quinn also wrote the name of the company where her friend had lived and worked. She would research the pharmaceutical company later.

"Got it. I'll leave first thing tomorrow morning."

"And, Quinn...there's something else."

Quinn waited for Maya to tell her. There was an air of danger to the silence.

"I should have told you this already. I don't know why I didn't. Maybe because I was scared. Or maybe I just didn't trust you as much then."

"It's okay, Maya, you can tell me anything."

"The guys who broke into Novac...they stole a lot, but they seemed interested in two particular materials. They specifically asked about them. Rare materials that we don't keep much of in the US. They filled their bags with those ingredients first, then they just shoved a whole lot of other stuff in. Almost like they were trying to cover up what they really wanted."

"Can you recall the materials they asked for?"

"Yes." Maya recounted the names of two pharmaceutical components Quinn had never heard of. She asked for the correct spelling, not wanting to make any mistakes.

"Those materials are in such short supply, there are very few labs that stock them. New York, Alabama, and Salina all did." Maya paused. "If you can find the last labs that stock them, I think they'll be the next targets."

CHAPTER 10

*Q*uinn studied the sky through the bakery window.

It was dark. Dark and gloomy.

There was a storm due this evening. Buckets of rain and heavy winds were expected. Based on the gray clouds, the storm wasn't far off.

Quinn couldn't wait. She loved storms. She was already picturing herself snuggled under some blankets on the couch, hot chocolate in hand. Or better yet, snuggled under Wyatt's big, muscular arm.

Maybe, if the guy agreed to another movie night, this one might go a little smoother.

When the door to the bakery opened, Quinn moved behind the counter. Mrs. Potter was in the back baking, and Quinn only planned to disturb the woman if she absolutely had to.

Two men and two women entered the café, one of the women holding a baby.

The women were beautiful. The first with radiant red hair and the second with a unique splattering of freckles across her nose.

The men were just as large as Wyatt and Mason. Quinn

wouldn't be surprised to learn they were part owners of Marble Protection. After all, there were still three men who she had yet to meet.

"Hi there, I'm Quinn. What can I get you today?"

The girl with brown hair and freckles was the one to answer. "Hey! I'm Shylah and this is my boyfriend Eden." She touched the arm of the tallest man before turning to the other two. "This is Asher, the baby dada, and Lexie, the baby mama, holding their little smoosh-face, Fletcher."

Quinn couldn't stop the smile that spread across her lips at the sight of the chubby infant. She wasn't typically a baby person, but she had to admit, he was damn cute.

"Nice to meet everyone." When Quinn looked up, she was again taken by Lexie's long red hair. "Your hair is stunning."

The woman smiled. "Thank you. All natural. Although I wouldn't be surprised if a few grays have snuck in since Fletch here was born."

Asher wrapped his arm around her waist. "Red hair, gray hair, it would all look beautiful on you."

Quinn wanted to melt to the floor at the man's words. How. Freaking. Sweet.

"And you're Eagle's sister?"

Quinn looked up at Eden. He wore the most intense expression. "That I am. I guess he told you?"

Shylah leaned forward. "They all know everything about their team. I wouldn't question it."

Yep. Quinn knew that was true. That was why, the moment Wyatt had left her place last night, she'd gotten on the phone to tell her brother about the bruise on her arm.

No way did she want Wyatt to rat her out again. He would probably make the entire thing bigger than it was.

Luckily, she was also able to tell Mason that Darren was leaving that night so there was no need to worry.

The last thing she needed was Mason marching into town and

forcing answers out of her. He was well-trained. But he was no match for men with superspeed and strength. And if she told him about her research, there was a definite possibility he would put himself in danger.

Pushing the thought to the back of her mind for the moment, Quinn gave her full attention to the people in front of her. "If you're here for coffees, I should warn you, I'm not the best barista. If there were learning plates for people in my position, I would be wearing them. I could ask Mrs. Potter to come out—"

"Don't be silly," Lexie cut in. "As long as there's caffeine in the cups, we'll be fine."

Quinn was liking these people already. "Done. So, four coffees. Anything else?"

The women laughed like Quinn had just told a joke, whereas the men shook their heads.

Asher turned to Eden. "Imagine if the women came to Mrs. Potter's Bakehouse and *just* ordered coffee."

"I would die of shock," Eden muttered.

Lexie looked up at the big men with a stern expression. "You mock all you want. I've never seen either of you step out of here without food in your hand or full bellies."

Asher shrugged his shoulders while Eden grunted. Quinn hid a chuckle at the alpha men being put in their place.

The women pointed out the pastries they'd like and Quinn began plating them. When Lexie and Shylah were done, Quinn tried to hide her shock. Tried and failed.

Twelve. They'd chosen twelve different pastries to share between the four of them. "Are you guys going to be able to finish all these?"

If they said yes and followed through, she would be surprised. Surprised and impressed.

Shylah threw her head back and laughed. "Good heavens, no. What we don't eat now becomes dessert tonight."

Asher scoffed. "If it lasts the trip home."

"Women who don't count their calories. I think you're my kind of people," Quinn joked.

Lexie chuckled as she shifted Fletcher in her arms. "Life's too short to count calories."

Shylah nodded. "Damn straight."

That had always been Quinn's thinking. "Take a seat. I'll get the coffees ready, then bring it all out to you."

As Quinn made a start on the drinks, Mrs. Potter stuck her head out of the kitchen. "Do you need help?"

"I'm okay, but I'll come get you if that changes."

Which was a likely scenario. But, who knew, maybe she would make four coffees without so much as burning the milk.

Mrs. Potter nodded and disappeared again.

"Need any help?"

Quinn almost jumped a whole foot at Shylah's voice right beside her. It was lucky the milk had remained in the pitcher. "You move just like my brother. Silently."

"I wish I was that slick."

Yeah, Quinn too. "I should be okay. Thanks for offering."

As Quinn went back to making the coffees, she expected Shylah to move back to the table. Instead, she leaned her hip against the counter.

"How are you finding Marble Falls?"

A heck of a lot better than she'd expected. "Surprisingly, I'm really enjoying it."

Shylah tilted her head to the side. "Surprisingly?"

"I thought I'd be so bored in a small town. Not just that, I thought I'd lose my mind without my job as a journalist." Yet here she was, mind fully in place.

"Bet you investigated lots of awesome stories while in New York." There was excitement in the other woman's eyes.

Quinn lifted a shoulder. "I don't know if I'd use the word awesome. I worked the crime beat, and it always frustrated me how often the bad guys got away. Sometimes, catching the perpe-trators of the crimes seemed near impossible for police."

Actually, more than sometimes. Quinn always wanted to see justice follow an injustice. Unfortunately, that wasn't always the case.

The smile fell from Shylah's lips. "Oh, I bet. The guys are always frustrated that they can never quite catch their enemies. It's heartbreaking to watch. At least your bad guys don't have superhuman speed, right? Wouldn't be able to get away so easily."

At those words, Quinn almost dropped the pitcher of milk. Swinging her eyes to Shylah, she studied the other woman. "Did you say superhuman speed?"

"Yeah, because..." Shylah paused, a frown marring her brows. "Don't you...I mean, I thought..." A moment of panic crossed over the other woman's face as she struggled with her words.

Placing the pitcher on the counter, Quinn took a step toward her. "Shylah, did you just say that the guys are chasing an enemy with *superhuman speed*?"

Shylah opened her mouth but no words came out.

"Shy!" They both swung their heads around at Eden's voice. "You got a message on your phone."

"Coming." Shylah gave Quinn an apologetic look before moving back to the table.

Quinn was slow to get back to what she was doing. Shylah's statement was rolling around in her mind, creating more ques-tions than answers.

Had her words just been a figure of speech? Or was it possible that Mason and Wyatt knew that men with superspeed existed?

Not only existed, Shylah had used the word "enemy."

Did her brother have enemies that he was hunting? Could those enemies be the same people who broke into the pharma-ceutical companies?

Turning back to the coffees, she finished what she was doing, surprisingly not making a single error. Surprising because her mind was anywhere but on the task at hand.

A couple minutes later, Quinn carried the first two coffees to the table. Asher immediately jumped up and grabbed the remaining drinks from the counter. He also helped Quinn carry the pastries.

Pushing what Shylah had said to the back of her mind, Quinn plastered a smile to her face. "Thanks for the help. Marble Fallers are crazy helpful. Wyatt helped me with his order the other day, Shylah just offered to help make the coffees, and now you've helped me serve."

"What can I say," Shylah shrugged, "we're a friendly bunch."

Lexie shook her head. "Don't be fooled, Shylah has no idea how to use that machine. She would have been zero help."

Shylah leaned back like she was offended. "Maybe that's true, but I would have given it a crack. I have a can-do attitude. Anyway, Quinn, how's your brother? We miss him and Sage."

"He's okay. We've texted each other a bit, but that's it. I think he's pretty invested in making sure Sage spends time with her brother. I don't know the entire story there. Just that they've been separated for a while."

The entire group nodded.

Shylah leaned forward. "Did he tell you that Eden and I have Nunzie and Dizzie?"

He definitely did. When her brother had told her he wouldn't be in town, the first question she'd asked was who was looking after the dogs. Because she was *not* a dog person. Far from it. She had zero faith in her ability to keep animals alive.

"I'm glad it's you and not me."

Eden shook his head. "I'm not."

Shylah hit him lightly on the shoulder. "They're cute."

"Is the mess they make cute?"

And that right there was another reason she did not want to look after them. She could barely clean up after herself.

Asher put his hand on Eden's shoulder. "This is why I live in an apartment, my friend." He glanced out the window, then at Quinn. "I hope you're getting home before the storm comes in."

Quinn looked out the window again. If possible, the sky had gotten even darker. "The storm is supposed to hit around six. I'm hoping to get out of here at five and hightail it home."

Boy, was she glad that she'd driven to work today.

"Well, I'm going to start cleaning up. Call me over if you need anything."

Smiling at the group, she made her way back. The moment she stood behind the counter again, her thoughts went back to Mason. To Wyatt. To the men who were strong enough to throw an adult across a room and kill them on impact.

Quinn was almost certain that her story and what Shylah had said couldn't possibly be related. She was probably just so invested in this whole thing that she'd misunderstood what the other woman meant.

Then why did she have this uneasy feeling in her gut?

Nibbling on her bottom lip, Quinn eyed her bag for a few seconds before moving to it. Pulling out her phone, she dialed Mason's number. She'd ask him if he knew anything about men with superspeed. About whether he had superhuman enemies. He would say no, call her crazy, and that would be that. Easy.

Only Mason didn't answer. The call went straight to voicemail.

Okay. So she couldn't ask Mason. Not right now, anyway. And even if she did ask him, there was a possibility, a huge possibility, that he wouldn't tell her the truth. The man had spent most of his life trying to shield her from danger.

Wyatt might be the same.

Maybe there was another way to find the information she needed…A possibly dumb way, considering the current weather. But when the hell had bad weather stopped Quinn from getting to the bottom of a story?

WYATT WAS JUST PUSHING through the door to his apartment when his phone began to ring. Dropping some grocery bags on the kitchen counter, he fished it out of his pocket. Mason's name flashed across the screen.

"Eagle, what's going on?"

Just as the words left his mouth, loud thunder echoed through the apartment. The storm was rolling in early.

"That sounded close," Mason said across the line.

He wasn't wrong. "It was. Has it hit Lockhart yet?"

As if on cue, more thunder sounded, followed by heavy rain.

"It has. We're in the thick of it." There was a small pause. "Have you seen Quinn this afternoon?"

Wyatt frowned at the concern in his friend's voice. "No. I've been at Marble Protection all day and am only just getting home now."

"Okay. Hunter called to give me a heads-up that Shylah might have accidentally told Quinn we have enemies. Less-than-human enemies." Wyatt cursed under his breath. "I also had a missed call from her. I tried calling her back, but the calls are going straight to messages. I called Kye, because you mentioned he was trailing her today. He was following her car at the time and said she looked like she was heading to my place."

Wyatt immediately went on alert. He hoped like hell she was safe in her apartment, because there was no way she should be out driving in this weather.

"Give me a sec, I'll check if she's back."

"Thanks. I never got around to taking my spare key back. Do you still have it?"

Damn, Wyatt had almost forgotten about that. He'd meant to return it to Mason when Quinn moved in, but had never gotten around to it.

Moving to his study, he opened the safe and spotted the key

immediately. Grabbing it, Wyatt headed across the hall. He knocked on the door, then stopped to listen. There were no sounds coming from the other side. But then, the rain was pelting down, drowning out a lot.

He lifted the phone back to his ear. "I can't hear her, but the wind and rain are loud. I'm going to check to be sure."

"Thanks."

Unlocking the door, he walked inside and did a quick check of every room.

No Quinn.

"She's not here."

Mason cursed across the line.

Kye was with her, and Wyatt trusted his friend. He still wanted eyes on her himself, though.

He was about to walk out, only to stop when something on the kitchen counter caught his attention. Taking a step closer, a frown marred his brow. It was a piece of paper with Salina Pharmaceutical Drug Lab written on it, as well as a couple of words Wyatt had never seen before. Pharmaceutical ingredients, maybe?

What the hell is this? Does it have something to do with the story she's working on?

"Eagle, has Quinn mentioned anything to you about the story that lost her her job?"

There was a brief pause before Mason answered. "Just that it involved a theft. She said she'd stopped looking into it."

"Did you mention anything to her about John or Salina Pharmaceutical Drug Lab?"

"No. I don't talk to Quinn about Project Arma. What's going on, Jobs?"

Was it possible the story she was working on, the one that she got fired for, was connected to them?

"She scribbled the name of the lab on a piece of paper."

Mason was silent. Wyatt started moving.

"I'm going to your place. Make sure she's okay. Later, I'll get answers."

"Make sure she's safe, Jobs. Safe from the storm...and also, from our kind."

It was rare for Wyatt to hear his friend nervous. But he was. Probably as nervous as Wyatt.

"Already done."

Hanging up, Wyatt went back to his place and grabbed his keys. He had a whole lot of questions that needed answering. But first, he had to know that she was okay.

CHAPTER 11

*S*witching off the engine, Quinn watched the rain fall.

Okay. She was here. Here at her brother's house to snoop through his things. To find out if he knew anything about these not-quite-human men.

She wasn't sure if she was hoping to find something or not.

Instead of getting straight out, Quinn spent a full minute watching the downpour outside. She would like to think it was because she loved the sound of the rain, but really, she was working up the courage to get out and walk through it.

Maybe if she moved fast enough, she wouldn't get wet. Was that how it worked?

Or *maybe*, if she sat and watched the rain long enough, it would stop. That seemed like wishful thinking. And the weatherman would probably agree. He'd predicted torrential rains until morning.

Glancing at her phone, she let out a sigh. Still dead. It died just before her shift had finished. She really needed to grab a car charger. Either that, or just charge her phone before work and not try to rely on twenty percent to get her through the day.

Glancing back at the house, she sucked in a deep breath.

Okay. Suck it up, Quinn. A little rain never hurt anyone.

The spare key was kept in a lockbox on the side of his house. The very *unshaded* side of the house. There was no way she could save herself from getting soaked.

When she'd first arrived in town, Quinn had needed to get into his place to grab the key to the apartment. Her brother had explained where the key was hidden over the phone, since he'd left for Lockhart just before her arrival.

She laughed when she saw it. No one would have known it was a lockbox. It was recessed into the wall and positioned behind a bush.

She still remembered wondering if he really needed *that* much security. At the time she hadn't thought so. If it turned out these men were enemies of her brother's, then yes. Yes, it was needed and probably more.

Placing her hand on the door handle, she said a silent prayer that she wouldn't be drowned, then climbed outside.

The rain hit her like a freight train. It was fast and frenzied and threatened to push her to the ground. Gritting her teeth, Quinn ran to the side of the house. She stumbled twice along the way, barely saving herself from landing in pools of mud.

Lifting wet fingers, Quinn took her time typing the password. Knowing Mason, if a mistake was made, something terrible would happen. The place would probably become impenetrable. Maybe a huge alarm and sirens would sound.

Thankfully, she didn't make a mistake. The pad opened and Quinn swiped the key. Good. One more run through the storm, then she would be in.

She was almost at the front door when her foot slid and she hit the ground with a thud.

Dammit.

Her hip took the brunt of the fall. It hurt like hell. Ignoring the pain, she pushed to her feet and ran the few remaining steps to the door. Unlocking it, she pushed through.

Once inside, she stepped up to Mason's home alarm and typed in the code. Another layer of security.

Once the door was shut, Quinn shook her arms. Water dripped from every inch of her body. Anyone looking at her would think she'd just stepped out of the ocean. As well as being wet, she was damn cold.

Switching on the light, she went to the kitchen and grabbed the towel off the oven. A tea towel wasn't optimal, but at least it would partially dry her until she got upstairs.

Stripping off her heavy, wet sweatshirt, she dried as much of her body as possible. Her T-shirt stuck to her chest. Jeepers. The moment she got home, she would be stripping off every piece of clothing and climbing straight into a warm bath. Maybe with a glass of wine. The couch with a blanket just wasn't going to cut it anymore.

She'd only visited Mason's home the one time. Just like last time, she was in awe of the space. She could not for the life of her figure out why the man needed two stories, five bedrooms and a ton of acres.

Did he plan to have four kids and a farm full of animals?

Hanging the towel back on the oven, Quinn moved to the living room. Okay, so the question was, where would Mason keep top-secret information on superhuman enemies? Office, right? Wasn't that where everyone kept important information?

Moving up the stairs, Quinn stepped into the office. She would be quick and efficient. She needed to get home before the storm got worse and the roads became undrivable. Starting with the desk drawers, she systematically worked her way through the room.

Drawers, cupboard shelves, little nooks in the furniture...she checked everything.

Ten minutes later, she had nothing. Nothing but bills, receipts, and home documents. None of which meant anything to her. She had discovered a wall safe but there was no way she'd be able to access the thing. What a waste of a trip.

To make matters worse, this entire misadventure made her reflect on just how vague Mason had been about the details of his life since getting out of the Navy.

Including—why had he left the Navy in the first place? Why his whole team had left?

He'd told her it was because their missions had taken a toll on him—emotionally and physically. Which made sense. She couldn't imagine what those guys might have gone through. The things they would have been required to do for their country.

At the same time, he'd always loved that stuff. And he was the kind of guy who rose to a challenge.

Quinn had meant to look into it. Question him further. Make sure everything was okay. Only, she hadn't. She'd been thousands of miles away and her job had all but consumed her life.

Guilt ate at her that she hadn't made time for Mason. He was the only family she had left.

When he returned, she would make sure she talked to him. *Really* talked to him. About him leaving the Navy. About this whole enemy with superspeed thing. With no distractions. She wanted to see his face when he spoke to her. He thought he was good at keeping his emotions masked, but he wasn't. Not from her, at least.

Since their parents had passed away, Mason and she had never lived in the same state. When their mother passed, he'd wanted to return home. But he'd been nearing the end of his BUD/S training. There was no way she or their father was letting him walk away from that.

Only a few years later, their father had his heart attack.

Losing a second parent, her last parent, was the hardest time in Quinn's life. That's when she'd moved to New York. Immersed herself in her work. In her new life.

Mason had visited a few times, but the stays had never been

long enough. And they'd barely talked about the important stuff. Like the passing of their parents. His leaving the Navy.

Now was time. Past time.

Quinn ran her hands over her chilled arms. She hadn't turned on the heat because she hadn't wanted to be here long. The cold house, in combination with her wet clothes, did nothing good for her body temperature. But thankfully, she was done. Done searching for things she wasn't even sure were here.

And that meant she could go home. Have a bath. Maybe bug Wyatt.

Once downstairs, Quinn reset the alarm, then stepped back outside. As she stood under the awning, she eyed her car. She'd thought the rain was falling hard when she'd arrived. That was nothing compared to now.

Well, Quinn, you're going to be one soaked rat, aren't you.

She was about to step into the downpour when a car stopped beside hers. She could just make out the face of the person behind the wheel.

"Wyatt?"

There was no way he would have heard her. *She* could barely hear her.

He hadn't gotten out of his car yet. The moment he did, he'd be just as soaked. She stepped into the rain and immediately felt the heavy water hit her body. Hunching her shoulders, she jogged across the yard.

Hopefully, she would get to him before he got out. Then she could find out what the heck he was doing here.

She was halfway to the car when deafening thunder sounded, and lightning sizzled from right beside her.

Screaming, Quinn fell to the ground—and looked up just in time to see a huge nearby tree falling.

She couldn't look away. She couldn't move. Her breath stopped.

The tree was a moment away from crushing her when Wyatt suddenly appeared beneath it, holding it up with his back.

A moment later, he was joined by Kye.

Kye—who had come from seemingly nowhere.

Quinn's mouth opened to scream again, but no sound came out. Her blood rushed through her veins.

That was no *human* strength they were using. It would take ten normal men to hold that thing. And the speed Wyatt would have had to use to reach her...

Who the hell were they?

Now her breaths were coming out quickly. So quickly, she was almost light-headed.

Crawling backward, she attempted to put space between them.

Wyatt's mouth opened and shut. Although she couldn't hear him, she knew he said her name.

She shook her head. An all-consuming need to get away took over her body. Her brain was struggling to comprehend what was right in front of her. That Wyatt and Kye were the same as *them*. The men Maya had spoken about. The men Darren had warned her about.

She stared at Wyatt, terrified. "You're one of them."

She wasn't even sure if she spoke the words or just mouthed them. Icy fear and confusion were stealing her breath and her clarity.

Without another thought, Quinn pushed to her feet and ran. She wasn't sure where she was going, just knew that she needed to get away.

WYATT PARKED his car beside Quinn's. On the drive over, the sky continued to light up with thunder as the rain steadily grew heavier.

The paper that sat on Quinn's kitchen counter was the furthest thing from his mind right now. Her safety took precedence. This weather was dangerous. No way did he want her out in it. He didn't even like driving in it.

Just as he undid his seat belt, he saw Quinn exit the house. He could see that her hair and clothes were already wet. She wasn't even wearing a sweater.

The woman must be freezing.

A noise behind his car pulled his attention. He barely heard it over the storm. Glancing over his shoulder, he could just make out Kye standing in the distance.

At least she'd had someone watching her.

He knew the moment she noticed his car. A small smile tugged at her lips. She said his name. He saw it form on her lips. With the storm raging around them, he barely heard it.

His hand had just touched the door when she began to run across the yard.

Damn it to hell. There were puddles everywhere. The woman was going to fall down and hurt herself.

Throwing the door open, Wyatt had only taken a couple of steps when lightning lit the yard.

He watched in horror as it hit a huge oak tree only a few feet from Quinn.

As Quinn cried out and fell to the ground, Wyatt took off.

The tree was a few feet from her body when he caught it, holding it up with his back.

It was damn heavy. Likely over five tons. If it had hit her, she would be dead. No question.

A second later Kye was beside him. Taking half the weight.

He scanned her body, needing to make sure she was okay.

Relief flowed through him when she appeared unharmed. When his gaze stopped on her face, the concern returned. Her expression was a mixture of confusion and uncertainty and utter fear.

Her chest began to rise and fall in quick succession. Then she began to crawl backward, putting distance between them. Like he was an enemy.

"You're one of them!"

Before he could question her words, she was pushing to her feet and running.

Cursing under his breath, Wyatt and Kye moved quickly to shove the tree to the side before he took off after her.

It took him three seconds to catch her. Wrapping his arms around her middle, he tackled her to the wet ground.

She immediately lashed out. It was a good move. On most men, it would likely injure and stop them. Not Wyatt.

"Quinn, don't fight me. You know I'm not a danger to you."

Surprisingly, she did stop. Fire raged in her eyes, replacing the confusion and fear of moments ago. "Who the hell are you? And don't bother lying to me."

Rain pelted them, almost drowning his words. "I'll tell you everything once we get back to the car."

"I'm not going anywhere with you, you lying asshat!" Again, she attempted to kick at him.

There was no way Wyatt was going to attempt a conversation in this weather. He was surprised she'd even heard him. Lifting her body, he hunched over, attempting to protect her from the worst of the weather. Her skin was icy cold and he could feel her shivering. Still, she fought him.

"Get your hands off me!"

Ignoring her anger, Wyatt went to the place she'd fallen to grab the key, only to find it was gone. Looking up, he noticed Kye standing by the open door.

Good. That would save him the hassle of unlocking the thing and keying in a code, all while subduing the woman in his arms.

Firming his hold, he moved the final distance into the house.

The moment he set her down, Quinn took off, running straight past Kye, not even sparing him a glance.

The only reason Wyatt didn't immediately follow was because she went upstairs. Maybe she needed a moment to process what she'd seen. Hell, any sane person would.

"Thanks for your help tonight, Cage."

He indicated to the stairs with his head. "Need more help?"

He needed a lot of help. But it wasn't the kind Kye could give. He needed to figure out how to explain things to Quinn without terrifying her further.

"I'll be okay. I think it would be better if it's just me here."

He dipped his head. "You got it. Take care, brother."

After Kye stepped out, Wyatt took a moment to turn on the heat before heading upstairs.

He had a feeling there was more to her fear and anger than simply witnessing his and Kye's strength and speed. And it probably had something—or everything—to do with that story she was working on.

When he reached the top of the stairs, he heard rummaging noises from the master bedroom. Light shone from the bottom of the door.

Walking to the room, he opened the door, only to stop immediately.

Quinn stood in front of him, gun in hand, trained directly at his chest.

CHAPTER 12

Quinn was aware that her hand trembled. She was also aware Wyatt was likely fast enough to dodge a speeding bullet. But the gun was her only layer of protection.

She'd thought Wyatt was normal. Average. He wasn't. He was something else completely. What, exactly, she wasn't sure.

Was he one of the killers Maya had seen? He certainly possessed the speed and strength.

"I know how to shoot, so don't even think about moving." Quinn was grateful her voice was steady. "How did you do that?"

Wyatt raised his hands. She almost scoffed at the action. If he thought that made him appear less threatening, he was dead wrong. It did nothing to ease her fear.

"Can we talk about this without the gun, Quinn?"

"No. Does Mason know what you can do?"

His veiled expression didn't change, but there was the slightest flicker of emotion in his eyes. "Your brother is just like me."

Shock rendered Quinn silent. Shock and disbelief. He was lying. He had to be.

"I'm not lying," he said, as if reading her thoughts. "Our whole team, all eight of us, are like this. We didn't choose to be this way. It was *done* to us."

He took a small step closer. She took a step back, causing her legs to hit the bedside table. "Explain this to me. Because right now, nothing is adding up."

Not the fact that her brother and Wyatt had superhuman abilities *or* that those abilities held a scary resemblance to the ones she was warned about.

"There was a program called Project Arma. It was government funded and supposed to teach us how to fight more efficiently. We were given drugs to help us recover quicker." His hands dropped to his sides. "The drugs weren't what they told us they were. They altered our DNA. Made us stronger. Faster. We can heal quickly, see everything, even if it's pitch-black. Hear things a mile away."

No. That wasn't possible. Was it?

If what he said was true, then there was a huge chunk of her brother's life that she knew nothing about. A trauma that he'd experienced, that he hadn't shared with her.

Wyatt took another step forward. "Your brother didn't want to tell you until it was over."

Her brows pulled together. "You're saying it's *not* over?"

Fury washed over Wyatt's face. It was an expression she hadn't seen him wear before. "It should be. It's not. Shylah was a nurse at the base. She discovered what was really going on and exposed the truth. Before the place was raided, the people working on the project ran and went into hiding. Our old commander, the head of the program, also went into hiding."

Thunder roared outside, echoing through the bedroom. The lights flickered. "How did they learn about the raid?"

Wyatt lifted a shoulder. "That's one of the great mysteries of Project Arma. They must have people on their payroll who could access that information. We just haven't been able to find any evidence to suggest who it might be."

Quinn was tempted to lower the gun. What Wyatt was saying fit the guy she'd thought she knew. It fit who her brother was.

Good people. Possible victims of a tragic situation.

But it didn't explain where he fit into Maya's story. She had to know. Even if she didn't like the answer.

"Do you have anything to gain from robbing pharmaceutical labs?" She searched Wyatt's face. Studied his body language. Waiting for any signs of deceit.

"No."

There was a ring of truth to the word. That, in combination with the fact he'd never given her reason to question his ethics, made her inclined to believe him.

Slowly, Quinn lowered the gun. The adrenaline that had been rushing through her system slowed.

"Can I have the gun?"

Quinn almost found it comical that he was asking, seeing as how easily he could take it. "Yes."

Lifting the weapon, she offered it to Wyatt. He approached and took it from her fingers, immediately turning the safety back on. "I didn't know Eagle kept this in his room."

She lifted a shoulder. "He's told me before he stashes one in the dresser."

And probably a million other places.

"Smart."

Quinn stepped to the side and watched as Wyatt put the gun back where she got it.

When he straightened, he didn't move closer or move away. Rather, just stood and watched her. Like he was trying to figure out whether he could touch her.

To be honest, she wasn't sure. A million different emotions swirled through her.

Wyatt was the same man he'd been this morning. The man she'd been craving to see and unable to get out of her head. But he was also different. So much so that she felt like she needed time to digest what he'd told her.

He must have read her hesitation, because he shoved his hands in his pockets. "I think we should stay here tonight. I'm not too comfortable with either of us driving in this weather."

As if on cue, the thunder sounded again through the room. It was deafening.

Quinn had all but forgotten the storm. Only minutes ago, she'd been seconds away from being crushed to death.

"I'll sleep in here."

Wyatt nodded. "I'll take the one across the hall."

He took a step toward the door, only to stop when Quinn touched his arm. The same zing of awareness shot through her body at the touch.

"Thank you. For saving me tonight."

If Wyatt hadn't been there, she would likely be dead. And in the process of saving her, he'd revealed his secret. Her brother's secret.

"If I hadn't been there to save you, Cage would have."

Quinn had questions about that, but right now she was too tired to ask them.

"Seeing that tree almost fall on you scared the hell out of me." He paused as if considering his next words. "I know you've had a lot to process tonight, and this probably isn't the best time for me to say this, but I care about you. I feel a connection to you."

Quinn wet her lips. She couldn't deny that she felt the same. "I feel it too."

A warmth filled his eyes. "Good. I'm going to go downstairs, fix us something to eat. You can have a shower and get warm—"

"I'm actually not that hungry. A hot drink would be nice though."

She felt abnormally tired. Probably due to the huge adrenaline dump.

"I'll bring you a hot drink."

She thought he was going to leave. Instead, his head lowered, and he pressed his lips to her forehead. She sucked in a long breath, giving herself permission to enjoy his touch.

When he stepped away, she had to stop herself from pulling him back. She went so far as to cross her arms over her chest as he walked toward the door. It wasn't until he was in the hall that he stopped.

"Would you have shot me?"

A smile tugged at her lips. Absolutely not. But there was no way was she telling him that. "I guess you'll never know."

A ghost of a smile appeared on his face, then he left.

Once she was alone, Quinn realized she was no longer shaking from the cold. Wyatt must have switched on the heat. She was still cold, thanks to her wet clothing, but not freezing.

Moving to the adjoining bathroom, Quinn turned on the water. As it warmed, she stripped off her clothes before stepping under the stream.

At first, the water felt like tiny pins pricking her skin. Quickly, the water turned from painful to warm.

She didn't know how long she stood there, just letting Wyatt's words swirl through her mind. She did know it was a long time.

She was consumed by a myriad of emotions. Shock. Surprise. Relief that it sounded like Wyatt was in fact one of the good guys.

Also, an overwhelming sense of sadness. Sadness because Mason hadn't told her about what he'd been through. That he'd experienced something that had no doubt altered his perspective of the world he lived in. Hurt him.

It was *her* fault he hadn't told her. She'd known that it was suspicious for him to leave the Navy. He'd damn well lived and breathed his job. Only, she'd been so absorbed in her own life, her own career, that she'd accepted his subpar explanation of "being done."

Heck, she'd barely checked on him—her own brother. Her last

immediate family member. She should have come down here and visited him. Put more time into ensuring he was okay.

She was an investigative journalist, dammit, and she hadn't even been able to see that there was a whole part of her brother's life that had gone wrong.

Closing her eyes, Quinn ducked her head. Maybe losing her job was a good thing. It had certainly given her more perspective. She needed to invest more time into people.

Maybe it was time for her to let go of this story. Leave it in Wyatt's hands. Even though she'd lost her job, she'd never stopped working.

Frowning, Quinn realized that Wyatt had never questioned her reference to lab break-ins. The man hadn't even seemed surprised.

Which was unusual. Unless, of course, he already knew something about it.

CHAPTER 13

*W*yatt tipped the delivery man before closing the door.

Hopefully, the two things in his hands would get the morning off to a good start. Bagels and coffee.

As expected, Mason's home was devoid of food. Luckily, Joan's Diner offered delivery.

Food was essential this morning. Not just because of the obvious—that breakfast was essential to *most* people. Also, because they had some big stuff to discuss. Questions needed answering, likely from both Wyatt and Quinn. It would be that much harder without sustenance.

On his way back to the kitchen, Wyatt heard Quinn moving around upstairs. Good. Hopefully, she wouldn't be much longer.

Placing the food on the kitchen counter, he got to work plating it.

Last night had been a lot. Not only had Quinn almost been crushed to death, which still made Wyatt feel sick to his stomach, but she also learned a hell of a great deal. About him. About her brother.

He wished she hadn't found out that way. But she had, and

there was no way to change it. It was no surprise that she'd been in a tangible state of shock and disbelief. Not to mention scared out of her mind. Yet, she hadn't fallen apart. Far from it. The woman had held him at gunpoint while looking him dead in the eye.

She'd impressed the hell out of him.

He hadn't asked her any of the questions he needed answers to. That's what this morning was for.

Although, he'd already discovered a bit himself.

Once Quinn had gone to bed, Wyatt researched the two words he'd found scribbled beneath "Salina Pharmaceutical Company."

They were the names of raw materials used to create drugs. Expensive materials that were in short supply in the US.

Popping the plates of food on the table, Wyatt went back to get the coffees.

If there was any positive to yesterday, it was that Jack's death was looking less and less like it was his fault. If the break-in was part of the story that Quinn had already been working on, then it was likely something much larger was happening than simply cutting off Wyatt's resources.

Some of the guilt in his chest eased. It wouldn't fade completely until he knew for sure, one way or the other.

Ten minutes later, Wyatt looked up to Quinn walking in.

His body immediately tightened at the sight of her.

She wore a light blue dress that ended just above her knees. He hadn't seen the woman in a dress before. She always looked beautiful, but now, he had to physically stop his jaw from dropping.

She looked sweet and seductive, rolled into one. Her long legs were toned, like a dancer's. Her skin a soft peach color. Her midnight hair was pulled up, but small wisps had escaped and were touching the sides of her face and shoulders.

The woman had an aura of strength and courage, crying at

him to reach out and touch her. He didn't know how any man drew their eyes away from her. For him, at least, it felt impossible.

"Many people would consider staring rude." There was a twinkle in her eyes as she said the words.

"Do you?"

She lifted a shoulder. "Depends who's doing the staring and what they're thinking."

Oh, Wyatt was thinking all kinds of things. And it was wreaking havoc on his body. "That you completely undo me."

Pink immediately tinged her cheeks. It was the first time Wyatt had seen any form of shyness on her. It increased his urge to reach out and touch her. Or better yet, pull her into his arms.

"Well, you certainly know how to make a woman's morning."

Wyatt couldn't restrain himself any longer. He took three steps across the room, landing him right in front of her. When Quinn didn't step back, he reached out and placed his hands on her hips.

"God, you're beautiful."

The word "beautiful" didn't even do her justice, but he had a feeling there was no word that would.

Quinn wet her lips. It drew his gaze to her mouth. "I definitely feel beautiful when you look at me like that."

Well, Wyatt was happy to look at her every second of every day, if that's what she required to feel good.

The moment her gaze lowered to his lips, he gave up the fight. Pulling her body firmly into his, enjoying the way they fit so perfectly, he lowered his head. Tasted her. She was sweet. Her lips were soft and pliant against his.

He felt her hands glide through his hair. At the same time, a soft moan escaped her throat, causing his blood to rush south.

Christ, the woman made fire burn through his veins.

Gathering her closer, he deepened the kiss. Giving her more of himself. Taking more.

Her hands moved down his neck to his chest. He felt the light pressure of her pushing him back.

Even though it took every shred of strength he possessed, Wyatt stepped backward.

For a moment, the only sound in the room was heavy breathing and pounding heartbeats.

Quinn leaned her head forward, pressing it to his chest. "We should talk."

She was right. They should talk. They *needed* to talk. That didn't make it any easier to let her go.

"We should."

Placing a long kiss on the top of her head, he slowly released her.

Once he'd stepped back, they both took a moment to gather themselves. Quinn's attention went to the food he'd set on the table. "Did you make this?"

"Would you believe me if I said yes?"

She scanned both the kitchen and dining area with her intelligent eyes.

Nope. He didn't stand a chance of fooling the woman.

"Unless you're an unbelievably clean and efficient cook, you ordered in." She moved to the table and took a seat. "Not that I'm complaining. I can see bacon in this bagel *and* a coffee. Those are the things I dream about."

The only thing Wyatt had been dreaming about lately was the woman right in front of him.

Taking a seat opposite her, he watched as she took a sip of her coffee. Her eyes closed, and she was the picture of serene.

He was beyond glad that she seemed herself again this morning. He hadn't known whether she would still be carrying some of last night's shock or fear.

"You even transferred the coffee into a mug," she said as she looked up. "That's commitment."

He lifted a shoulder. "Coffee tastes better in a mug. In my opinion."

Quinn laughed. "I would drink coffee from a ladle if I had to. It's quite a problem."

Not to Wyatt. He couldn't find anything about the woman that was a problem.

That was the problem.

"The weather's a lot better out there. We might just make it home."

The sun was even poking through the clouds. Although, they'd still need to be cautious on the wet roads. And be on the lookout for trees and branches barricading the streets.

"So, how fast are you exactly?" Quinn asked, clearly not interested in discussing the weather.

He lifted his bagel to his lips. "How fast do you think I am?"

"Maybe faster than a car. Not so sure about a bullet?"

He chuckled. "We've never tested it, but you're probably right. Rocket's the fastest, hence the name. Of course, he was the fastest before we changed."

Her head tilted to the side. "Changed. Interesting word choice. I would have said altered. Or enhanced. It had to be tough. Discovering the truth about what the project was. What was done to you."

Wyatt wasn't going to lie. One, because he didn't want to. And two, because Quinn was smart and would see right through him.

"Some people see the world through a rosy-colored lens. All light, no darkness. I wasn't like that. As a SEAL, I couldn't be. So I thought I was prepared for whatever was thrown my way. But *nothing* could have prepared me for what was done. It challenged my view of the entire world. I had to dig deep not to let the deception define me."

Sympathy flashed across Quinn's face. "Did you ever consider remaining a SEAL?"

"Not for a second. I lost faith in the system. I need my life to be in *my* hands now. I need choices. You don't have that when you're a SEAL. Now, I spend time helping people on my terms. I spend time with my team, who are my family. And I spend a lot of time researching Project Arma."

A shadow fell across her face at his mention of Project Arma.

He kept his voice casual as he spoke. "Have you heard of the project?"

She shook her head. "No."

He could tell she was being honest. At the same time, he felt like she knew *something*. Maybe she knew about the organization, just not what it was called.

"Have you heard about other men who can do what I can do?" Her eyes widened a fraction. It was subtle. He didn't miss it. "Will you tell me how?"

She cast her gaze down to her coffee, taking a small sip. "I will. If you tell me what you know about the pharmaceutical company break-ins first."

Ah. She realized he knew *something*.

"Okay. That's fair." He leaned back in his seat. "I had a friend named Jack. We went to high school together. Incredibly smart guy. Also very trustworthy. He studied pharmaceutical science at college and got a job at the Salina Pharmaceutical Drug Lab."

Quinn didn't speak or move, but he heard the slight hitch in her breathing.

"He's helped me with a few things over the years." Wyatt tensed before he said the next part. The words were damn hard to say out loud. "I just found out that he was murdered. When I researched his death, I found that some colleagues of his also died."

Quinn didn't appear shocked by his words.

"I assumed he was killed because the people running Project Arma connected him to me," Wyatt continued. "They wouldn't want anyone to help us because they know we're hunting them.

We also shut down their main facility less than a month ago. They lost a lot. They'd be angry."

"Would they have lost drugs? Materials to create their drugs?"

"Yes. They lost everything they kept at their main base. It was a significant loss for them."

"Makes sense now." She almost seemed like she was talking to herself.

"What does?"

Placing the mug on the table, Quinn leaned forward. "There's a pharmaceutical company called Novac, which I used to pass on my way to work. It was broken into. Lab technicians were killed. Active ingredients and raw materials were stolen."

The story she was working on. "The police told you that?"

Quinn scoffed. "No. I saw the dead bodies being wheeled out. No one would tell me squat. I researched other pharmaceutical companies around the country. I found one in Alabama where four lab technicians had all died on the same day."

Wyatt ran his hands through his hair.

If this was connected to Project Arma, it more than likely meant they were robbing pharmaceutical companies to try to recoup some of the materials they'd lost. The whole thing wreaked of desperation.

If that was the case, then surely the CIA would be on it and should have notified Wyatt's team.

"Why wouldn't these break-ins have made national news?"

Quinn nodded. "Exactly. It's likely someone, or multiple people, are being paid to keep quiet."

Made sense. Cover-ups usually came down to money.

"I contacted people from both companies, asking if anyone had information," Quinn continued. "One woman responded. Maya. She contacted me from a new email after she'd run. She was a witness to the New York break-in. The only living witness."

"There's a witness?"

Quinn nodded. "She was there. She survived the attack and

told me what happened. That the people who broke in are fast. And strong. And can hear a person's heartbeat."

Ah, hell.

"What exactly did she see?"

Wyatt had a feeling he knew. But he needed to hear it anyway.

For the first time that morning, a hint of fear flashed over Quinn's face. "Men broke in and systematically went through the room, killing scientists and stealing materials. They killed people by snapping their necks and throwing them against walls. She said they didn't seem human. Described them as 'unstoppable.'"

Wyatt cursed under his breath. It was confirmed then. Project Arma was stealing ingredients to create their drugs. They were also killing people across the country.

"There's something else. Maya said they were only really interested in two main materials. And those materials are rare. She said there wouldn't be many labs that kept them."

Wyatt was already standing and grabbing his laptop. He'd researched the materials that she'd written down but hadn't tried to pinpoint where they were stored.

That information wouldn't be available to the public, but there was a chance he could still find it.

When he returned to the table, he began typing. Quinn stood and moved behind him.

"How did you know which materials Maya told me about?"

"I went into your apartment to check if you were there yesterday. I saw them written down."

A hit to his shoulder had him looking up.

"That was for going into my private space without my permission." Even though she said the words with a hard tone, there was a smile on her lips.

"I've been meaning to return the key to you. I'm sorry. It won't happen again."

"Better not." She looked back to the screen. "Now, get back to work."

Shaking his head, he went back to typing. It took ten minutes, but he got the list.

Four. There were four labs that stocked those two ingredients. Alabama, New York, and Salina were three of them. That left one more. One pharmaceutical company, that as far as he was aware, had yet to be raided.

Leaning back in his seat, Wyatt breathed out a long breath. "Green Pharmaceuticals, Portland. The only lab remaining that stocks those ingredients."

He needed to tell his brothers. They needed a plan.

CHAPTER 14

Quinn smoothed the blue material over her lap. The dress belonged to Sage. She'd been low on options this morning. First she'd tried on a pair of jeans, which had almost been comical. They hadn't come close to fitting her long legs.

So, she was in a dress. Quinn rarely wore dresses. In fact, she couldn't actually recall the last time she'd had one on. Mostly because she didn't like them very much.

What she *did* like was the way Wyatt looked at her in a dress. Like he couldn't drag his eyes away.

But then, he always made her feel special when he looked at her. Like she occupied all of his attention. Like she was the only woman he saw.

She snuck a peak at him from the passenger seat. He'd insisted on joining her on the drive to Tyler to pick up Maya. She loved having him along for the drive, but knew he was giving up a day where he could be strategizing against his enemy.

"You didn't need to join me." That may have been the fourth or even fifth time she'd said those words. She didn't know why she kept repeating them. Guilt maybe?

"Like I've said a bunch of times, I don't mind. Besides, it's been more fun with me here, hasn't it?"

Heck yes, it was better with him. She'd been laughing so much that her cheeks hurt.

He'd also made a couple of stops along the way and forced Quinn to get out and stretch her legs. Something she hadn't done the first time she'd driven to Tyler, and probably wouldn't have done this time, had she been alone.

Each stop, she'd hurried Wyatt, though. Because, yet again, she was pushed for time. With everything that had happened last night, she'd almost forgotten her promise to go get Maya.

Her original plan had been to leave Marble Falls at the crack of dawn. That definitely hadn't happened. And it made Quinn nervous. Nervous that the other woman wouldn't wait for her. Nervous that she'd be too late.

Maya had sounded scared yesterday. The likelihood of her skipping town was high.

"I could have brought Maya back to Marble Falls myself," Quinn added. "You could have used the day to meet with your team and come up with a plan for the last lab."

He gave her one of his crooked smiles. It was the kind of smile that made her heart race.

"That's what teams are for. When one person can't make it, the others pick up the slack. I've told them what's going on. They'll meet and create a game plan. I'll get a rundown of what's happening when I get back. Plus, I have my phone right here if they need to get in contact with me."

Well, if it worked for Wyatt, it worked for Quinn.

"You're not planning on telling Maya what you can do, are you?"

"No. We don't tell anyone if we can avoid it."

That was good. Maya didn't know Wyatt from a bar of soap. If she found out that he could do what her attackers could do, she would likely react just as Quinn had. Only, where Quinn had been easy to talk down, Maya wouldn't be. Because she didn't know Wyatt. She hadn't spent the time with him that Quinn had.

"Maybe I should go in first." Quinn snuck a peak at Wyatt. "Alone."

It was possible Maya could try to take off at just the sight of Wyatt. He would easily be able to catch her, but the goal was to build trust. To help her, not scare her.

This time, Wyatt didn't agree so easily. "I'd prefer to be with you."

She frowned. "You think she'll hurt me?"

"I think she's a witness to a crime involving dangerous people. We don't know what we're stepping into. Once someone's been exposed to the evil of Project Arma, their safety isn't guaranteed. And neither are the people they come into contact with."

Okay. Maybe Wyatt was right. Maya had enemies. It would be best if he was there for protection.

"Yeah, you should come in. But you need to stay behind me." She studied his face for a moment. "And try not to look so big and threatening."

Wyatt put a hand to his chest. "Me? Big and threatening? I think you have me mistaken for Hunter or Cage."

She couldn't help but chuckle. "You all fit the bill. At a hundred feet tall with pounds upon pounds of muscle, you're walking Arnies."

"Arnies?"

"Arnies. Arnold Schwarzeneggers."

He chuckled. It was a deep chuckle that she felt right down in her core. "You didn't seem intimidated that first time we met."

That's because she was tough as nuts. Also, because the man was sex on a stick. "I don't scare easy. I've got balls of steal."

"With a job as an investigative journalist, that must be true. Your brother must worry about you."

He did. She still remembered the early days when Mason

would call her every other day. After some time passed, the calls had dropped off to weekly.

"Mason's a stress-head. I'm hoping Sage will bring some calm into his life."

"He has good reason to stress. Although, I think Sage lessened it to a degree. She's a very calm person. Some might say your complete opposite."

Quinn shoved his shoulder playfully. "Okay, funny man."

"I like to think I am."

He was. It was one of the things she liked most about him. Not that she would be telling him that and inflating his ego any further.

"Do you have any siblings?"

She'd never actually asked him about his family. When she thought about it, she actually knew quite little about the guy. Especially considering how much he knew about her.

"No siblings. My parents thought I was perfect, and their job was done at one."

Quinn laughed out loud. He actually did seem pretty perfect to her, so his parents wouldn't be wrong. "What are your parents like?"

"Awesome. Both retired but spent most of their lives working as high school teachers. Very hard-working people who love each other to death." He paused to look at her. "That's what I want. A love that lasts a lifetime."

There was an intensity in the way he looked at her. The smile slipped from her lips. "My parents were exactly the same. I would love to experience a love like that."

Reaching over, his hand wrapped around hers and squeezed. "I'm sorry you lost them."

"Thank you."

"And maybe you will one day." When she looked at him with confusion, he continued, "Experience a love like that."

That was the dream. To love someone so hard that it lasted forever. That not a day passed where she felt alone.

Just then, Wyatt slowed the car to a stop. For the first time in a while, Quinn looked out the window and studied her surroundings.

They'd pulled outside a large apartment building. It looked incredibly old and rundown. Dangerous. In fact, the whole area looked dangerous.

"Are you sure this is it? The place doesn't look safe for a single woman."

If she didn't have Wyatt by her side, no way would she feel comfortable being here.

Wyatt unbuckled his seat belt. "I'm guessing she left New York in a rush and wasn't able to take much with her. She's probably also paying in cash and not using ID. That would limit her options in terms of rentals."

Guilt hit Quinn hard. She wasn't responsible for the other woman—heck, she barely knew her—but if Quinn had realized Maya was living *here*, she would have at least tried to convince her to come to Marble Falls. Offered her a safe place to sleep.

Maybe the inside looked better than the outside. But Quinn wouldn't be holding her breath.

Stepping out of the car, Wyatt led them into the building. The moment they walked inside, she struggled not to gag at the overwhelming stench. It was a cross between mold, urine, and tobacco.

Her stomach rolled.

Wyatt reached for her hand and threaded his fingers through hers. His touch was instantly calming.

Making their way up the stairs, they moved slowly. Along the way, she heard muffled voices from behind closed doors. Some were raised. Some aggressive.

Her hand tightened around Wyatt's.

If she had to hazard a guess, she'd say the building was filled with deadbeats and drug dealers. And it made her feel sick to her stomach that Maya was living here.

Wyatt came to a stop in front of a door. Instead of knocking or trying the handle, he stood there for a few seconds, a focused look on his face.

A moment passed before Quinn realized what he was doing. Listening. Listening for people on the other side. Breathing. Footsteps. Possibly even a heartbeat.

"There's no one in there."

Quinn's heart sank. She was too late.

She was about to walk away when Wyatt's hand went to the door. He turned the knob and pushed it open.

She looked up at him in surprise. "She left it unlocked?"

"Yes."

Her heart sank further, but this time accompanied by a tinge of fear. Fear for the other woman's safety.

There was no way Maya would have left her door unlocked if she was still living there. Not a chance.

Wyatt took a step inside and Quinn followed. She closed the door behind them before stopping in the middle of the living room. She glanced around the apartment. The kitchen sat to the left, and a bedroom and bathroom were to the right.

The place was almost bare. A worn couch with dark stains sat beside her, and there was an old wooden table in the kitchen. She could see a sagging bed with a mattress in the bedroom. No sheets. No pillows.

Any thread of hope Quinn might have been harboring that the other woman had just popped out was dashed. No one was living here.

When she glanced up at Wyatt, she saw a frown marring his brow. Tension was coming off him in waves.

"What is it?"

His eyes settled on the doorway that led to the hall, his frown becoming a scowl.

Before she could even interpret his next action, he grabbed her arm and pulled her behind him. "A sensor."

She attempted to peer around his large body to see what he was seeing, but she noticed nothing unusual.

Suddenly, a loud bang echoed through the apartment as the door was kicked in. Two men entered. Large men, dressed head to toe in black.

Fear crawled its way up Quinn's throat. Her heart pounded so hard against her ribs, she was certain it would beat right out of her chest.

The men weren't carrying weapons that she could see. They probably didn't need to. They *were* the weapons.

Without missing a beat, Wyatt pushed Quinn behind the couch and stepped forward.

For a moment, no one moved a muscle.

Then she watched in horror as an explosion of violence erupted in the room.

Wyatt leapt forward, throwing punches. Deflecting strikes.

The men moved just as quickly. Blow upon blow was thrown, all in Wyatt's direction. He blocked each and every one. All three men moved like machines.

At one point, one of the men pulled out a gun. It was as if Wyatt knew what was coming. Before the other guy had a chance to use it, Wyatt swiped the weapon. In the process, he broke the man's arm.

The man cried out in pain and Wyatt took advantage, spinning him around and snapping his neck.

Quinn was too shocked to feel sickened by what she saw. A numbness had entered her limbs.

While Wyatt held the limp man in his arms, the second man dove toward her. He was less than a foot away when Wyatt grabbed him and pulled him back.

The two wrestled and grunted. Their movements almost lyrical. Whenever one man raised an arm, the other anticipated it. Blocked the move.

Finally, one of Wyatt's punches landed, sending the man in black to the floor. Wyatt then lunged at him. At the same time, the man in black whipped out a knife and slashed at Wyatt's midsection.

Quinn cried out as blood began to seep from his stomach.

The injury did nothing to stop him. Wyatt slammed his fist into the man's gut, the knife falling from his fingers and sliding toward Quinn. Without thinking, she lifted the knife and held it out in front of her.

She looked up just in time to see Wyatt punch the man's throat before grabbing him in a chokehold. Wyatt held him tightly until the man in black stopped moving, his body going limp.

The room suddenly shifted from chaos to stillness. For a moment, Wyatt remained on his knees. He didn't even appear to be breathing heavily.

When he stood and turned, his face was clear of any expression. He took a step forward. "Are you okay?"

Her? He was asking if *she* was okay? The man had just fought two assassins. He could have died...

"I'm okay."

He studied her face. Almost like he was assessing whether to believe her. "Can I have the knife?"

She looked down at her hand. The knife was still pointed forward. The fact that she'd been holding it was the furthest thing from her mind.

Wyatt could have easily taken it from her. He was asking for it to make her feel like she had control. To make her feel safe.

Turning the knife, she offered it to him, handle first. He took it from her fingers gently, before reaching for her hand. "We need to get out of here. Are you okay to walk or do you need me to carry you?"

"I'm okay to walk, Wyatt. I'm not about to break. Let's get out of here before any other lunatic murderers come."

CHAPTER 15

*W*yatt closed the door to his apartment.

Frustration sat like a rock in his gut. He hadn't wanted Quinn to see that part of him. The part that could kill a man with his bare hands. Choke the life right out of him.

But she had.

She'd said she was okay, but her silence on the way home had been deafening. Not only her silence; she'd also barely touched her dinner. It had only been drive-through, and they'd sat in the car to eat it. She'd simply fingered the food in the container.

Wyatt moved into the kitchen. Luckily, he healed fast, so the cut across his stomach was already looking a lot better than earlier. Dried blood matted his skin. He needed a cold, hard beer followed by a long shower.

Opening the fridge door, he pulled out a bottle and uncapped it.

When Wyatt had offered to stay with her, Quinn had said she was tired. But a fear had started to unfurl in his gut, that her wanting to be alone had more to do with wanting space from *him*.

Quinn had probably written about death a hundred times, but

never witnessed the act herself. Seeing it was completely different.

And he hated that the death she saw had been at his hands.

Wyatt downed half the beer in one go. He'd called his brothers on the drive home to let them know what had happened. He'd also found out that Kye, Oliver and Bodie, were flying over to Portland to take first shift watching Green Pharmaceuticals. They were probably already there.

Wyatt needed a shower. He needed to wash away the stench of death. Placing the half-empty beer on the counter, he headed toward the bathroom.

He was partway there when he heard the door across the hall opening. Then footsteps. A light knock sounded.

Moving to his door, he pulled it open and his gaze collided with Quinn's.

She looked exactly the same as when he'd left her. The blue dress still flowed around her body, her hair was still pulled up into a high ponytail, and she still wore the same unreadable expression on her face.

"Are you okay?"

Quinn's concern took Wyatt off guard. She was asking him if *he* was okay, when *she* was the one with shadows under her eyes?

"I wasn't ignoring you. In the car, that is. I was in my own world." She spoke quickly. Like she was trying to get all the words out as fast as possible. "I didn't think. I should have thought. I mean, you have a huge gash on your stomach, for Christ's sake. If I had a cut that size, you would have checked on me the moment we were safe. And then there's everything else that happened. I didn't even ask how you were feeling—"

"Quinn."

She abruptly stopped speaking.

"Would you like to come in?"

She opened her mouth, then shut it. "I...no. I just wanted to check that you were okay."

Disappointment swirled in his gut. He was careful to keep his features masked. Just because he wanted to be close to her, didn't mean she wanted to be close to him. "I'm okay."

She nibbled on her bottom lip. Her arms folding across her chest in a defensive stance. "Are you sure? There was a lot of blood on your shirt. Actually, there still *is* a lot of blood on your shirt. We didn't even put a bandage over it after…" She waved her hand around. "We just got in the car and started driving. Maybe we should have stopped at the hospital. Can you do that? I don't know—"

"Quinn." Wyatt interrupted her again, unsure when her nervous rambling would end. "I'm okay. It wasn't a deep cut and my body heals quickly."

He peeled the shirt from his skin, lifting the material.

She took a step closer, surprise flashing across her face. She went to touch his skin, but pulled her hand away before she made contact. "There's barely a mark."

"The wonders of altered DNA." He lowered his shirt but kept his gaze fixed on her. "Come in. I'll make us a drink. We can sit in front of the TV and keep each other company."

And my desperate desire to check that you're okay—that we're okay —can be fulfilled.

It wasn't just that he wanted to figure out where he stood with Quinn. Twice now, she'd almost died. Two times in less than twenty-four hours, she would have died had he not been present. And that was terrifying.

Her tongue peeked out of her mouth and wet her lips. She seemed to consider his words, and for a moment, Wyatt was hopeful.

Then she took a step back. "I should get home. I have an early shift tomorrow."

The blank mask remained on his face. Not an ounce of the disappointment that tore at him showed.

He watched as Quinn turned around and walked back inside her apartment.

Cursing under his breath, he headed to the bathroom. He hoped this wasn't the end for them. Hell, their relationship had barely begun.

He didn't know what thoughts were running through her head, whether it was shock at what she'd seen, fear for her life, disgust at what he'd done.

For all he knew, it could be a combination of all three.

Stripping off his clothes, he stepped under the spray of water and immediately began scrubbing the blood from his body. The water below his feet turned a light shade of crimson.

The color of pain. Death.

Killing had never come easily to Wyatt. It was an unfortunate necessity in his field of work. He'd enlisted when he left high school because he'd wanted to help people. Save lives. Studying IT, like his parents had wanted him to, hadn't felt like enough for him. He might have been happy in the short term, but unfulfilled in the long term.

Unfortunately, to save lives, you sometimes needed to take the lives of others.

Wyatt was good at fighting. Good at killing. That didn't mean he enjoyed it.

QUINN CLOSED the door and pressed her forehead to the wood.

The last twenty-four hours had been a lot. She'd thought she was okay. Leaving that apartment, she'd *told* Wyatt she was okay. But every minute that had ticked past in the car became heavier.

The haze of death and danger in Maya's apartment was one she was sure she'd never forget. Wyatt had killed two people right in front of her. To save her. To save *them*. If he hadn't, she wouldn't be standing where she was. She'd be dead.

Turning around, Quinn slid to the floor, wrapping her arms around her legs.

This was Wyatt's world. At least, until his enemy was destroyed. Did it get easier for him? At a certain point, does a person just become numb to the violence that stalks them?

Scrubbing her hands over her face, Quinn took a few deep breaths.

If there was anything she could take away from today, it was that life was short. Tomorrow wasn't guaranteed. Hell, the next *hour* wasn't guaranteed.

So then what the heck am I doing sitting in this apartment by myself?

Quinn didn't want to be alone. Not after she'd come so close to death. She wanted to be with Wyatt.

Not just talking to him. She wanted to touch him. Feel the heat of his skin against hers. Remind herself that they were both there. Living and breathing.

Screw it.

Standing, Quinn left her apartment and marched up to Wyatt's door. The knock sounded loud in the evening quiet.

While she waited, the nerves tried to sneak in, but she pushed them down.

When the door finally opened, her jaw dropped. Wyatt no longer wore the stained white shirt and jeans. Instead, a towel hung low on his hips, water droplets running down his body... down his thick chest and wide shoulders and the toned muscles lining his arms.

Every inch of Quinn's body heated with awareness. Any part of her that had still been wondering if this was a good idea vanished.

"Quinn—"

"Kiss me."

Shock washed over his features. Then a hand brushed through his hair. "Maybe we should talk about—"

"I don't want to talk. Or worry. Or strategize. I want you to grab me. Pull my body against yours. And kiss me."

Wyatt's gaze heated. A few seconds passed while he remained still. They were nervous seconds. Seconds where Quinn wondered if he might just turn her down flat.

Then, with lightning reflexes, he lifted her from the floor and into his arms. His lips landing on hers. Firm and sure.

Her nerves turned into passion. And she was lost. Lost in a sea of Wyatt.

Locking her feet behind his body, she ran her fingers through his silky hair.

Quinn was vaguely aware of the air moving around her. Of the click of the door closing. But it was all background noise. Everything was. Except him.

Wyatt's big, warm body wrapped around her like a jacket. His lips wreaking havoc on her insides.

Soft moans filled the air. Moans from deep in her throat.

He kissed her passionately and fiercely. As if he was claiming her. Like they were claiming each other.

As desire rippled through her, she became aware that there were too many barriers between them. She wanted to feel his skin on hers.

As if reading her mind, Wyatt lowered her to her feet. She was vaguely aware that they were in the bedroom. Standing beside his bed.

Reaching for the hem of her dress, she pulled it over her body. At the same time, Wyatt removed the towel.

He stood in front of her, completely bare. A warrior. *Her* warrior.

Reaching behind, she removed her bra, then her underwear.

Wyatt's eyes didn't shift from hers. He stepped closer. Hand moving to the side of her face. "You sure you want this?"

"This is the *only* thing I want."

She burned for the man in front of her.

His lips returned to hers, sending electric waves of awareness through her body. Lifting her like she weighed nothing, Wyatt placed her on the bed. His weight quickly settling above her.

Every inch of him touched every inch of her. It set her body ablaze.

His soft kisses never ceased.

She released a strangled moan as his hand went to her breast. He massaged and played. Pinching and rubbing her sensitive peak.

She latched onto his shoulders. Needing to anchor herself.

Instead of switching his hand to her other breast like she expected, he began to trail soft kisses down her jaw, then her neck. He landed on that other breast and sucked.

Quinn's breaths came out short and raspy. Her fingers scraped down his back.

The man was torturing her. Igniting an almost unbearable need inside her.

After minutes of the torture, Wyatt's mouth came off her nipple with a pop before trailing farther down her body. It wasn't until he hovered over the apex of her thighs that he paused.

Quinn's breathing stopped as she waited. His head lowered and his tongue slid across her clit.

Her entire body jolted and then trembled at his touch. Flinging her head back, she pushed her hips upward.

His tongue began to move in firm, even thrusts. Desire swirled through her core like a storm.

She felt alive. Alive and on fire. Her body throbbed with need. His hand held her hips firm, anchoring her to the bed.

Quinn was almost at the breaking point when Wyatt lifted his body, and his face returned to hover over hers. She could feel him, hot and hard against her thigh.

"One last time, Quinn. Tell me you want this."

"I want this, Wyatt. Take me."

A soft growl tore from his lips before he reached to the side of the bed, then quickly donned a condom. When he returned to her, he positioned his hardness at her entrance.

For a moment, he didn't move. Instead, he looked at her. *Really* looked at her. Like he saw every little part of her, including the hidden crevices that the rest of the world missed.

"You're perfection."

"Only for you, Wyatt."

He lowered himself, filling her inch by inch.

She didn't move a muscle. Wanting to feel everything. Her muscles stretched around him.

Once he was seated inside her completely, he lowered his head and pressed his lips to her ear. "It's like you were made for me."

They were made for each other.

When he began to move, she struggled to breathe through the sensations. He rocked inside her, over and over again. Thrusting in and out.

His teeth nipped her neck, and a small whimper escaped her lips.

Soon, she rose to meet him, thrust for thrust.

Every time their bodies clashed together, her sensitive breasts crashed against his hard chest. Throwing her head back, Quinn let out a cry. Everything about the man was overwhelming. Intoxicating.

Her heart thrashed against her ribs. The need inside her building.

When his hand lowered to her clit, another whimper escaped her lips. He used his thumb to rub her sensitive bundle.

That was it. Quinn's body spasmed as she soared over the edge.

Her breathing came out as erratic gasps. Her core throbbed around him. Wyatt thrust a few more times before tensing above her. He let out a growl of passion low in his chest as his orgasm took him.

For a moment, they both stilled. Breathing through the intensity of what they'd just experienced.

When he lifted his head, he touched a finger to her face and traced her cheekbone. "I could lie here with you forever."

"Forever sounds pretty damn good to me."

It seemed infinitely better than anything else in the world.

Dropping next to her, Wyatt pulled her against his side. She snuggled into him, knowing what they'd just done was anything but ordinary. Nothing about their relationship was ordinary. It was better. And she wanted to hold on with two hands and not let go.

CHAPTER 16

*W*yatt watched as a man entered the Green Pharmaceuticals building. It was close to midnight, but that didn't make the guy any less clear to Wyatt.

He wasn't one of the men Wyatt was waiting for. Not even close. This guy was too short. Too slim. Likely a lab technician arriving for shift changeover.

No. The men Wyatt wanted to see would no doubt be larger. Hardened. And there was a good chance they would be ex-military.

Wyatt had been sitting in his car for over two hours. He could easily last all night if he had to. He'd done it the previous night, no problem.

Luca guarded the back of the building while Eden was a street away, in a motel. Although he slept, all it would take was one message to have him at the building within minutes, ready to go.

The men were rotating shifts. Even though all the break-ins had occurred under the cover of night, they wanted to cover days as well. They didn't want to miss their one opportunity.

The three of them had flown over to Portland yesterday.

Oliver, Kye, and Bodie had returned to Marble Falls after covering the place the previous four nights.

Even while back home, no one was ever "off duty." They wanted eyes on the women. Particularly Quinn.

Evie was currently trying to locate Maya. If the woman was alive, and not already taken by Hylar's men, they hoped to find her—and find her soon. Evie was hacking into facial recognition software in the towns that surrounded Tyler, and specifically watching buses, car rental stores and airports. She had already hacked the woman's phone, email, and credit cards, but it looked like Maya had already abandoned them. Smart.

Wyatt leaned his head back but didn't take his eyes off the building.

He couldn't let Hylar's men kill more people. And he certainly wasn't going to let the guy get his hands on the materials he needed. The last thing he wanted his old commander to do was create more drugs and alter other men.

At the thought of his old commander, Wyatt's fists clenched. Even if he lived a hundred years, he would never forgive himself for trusting that man. For not seeing the greed that must have been there all along.

Wyatt had viewed the man as a father, whereas Hylar saw Wyatt and his team as weapons. Tools in the army he was building.

Once they found Hylar, he needed to die. There was no other way.

A ding from his phone pulled Wyatt out of his thoughts. Shooting a quick glance at the screen, a smile touched his lips before he drew his attention back to the building.

Quinn.

The woman had sent him a message with no words. All it contained was emojis. Because Wyatt had made a comment about being able to hack any code.

Big mistake. Quinn had taken that as a challenge, sending him nothing but emojis, requiring him to crack the meaning of each text. So far, he'd failed twice.

This time, it was easy. She sent him a bed, a snowflake, and a sad face.

She was telling him she was in bed. Cold and alone. He used voice activator to send her a message back. Four words—I miss you, too.

It wasn't a lie. He missed the woman like crazy. She'd literally just walked into his life one day and now he couldn't live without her. She'd changed everything.

And there wasn't a single part of him that wanted to go back.

Mason was due home in six days. That was when Wyatt planned to discuss his relationship with Quinn. If Mason ended up punching him in the face, Wyatt wouldn't stop him.

He hadn't set out to date his friend's younger sister, but he wasn't sorry. Far from it. He felt happier than he had in a long time. Possibly ever.

Wyatt sat a little straighter when a movement caught his eye.

His body tensed at the sight of three men exiting a side alley.

All three of them were tall and muscular. Clearly very physically capable. Just as Wyatt expected.

Without taking his eyes from the men, he hit dial on his phone.

Eden answered. "Jobs?"

"Call, Rocket. It's time."

Eden didn't respond. He didn't need to. Both he and Luca would be there within minutes.

Even though the men walked in the shadows, Wyatt could see every inch of them. They wore black and were clearly armed. Not one of them held weapons in their hands, but Wyatt could see the outlines of guns concealed under the men's clothing.

They probably only wore the weapons as a backup. After all, it was lab technicians they were expecting to face. Not trained former SEALs with altered DNA.

Wyatt knew the door to the building was locked. Each worker who entered had used a key to access the place. So when one of the men pushed it open with the simple turn of his hand, it was the last confirmation Wyatt needed.

They were Hylar's men.

It wasn't until they slipped into the building that he exited his car. He was halfway to the door when Eden and Luca appeared beside him. Even though they would have sprinted the distance from their locations, neither man breathed heavily.

The three of them entered the building without making a sound. They didn't speak because they didn't need to. They knew exactly what to do. What was about to happen.

Wyatt had already studied the blueprints of the building. Inside was a long hall. Down at the end was the main lab. That was where the majority of the supplies were kept.

As they neared the door, they heard gasps from the scientists. Accelerated heart rates. Wyatt could almost smell the fear.

The men would also hear them coming, but would likely assume they were more lab technicians. They were wrong.

Wyatt put his hand to the door and pushed inside.

The moment they entered, the three men in black looked up, a mixture of shock and anger on the faces.

One of the thugs already held a lab technician by the throat. The other two paused mid shoving materials into a bag. Scientists fanned across the room. Three men, two women. Each looking more scared than the next.

High-tech devices filled the space, while liquids, bottles, and trays covered the counters.

"Don't tell me you weren't expecting us?" Wyatt asked, directing his words at the man holding the technician.

He scowled, shoving away the guy he'd been holding. "Who the fuck are you assholes?"

Eden took a step into the room. "We're the assholes who are going to kill you."

One of the men holding supplies laughed as if Eden had just told a joke.

"Don't believe us?" Luca asked. "Good. I like taking people by surprise."

Wyatt scanned the room, making eye contact with each scientist. "Get out of here."

For a moment, no one moved, too scared to know whether they would die for doing so. Then one man took a step toward the door. And another.

Slowly, the rest followed. One of the men in black took a step toward a woman.

Wyatt was between them before the guy could blink. "Going somewhere?"

His eyes widened. Clearly he wasn't expecting an even fight. A look of fury came over his face. "So you're like us. You think that means you can stop us?"

He didn't *think* he could stop them. He knew he would.

A second of dead silence passed before the man pulled his arm back and shot it forward. Wyatt caught the fist in one hand.

That was all it took for the room to break out into violence. Around him, Wyatt could hear fists colliding with skin. Grunts of pain. Quick movements.

Wyatt twisted the fist in his hand, but the man wrenched it free, showing his strength.

"I'm looking forward to making you hurt," the man sneered.

Wyatt was looking forward to silencing the guy permanently.

The man grabbed a knife that was sheathed to his ankle, swiping in Wyatt's direction. Once, twice, three times. Wyatt dodged every strike. On the fourth, he kicked the knife out of his hand.

He didn't stop there. Wyatt immediately kicked the man in the gut. He hit the floor, sliding across the room. His large body hit a table and sent chemicals and test tubes flying.

Wyatt followed. "Where's Hylar hiding?"

The asshole jumped to his feet. "I'm not telling you shit."

He lunged at Wyatt, who stepped to the side just before the man made contact, grabbing him from behind. Snaking an arm around his throat, he immediately tightened his grip.

"Where's Hylar?"

The man spluttered in Wyatt's grip. Struggling for air.

A sharp pain bloomed in Wyatt's ribs. An elbow. Wyatt used his body to push the man to the floor. Disabling him.

He looked up to see Eden shoving a knife through his man's neck. Luca's guy was already dead.

Good. They only needed one man alive.

Luca gave both Wyatt and Eden a nod before lifting the bag of materials. The bag the men had just filled. He left, moving so quickly he was a blur.

Eden walked over to where Wyatt still held the man to the floor. Wyatt was about to stand when noise sounded from the front of the building. The door opened and footsteps followed. Many footsteps.

Wyatt remained where he was, not willing to release the man in his grasp.

A moment later, the lab door opened and police entered. Guns were immediately trained on them.

The man below Wyatt bucked. Wyatt firmed his grip—

And a second later, a bullet hit the man between the eyes.

Blood sprayed, splattering Wyatt's face and arms.

What the hell?

Rolling to the side, he raised his own gun. Eden already had his trained on the man in front of him.

That's when he saw who it was. Agent Sinclair. Member of the CIA. The man heading the Project Arma shutdown.

He was standing in front of the officers.

Sinclair holstered his gun. "Weapons down, boys, these guys are working with me."

When the officers dropped their weapons, Wyatt and Eden slowly lowered theirs.

Sinclair walked farther into the room, stopping a foot away from Wyatt.

Frustration clawed its way up Wyatt's throat. "Why the hell did you shoot him?" That was him being polite. What he *really* wanted to do was push Sinclair against the wall and take out some of his anger. Any hope of acquiring answers was lost.

"The guy was about to show the boys in blue what he could do. I did what I needed to."

Except that wasn't true. Wyatt could have easily subdued the man, particularly with Eden's help. And Sinclair knew that.

The team had researched Sinclair. They'd researched him *thoroughly*...and always came up with nothing. No prior connection to Hylar. No prior connection to Project Arma.

It was frustrating. They sensed more and more that something was off about the guy. His actions tonight just strengthened Wyatt's suspicion.

The same rage was bouncing off Eden. "We had it handled."

Sinclair's eyes narrowed. "How about you guys tell me what you're doing here?"

"We've been following the pharmaceutical lab break-ins across the country," Wyatt lied. Not willing to implicate Quinn. "We pieced together that this would be the next target."

"The fact that *you're* here means you knew Project Arma was behind it. Why didn't you tell us about these break-ins?" Eden asked.

Sinclair's jaw tightened. "By the way the scientists were killed, I had an idea that men from Arma were responsible. I couldn't be sure though. I can't just share every file with you unless I know for certain it involves Project Arma."

Wyatt crossed his arms. "But you *would* have told us. If you knew it involved them. Right?"

"Yes."

It was a lie. The asshole didn't even try to hide it. Even though Wyatt's team was supposed to be helping the government shut down the program, this guy was doing everything possible to keep them out of it.

They needed to keep looking into Sinclair. Find whatever it was that they were missing. Because they were missing *something*. They had to be.

"We appreciate your help on the matter." Sinclair turned, all but dismissing them. He'd only taken a couple of steps when he stopped and looked back. "There was a surviving witness at one of the other break-ins—a Maya Harper. We can't locate her. You wouldn't happen to know where she is by any chance?"

Wyatt shook his head. "No clue."

And if he did know, he wouldn't be telling this guy.

CHAPTER 17

*Q*uinn's cursor hovered over the delete function. She hated deleting research. It meant washing away hours of work that she'd dedicated time and energy to.

To be fair, the work she was deleting right now barely amounted to anything. Not that it made it easier.

Blowing out a long breath, she darted her gaze around Joan's Diner one last time before clicking "delete."

There. Done. No more research about laboratory break-ins, murdered scientists, or men with super strength. She was leaving it all in Wyatt's hands. Trusting him and his team to save the technicians at the final lab.

He'd assured her he would do everything in his power to do just that. That's why he was there right now, stopping the next crime.

There was a time where Quinn wouldn't have given up writing the story. The belief that all people should have access to all information had been firmly ingrained in her.

Now, Quinn's beliefs weren't so black and white. Her opinion on the matter was changing. Maybe not everyone wanted to know about the world's darkest and ugliest secrets. Maybe it was actually safer that they didn't know.

A lot of people just wanted to feel safe and were happy to leave that safety in the hands of people like Wyatt and his team.

Closing her laptop, Quinn sat back. She could have done this in her apartment, but the place was quiet and empty. With Wyatt out of town, it just highlighted the fact that, apart from Mrs. Potter—and Mason when he returned—she really didn't have anyone else here.

By nature, Quinn was a social person. She liked to be talking. Interacting.

Just then, she noticed two familiar faces stepping into the diner. Both women caught sight of her and immediately started weaving their way through the tables.

"Hey, Quinn!" Evie smiled as she and Shylah stopped beside her table.

"Hey! Fancy seeing you ladies here. How are you?"

"Why hello! We're good," Shylah said. "You'd be surprised how often we come here when the boys are away. And every other place in town."

Evie nodded. "Although, I have no doubt someone is trailing us."

Quinn understood that. "I'm pretty sure Wyatt has one of the guys watching me. He thinks I don't know, but I can just sense them."

Not just here and now. She sensed them constantly.

Evie smiled. "The boys are very safety conscious. It's nice to feel protected. Although, a bit of freedom at times is bliss."

Quinn didn't think she was in any danger, but if someone wanted to trail her, they were more than welcome.

Waving her arm, she signaled to the other seats. "Join me, please. Save me from my loneliness."

Shylah dropped into the seat opposite, while Evie sat beside her.

"It's nice to have another girl in the gang." Shylah smiled.

Evie nodded. "It is. And this girl gang needs coffee."

Oh yes. Quinn had already finished a cup, but more coffee always worked for her. "Woman, you are speaking my language."

When the waitress came to the table, all three women ordered large coffees. The waitress was quick, barely a couple minutes passing before they each had their drinks.

"This is my third for the day," Quinn admitted, for no reason other than to be open.

A surprised expression crossed Shylah's face. For a moment, Quinn thought she was about to receive judgment.

"Snap! This is my third, too. Coffee is life."

Evie lifted a shoulder. "This is my second, but I think I deserve a place in the coffee addict club."

Yep. It was official. These were definitely her people.

"We'll give you a spot," Shylah said, before eyeing the laptop in front of Quinn. "Working on something?"

"The opposite, actually. Deleting something."

Evie's forehead furrowed. "Something important?"

Very important. But not something that she needed to write and publish to the masses. "You know what Eden, Luca, and Wyatt are doing right now, don't you?"

Both women looked unsure how to respond. As if *they* knew what the men were doing but weren't sure if *Quinn* knew.

"It's okay. I know. I was actually working on a story about the break-ins before I learned about Wyatt. That's why I'm deleting the file. He said he's going to take care of it."

And Quinn was going to trust him.

Both women looked relieved. They clearly hadn't wanted to lie to her. Another tick to their names.

"If there were ever people you wanted to 'take care' of a situation, it's those guys," Evie said warmly.

Shylah lifted her coffee. "Heck yes. No one else comes close to their bad-assery."

A chuckle escaped Quinn. "Bad-assery. My brother would love that description."

"Oh, I keep forgetting you and Mason are siblings. What with you dating Wyatt and all. How silly of me."

They weren't officially dating. They hadn't put a label on their relationship. "We're still fairly new."

Shylah waved her hand. "Semantics."

"You got a good one." Evie leaned closer. "I mean, all the guys are amazing, but Wyatt's pretty special. Him and I spend a bit of time together working on Marble Protection's IT, and I have yet to find a flaw in the guy."

Quinn had yet to find a flaw with the guy as well. She was still racking her brain on how that was possible. No one could be that perfect, surely.

"Maybe he's one of those guys who leaves the dishes in the sink to 'soak.'" Quinn used air quotes when she said the last word.

Shylah's eyes widened. "Oh, I hate that. The lazy buggers. Or he could be someone who throws his clothes at the laundry basket rather than just walking the two feet to put them in. Dirty clothes end up everywhere."

"Yeah, everywhere but the basket." Quinn hated that.

Evie smiled. "I love Luca, but there's one thing he does that really grinds my gears. When he empties the trash, he never remembers to put a new bag inside. I usually have my hands full of garbage when I realize."

Quinn shook her head. "I guess I'll have to wait and see what Wyatt's is."

It had to be something.

"Then report back to us." Shylah looked much too excited by the prospect.

The women chatted for another ten minutes. Mostly about the boys and the crazy things they said and did.

When Quinn glanced down at her phone, she realized it was

almost time for her shift at the bakehouse. "I've got to get going. It was really nice seeing you both."

Shylah reached over and touched her hand. "We should organize a time for us all to go out together."

"I would love that."

"That would be lovely," Evie agreed. "I'll be away with Luca this weekend, but maybe the one after?"

Shylah leaned back again. "Lexie and I think he's going to pop the question."

Evie's cheeks went a rosy pink shade. "I disagree. We haven't been dating long enough."

Quinn stood and began packing up her belongings. "If there's anything I've learned since meeting Wyatt, it's that time is inconsequential when it comes to relationships. When you know, you know."

And Quinn definitely knew.

"So, you *are* in a relationship." Shylah's eyes twinkled.

Quinn pulled the strap of her bag over her shoulder. "I'm infatuated with the guy. But don't go telling him that. He'll get a big head."

All three women laughed before saying a quick goodbye.

God, this town was just getting better by the day. She had a job she was enjoying, a guy she was swooning over, and the women seemed to be people she could easily become good friends with.

Quinn was just stepping outside when a message came through on her phone. Pulling it out, her heartbeat picked up a notch when she saw it was Wyatt. No words. Just four emojis. Two coffees, a couple holding hands and a sun.

Quinn smiled. If she was interpreting the message correctly, he was saying he'd be back in time for breakfast.

Gosh, she hoped she was right. She missed the guy like crazy. Missed talking to him. Touching him. Seeing his forehead furrow whenever she did something that confused him.

Which was far too often.

Quinn was just about to respond when her phone started ringing.

Tanya.

Crap. She hadn't spoken to her friend in several days…and she certainly hadn't told her about the last time she'd seen Darren. She'd been distancing herself from Tanya because it was too hard to maintain a friendship with the way her husband had treated her.

Reluctantly, Quinn lifted the phone to her ear. "Hey, Tan."

"Quinny. How are you?"

She felt a tenderness at the use of the nickname. Tanya was the only person who called her that.

Quinn continued down the street. "I'm good. Just settling into small-town life. Did I tell you I got a job at a bakery?"

Tanya gasped through the line. "No. I don't believe it."

Quinn wouldn't have believed it a few months ago, either. "It's true. I make coffee with an actual coffee machine and everything."

"Quinn. You're an instant-coffee woman."

She *used* to be an instant-coffee woman. "What can I say, now I'm a changed woman."

"Wait until I tell Darren, he'll lose his marbles."

She laughed, but it was forced. "Is he at work?"

"Actually, no. That's why I'm calling."

Quinn stopped. She tried to ignore the dread that was pooling in her stomach. "What is it, Tan?"

"He's still in Marble Falls. I tried to convince him to come home, but he said you weren't okay. *Are* you okay, Quinn?"

It took her a moment to wrap her head around what Tanya had just said. She had one glaringly obvious question—why was he still here? To convince her to drop the story again? Dammit, why hadn't she just told him it was done?

"Have you spoken to him?" Quinn asked.

"A few nights ago. He hasn't been answering my calls today or yesterday. Just sending quick text messages. I miss him."

So, he hadn't told his wife the real reason he'd come. Quinn had no idea where he fit into this whole Project Arma and drug theft problem, but if Tanya didn't know about it, Quinn was still dead set against involving her.

"The next time I see him, I'll try to convince him to go back to New York."

She intentionally left out the fact she hadn't seen the man in over a week, not wanting to raise alarm in his wife.

Tanya sighed. "Thank you. I already lost you and our weekly coffee dates. I'm going crazy without him, too."

Quinn smiled at the memory of their coffee dates. They went every Wednesday and basically spent the entire time complaining about men. It was very therapeutic.

"I miss our coffee dates, too. Maybe we can do a phone date next Wednesday."

"Yes! And we can FaceTime it with coffees in hand."

Quinn chuckled, even though concern about the Darren situation still clouded her mind. "It's a date."

"Good. And thank you, Quinn. You're a good friend. Chat again soon."

"Bye, Tan."

Quinn hung up and shut her eyes.

Good friend? She felt like the furthest thing from a good friend. She hadn't told Tanya about the real reason Darren was in town because she hadn't wanted to endanger her. Now, she was basically lying to her.

The moment Wyatt returned, she needed to tell him about Darren so they could find him. They had to find out what his motivation was for trying to convince her to keep quiet about the story.

They also needed to know how he knew about the killers' genetic enhancements.

Blowing out a long breath, Quinn continued walking to work. She hoped like hell Darren hadn't involved himself too deeply in this mess. For Tanya's sake, the guy better be redeemable.

CHAPTER 18

Quinn handed the coffees to her customers. The older couple thanked her before heading out. She was just about to turn around and begin cleaning when one of the customers stopped; the lady, who was halfway out the door.

"This is fabulous coffee."

A smile a mile wide spread across Quinn's face. "I'm glad you like it!"

She remained composed right up until the door closed behind the couple. Once it was just her, she pumped both fists into the air and let out a squeal. Then, of course, she followed it up with a little happy dance.

Finally. She could make a cup of coffee that didn't taste terrible.

Quinn was kicking goals today. First, she'd said goodbye to a story that she'd previously been determined to write. Now, she was making coffee so good it warranted compliments.

Win-win.

"You look happy."

Quinn spun around to see Mrs. Potter standing behind her.

Jeez, the woman moved like a cat. And she'd probably caught Quinn's cheesy dancing. "She liked my coffee."

It sounded like a trivial reason to be so happy. But not for her. Because for Quinn, it was a small step forward in this new life she was building for herself.

A life that entailed new friends, a guy she really liked, and learning new skills. She hadn't lied to Tanya, she really was a changed woman.

Mrs. Potter nodded. "I heard. How wonderful. I hope you're enjoying it here. Not just in the bakery, but in Marble Falls in general."

"I am."

At first, Quinn had seen the job as just that. A job. Something to earn her some money until she could get back a semblance of the life she'd lost.

At some point, Marble Falls had started to feel like home.

"There's something peaceful about Marble Falls."

Mrs. Potter patted Quinn's shoulder. "The town draws you in, doesn't it?" She took an apron from the shelf and handed it to Quinn. "Would you like to help me make some cinnamon rolls?"

Quinn's eyes widened a fraction. Last shift, Mrs. Potter had shown her how to make apple pies. Quinn had loved it. But *watching* someone bake something was very different than *helping* them bake.

Plus, the cinnamon rolls were the most popular item sold at the bakehouse. No way did she want to mess them up.

With tentative fingers, Quinn took the apron. "Are you sure? I could put a dent in your bakery's perfect reputation."

"Nonsense. Baking is like math. There's a process. And once you learn the process, it's easy."

That analogy did nothing to curb Quinn's apprehension. She was also terrible at math.

Mrs. Potter went to the cupboard and took ingredients out to place on the prep bench.

"It's great that you have work space and an oven out here, as well as in back."

Mrs. Potter nodded. "I designed it so I can bake in the back in the morning but also in the front, during the day, in between serving."

The woman was clearly a genius.

Quinn tied the apron around her waist. "Just promise me you won't sell these rolls if they suck."

"Nothing that is ever made in this store has ever 'sucked,' and I don't anticipate today being the first."

Well, at least one of them had confidence.

Quinn watched as Mrs. Potter got started. The woman explained every step. She also explained why each step was important, which helped cement it into Quinn's brain.

After a few minutes, Mrs. Potter placed the dough in front of Quinn. "If you kneed this for a few minutes, we can place them on the tray."

As they continued working through the process, Quinn found she was actually enjoying herself. "I can't believe I'm saying this, but baking actually seems kind of therapeutic."

"Oh, yes, it is. There's a calmness in the repetitive motions and the step-by-step process. It forces you to be mindful."

"I guess it also takes your mind off anything that's happening in your life. Things you may not want to think about."

Mrs. Potter paused to give Quinn her full attention. "Funny you say that. That's exactly why I began baking so many years ago." She turned back to what she was doing, a reflective expression on her face. "You may not believe this, but I used to be a criminal defense attorney."

Okay, if that wasn't a knock-her-socks-off kind of surprise, nothing would be.

Mrs. Potter was right. It was pretty unbelievable. The woman looked about as far from a defense attorney as possible. "No..."

"Oh, yes. My old life involved long working days and even

longer nights. I had a complete absence of work-life balance. My job was my world. And I loved it."

It sounded like Quinn with her job at *The New York Times*.

"What happened?"

"I baked a cake."

Quinn chuckled, unsure if she was being serious.

"I don't even remember why now. I'd barely baked a thing in my life, but one day, I saw some bananas in a bowl, the eggs in the fridge, and decided to make a banana cake. It was fun. So, a few days later, I made another. Soon, I was baking every other day. I shared what I baked with friends and family. No one seemed to hate it. One day, I realized I enjoyed being in the kitchen more than the courtroom. And that was it. I left the high-stress job, moved here and started Mrs. Potter's Bakehouse."

"Just like that?"

"It seems odd, doesn't it? I guess when something feels right, you just need to follow it. We only have a limited time on this Earth. Why not follow what makes us happy?"

There was so much truth to that statement. "Do you ever regret it?"

"Leaving my job? Oh, no. Not for a second. Don't get me wrong, it was scary. The corporate life was all I'd ever known. But at some point, I started needing something different. Something quieter. Something to feed my soul."

It was like the woman was speaking every little whisper that had been floating around Quinn's brain for the last couple weeks.

Never in Quinn's life would she have been able to picture herself feeling at home in a small town. Never would she have been able to picture herself *baking*.

And yet, here she was, living in Marble Falls, baking cinnamon rolls. Happy.

"Sometimes our lives take unexpected turns," she continued. "I've found it's best just to roll with it." Mrs. Potter lifted the dough. "This looks fantastic."

Quinn smiled, then glanced at the clock. "Will they be bought? It's already afternoon."

She laughed. "No. We're making these purely for you to learn. What doesn't get purchased are for you to take home. Wyatt loves these."

Yep. Quinn knew that. Wyatt raved about the rolls a lot. She loved the guy's sweet tooth. It was just one of the things that set him apart from the men she was used to.

Quinn and Mrs. Potter spent the next half hour finishing the rolls. It wasn't until they were baking that Mrs. Potter headed home for the day. At that point, Quinn found herself unable to take her eyes from the oven.

If these rolls turned out good, she would be doing more than a happy dance. She would be raving from the rooftops to anyone who would listen that not only could she make a mean cup of coffee, but she could also bake the best cinnamon rolls in town.

Maybe Wyatt could be her taste-tester. Let her know if they were as good as they usually were.

No. Scrap that. The man would never tell her the truth. He'd probably say he loved them even if they tasted like ash, just to make her happy.

Someone who *would* tell her the truth was Mason. Five days left until he was due to return. Maybe she'd bake some more rolls then. He would be the perfect test subject.

He'd wanted to return earlier, but had agreed to continue their visit with Sage's brother once Wyatt assured him Quinn was safe.

Quinn took a step toward her phone...only to stop and press a hand to her temple. She felt the beginnings of a headache. Strange, she never got headaches.

Not only that...was she also feeling a bit dizzy?

Frowning, Quinn was about to grab a glass of water when the dinging of the timer went off.

The cinnamon rolls were ready!

Turning back to the oven, she switched it off and opened the door.

Sweet scents immediately bombarded her. Now she just had to hope they tasted as good.

Quinn was placing the rolls on the counter when the door opened. Swinging her gaze to the front of the store, her heart clenched at the sight of Wyatt stepping inside.

An excited squeal escaped her lips before she ran around the counter and propelled herself into his waiting arms. He caught her easily.

God, it was good to have the man's strong arms wrapped around her again. They'd only spent a couple days apart, but it felt like a lot longer.

Her lips went straight to his. The kiss was firm and knowing. She groaned deep in her throat. Oh, how she'd missed these kisses. Missed his touch. Missed every little thing about him.

After a minute, Quinn finally lifted her head. "I thought you were getting home tomorrow."

Not that she was complaining. Not. One. Bit.

He nuzzled her neck, causing shock waves of awareness to filter through her body. "No. The sun, coffee, and couple meant I was looking forward to waking up with you."

She threw her head back and laughed. "Well, you definitely needed to put a picture of a bed in that text somewhere."

He raised a brow. "I didn't want you getting any ideas."

Oh, she definitely would have gotten ideas. Actually, those very thoughts were running rampant right now. "Too late."

Wyatt lifted his hand and grazed a finger down her cheek. "I hope those ideas include dinner at my place."

Amongst other activities. "Dinner, dessert, then the other stuff. I'll bring dessert."

His eyes widened in shock.

She couldn't blame the guy. She had told him on numerous

occasions that anything she prepared in the kitchen would likely poison the consumer.

"Don't look so surprised. Mrs. Potter has shown me a few things while you've been gone. One of those things just happens to be her famous cinnamon rolls. Although, they both still need to be glazed and frosted. That only consists of a couple of ingredients, though, so should be foolproof."

But hell, even if the plain roll tasted as good as it smelled, Quinn would feel amazing.

"I'll eat anything you make. And it's no surprise you're picking up new skills while I'm gone. You had to fill your time with something to stop missing me."

Quinn playfully hit his shoulder before kissing him again. She couldn't help it. She needed her lips to be on his.

Even though she wanted to know how his trip went, that could wait. At the moment, the only thing she wanted to do was refamiliarize herself with the man.

"I missed you," she said, finally coming up for air.

"I think I missed you more."

"Not possible."

Pressing her lips to his a final time, Quinn slid down his body. Moving back to the prep area, she placed the unglazed cinnamon rolls in a bag before sliding them across the counter. They'd only made two, luckily.

"That's dessert. Well, an almost-complete dessert."

"I had something else in mind."

Jeez, he was going to be the death of her. "Get your mind out of the gutter, buddy. You get that *after* you tell me my cinnamon rolls are amazing."

Wyatt opened his mouth to say something—only to stop. A frown marred his brow.

"What is it?"

"Can you smell that?"

Quinn's own forehead furrowed as she sniffed. She couldn't

smell anything. "No."

When Wyatt's eyes shot to the door leading to the back kitchen, Quinn moved in that direction.

Oh crap. Had Mrs. Potter left something on and forgotten to tell her?

Moving to the back, Quinn pushed through the door, but immediately pulled back.

Gas. It hit her hard.

Where was it coming from? The room was pitch-black, which was normal. All the blinds were closed, as well as the back door.

Reaching for the light switch, Quinn was about to flick it on, but was stopped by Wyatt's hand on her wrist.

"If you turn the switch on, it could cause a spark and ignite an explosion."

Holy heck. She didn't know that.

She could have just caused the entire kitchen to blow up.

Wyatt took hold of her hand and pulled her back toward the front of the store. He didn't stop at the counter though. He kept going.

Once they stepped outside, Wyatt led them to the back of the building. Stopping at the gas meter, he opened it and immediately rotated a valve.

"I'm turning the gas off," Wyatt said quietly.

Suddenly, her earlier headache and dizziness made sense.

Wyatt pulled his phone out and pressed it to his ear. "Ax. I know I just sent you home, but I need you back here."

Oliver. He must have been the one watching her today. Although she hadn't seen the guy once.

"Ax was in a car across the street," Wyatt said, confirming her thoughts. "He only would have come into the store if someone who posed a threat had entered, or if you'd gone into the back."

And if she had gone into the back, Oliver never would have made it inside in time.

Wyatt's arm tightened around her waist as they waited for

Oliver. He was quick, taking only a couple of minutes. When he arrived, his brows immediately drew together.

"Gas."

"Yes. I've turned the main switch off. We need to air the space out, then we can see where the leak is coming from. I didn't want Quinn breathing it in, but also didn't want to leave her out here alone."

Oliver nodded before moving to the back door, disappearing inside.

It didn't take long for him to open the place up. Less than five minutes later, Oliver returned, the grim look on his face telling Quinn she wasn't going to like what he said next. No doubt Wyatt wouldn't, either.

"The gas hose was disconnected from the stove."

Wyatt's body tensed as much as hers.

Crap. That meant this was no accident, right?

Oliver turned and checked the door. "The lock wasn't broken."

That's because it was never locked during open hours. "Mrs. Potter likes to keep it unlocked. She mentioned something about locking herself out before." Tiny goose bumps rose along Quinn's arms. "Do you guys think someone was trying to kill me?"

God, saying those words out loud felt like she was in the middle of a dream. Or more accurately, a nightmare.

Oliver's expression remained impossible to read. When she looked up at Wyatt, she saw his features immediately smooth, as well. "Let's get you home. Ax, you okay to wait for the kitchen to air out before locking up?"

The big man nodded. Then Wyatt was moving her away.

Quinn was very aware he intentionally hadn't answered her question. And she knew why. She'd come very close to dying. That was no accident.

CHAPTER 19

$\mathcal{W}$yatt shook a decent amount of garlic powder into the pasta sauce. While Quinn was busy getting changed, he was cooking dinner. Although she was in her own apartment, he was listening to her movements across the hall. Stopping at any new sounds that passed their doors.

That wasn't the only thing he was doing. While the pasta cooked on the stove, his laptop sat on the counter. On the screen was every bit of information he could find on Darren Hoffman, Quinn's former boss.

Thirty-eight years old. Married. No kids. That was the surface information. The stuff that was easy to find.

There was other information. Information Wyatt had needed to dig for. Unfortunately, none of it raised any red flags.

No suspicious emails in his inbox, no unusually large payments into his accounts, and no background in military or pharmaceuticals.

As far as Wyatt could tell, the man was squeaky clean. Which was annoying as all hell, because he was the only person Wyatt could think of who might have reason to harm Quinn. Or, at least, the only person Quinn had mentioned.

Plus, he'd found no return flights to New York bearing his name. Which meant, it was likely he was still in Marble Falls. The question was, where?

Wyatt wanted to find him. If Darren was responsible for the little setup at the bakery tonight, Wyatt wanted the guy to pay.

Rage pumped through his veins at what could have happened if he hadn't been there to stop Quinn from switching the light on.

As the pasta water began to bubble over, Wyatt quickly turned down the heat. He was making beef ragù with fettuccine. The table was already set and candles lit.

He'd wanted tonight to be romantic. Regardless of what had happened, he was still going ahead with the dinner. The only problem was, he couldn't get today's incident out of his head.

If it wasn't Darren, the only other person Wyatt could think of who might have reason to want her dead was Hylar. And that was only if he'd somehow discovered it was because of *her* that his last attempt to rob a lab was stopped. The man shouldn't have access to that information.

Wyatt didn't think it was Hylar. Or anyone who was part of Project Arma. They would have gone a more direct route. The whole bakery sabotage was amateur. And Arma was anything but amateur. If they wanted her dead, they would have just walked in and killed her before hightailing it across the country.

Wyatt paused as movement of Quinn leaving her apartment sounded.

Shutting his laptop, he was opening the door before Quinn had a chance to knock. At the sight of her, heat slammed into his gut.

Quinn's thick black hair was down, flowing over her bare shoulders. She wore a black top with thin straps and jeans that hugged her legs.

He took a step closer. "How has no man claimed you yet?"

A smile lit her face, and it only made her more beautiful. "I didn't let any man claim me…because I was waiting for you."

Wyatt reached out and pulled the woman into his arms, loving the way she melted against him. Her body fit his like that was where she was meant to be.

A purring sound escaped her chest as he kissed her. It sent his blood pumping.

Perfect. The woman was perfect, and she was his.

When he pulled back, it was to see Quinn's eyes closed, but the smile remained. Her voice was like silk. "Mm, not only do you taste good, but you smell good too."

Wyatt chuckled as he pulled her inside and closed the door. "As much as I'd like to take credit for that, it's likely the pasta that smells good."

A short gasp escaped her lips. "It smells delicious. And there's wine. And candles…"

"And a sexy man who made it all possible?" he whispered in her ear before moving past her.

"Yes. And you."

"I hope you like beef ragù. It's my specialty." Wyatt lifted the pasta off the stove and strained it.

"Well, it certainly smells better than my specialty—steamed rice. Actually, I'm pretty sure the last time I made steamed rice it went clumpy."

He flicked her a quick glance. "You don't give yourself enough credit. By the look of those cinnamon rolls, you're better in the kitchen than you think."

She leaned her hip against the kitchen counter. "We shouldn't get too excited, I still need to glaze them. I'm actually finding baking to be kind of enjoyable though. Which is nuts, because I've never been that type of person."

"What kind of person?"

She lifted a shoulder. "The kind of person who bakes a cake."

"What kind of person are you?"

Wyatt knew the kind of person *he* thought she was. But he

wanted to hear what kind of person *she* thought she was. Because he wasn't sure the two were lining up.

"The kind who skips the grocery store and orders Uber Eats. The kind who prioritizes writing a story over any and everything else. The kind whose mind is moving at a hundred miles an hour because her life is so busy. At least, that's the person I used to be."

That sounded more like how her *life* used to be, rather than who she was. "Do you miss it?"

Her brows lifted. "My life in New York?" She seemed to consider her answer. "I thought I would. I thought I'd be so bored without journalism. But I'm really not. For the first time in my life, I feel...content. Like I don't have to push myself to the limit. I can just be."

Quinn probably didn't realize how damn happy that made him. A part of him had been worried that Marble Falls wouldn't be enough for her. Wouldn't be big enough. Busy enough. She still might need the busyness of a big town at some point. But for now, at least, she appeared comfortable.

"I'm glad you're happy."

Their gazes caught. Although no words were spoken, the silence was loud.

It wasn't just Quinn who was happy. It was him, too. They had each other to thank for that. They cared about each other. It was big and scary. And it was real.

"Thank you."

He dipped his head. "Ready to eat?"

"Yes. Feed me, please. I'm a starved woman."

Five minutes later, they both had a bowl of ragù in front of them and cutlery in hand. Over the meal, Quinn made him laugh and smile more times than he could count. Her stories about the crazy things she'd done to get to the bottom of the stories she'd written were mindboggling.

One time she'd dressed up as a man to get into a gentlemen's club. She'd lasted the entire evening without a single person catching her. Another time, she'd pretended to be the CEO of a tech company to get information from unsuspecting customers.

Wyatt could imagine her pulling off the CEO role—she definitely had the confidence—but not the man part. Not for a second. She was too feminine for that.

But it was the stories about her and Mason that really got him. She described the guy as a pain in the butt. Even though he nodded and agreed, he secretly loved the fact that her brother vetted all her dates. That he was a constant pair of eyes looking over her shoulder.

They didn't talk about the gas leak once. It wasn't until they were both almost done that she asked the question he'd been waiting for.

"How was Portland?"

Wyatt had been looking forward to the question. Because he knew she'd be happy with the answer.

"We saved them."

Quinn breathed out a sigh and dropped her head into her hands. After a few seconds, he started to wonder if he should be concerned, but then she looked up.

Relief. Gratitude. Serenity. It was all there on her face.

"That makes me happy. It would have killed me to see any more lab technicians die when they could be saved."

That was just one of the things about Quinn that drew him in. Her giant heart.

She leaned forward. "You're amazing."

Nope. One of them was amazing, but it wasn't him.

"You're the one who didn't give up on the story, even when you lost the life you knew. *You* saved their lives. You helped us prevent Arma from getting something they wanted. Thank you."

"Okay, I guess we're both pretty amazing."

Wyatt reached across the table and interlaced his fingers with hers. "I'll agree with that."

"Did you get any information from the men who broke in?"

Wyatt's muscles tensed. "No. The police arrived, alongside a CIA agent. The agent killed the last man." The fact still made Wyatt both angry and frustrated.

"I'm sorry."

He shrugged, playing it off as no big deal. When in reality, it was a huge deal. "There'll be more leads to help us locate the remaining Project Arma members."

Quinn paused for a moment, seeming to be considering her next words. "Do you think Maya's still alive?"

A muscle ticked in Wyatt's jaw. He wished he could tell her what she wanted to hear, but he didn't want to lie.

"I *hope* that she's alive. I really do. Evie's working overtime searching surrounding towns. If we do find her, we'll go to her. I promise."

It was entirely possible the woman was captured or dead. Both Wyatt and Quinn knew that. If she *was* alive, and only using cash, it might be almost impossible to find her.

Wyatt could see the guilt that ate at Quinn. Like she'd failed the other woman. For not convincing her to come to Marble Falls at their first meeting, and for arriving late the second time.

Quinn straightened in her seat. "I know you guys and Evie are doing everything you can."

They were. He hoped that she was on the run and they found her before anyone else did.

"Can I ask about Darren. Is there anything I don't know that I should?"

Quinn's face hardened. "Darren's an asshole. Always has been. Is there anything in particular you want to know?"

"Did you date?"

Quinn laughed but there was no humor behind it. "No. He's married. I'm good friends with his wife, actually. Or was. I've been distancing myself since Darren fired me. She's a lovely person. I have no idea why she married the asshat."

Wyatt would have used a stronger term than "asshat." "Did he ever give you any hint as to why he didn't want you to pursue the story about the labs?"

There was a subtle jolt to her hand.

"I wasn't trying to hide this from you, but with everything else, it just kind of slipped my mind. That night you found the bruises on my arm, Darren admitted to me that he knew about people with altered DNA. He wouldn't tell me how he knew or why he needed me to let go of the story. Just said they were dangerous."

No wonder Quinn had been so freaked out when she saw him use his strength and speed. She'd been warned not once, but twice that people like him were dangerous.

"I don't want to alarm you, but Darren might still be in town."

The total absence of any surprise on the woman's face told Wyatt that she already knew. "Tanya called me. This morning, actually. She wanted me to ask Darren to come home."

Everyone wanted Darren to go the hell home.

"Does his wife know about men with altered DNA?"

Quinn immediately shook her head. "I don't think so. When I asked Tanya if she knew anything about why I was fired, she said no. She doesn't like to involve herself in Darren's or my work. She suffers from anxiety. I think the research we do stresses her out. I also don't think Darren would have told her. He doesn't show her much respect. Basically sees her as the housekeeper."

Yeah. The guy sounded like a real gem in the husband department.

Quinn leaned across the table. "What did you find on him?"

Wyatt shook his head. She knew him too well already. "Nothing. Everything points to him being completely average."

Quinn lifted a shoulder. "Maybe he is. Maybe he's just a normal jackass who got caught up with the wrong people."

There was one problem with that. Normal jackasses don't usually try to kill people by causing their workplace to explode. "I looked up Tanya, too. Nothing."

Quinn didn't seem surprised. Lifting her wineglass, she took a sip. "Sorry. I shouldn't have brought any of this up. Curiosity tends to get the better of me."

"I love your curiosity. How about we talk about how beautiful you look tonight instead?"

She frowned. "Just tonight?"

Wyatt threw his head back and laughed. "Every damn second of every damn day."

"That's better."

Jesus, where had this woman been his whole life?

Standing, they both began cleaning the table. Half an hour later and they were on the couch. They were going to wait a bit before glazing the cinnamon rolls.

Quinn chose an action movie. But it was her body pressed against his that stole his focus.

"I've been thinking I might stay."

Wyatt tightened his arm around her waist. "I was hoping you would. I've missed you the last few nights."

Sleeping with her soft body against his made for the best damn sleep of all time.

She looked up at him. "No. I don't mean tonight. Although, I *am* staying the night. That's a given. You'd have to physically remove me if you wanted me out. I mean, I might stay here. In Marble Falls. For good."

For a moment, Wyatt didn't react. Because everything about what she'd said was life changing. "Really?"

She wet her lips. "Yes."

"I would like that." Not just like; it would be the best damn thing to happen. Possibly ever.

"That's good. Because we haven't talked about us or where we're headed. I didn't want to freak you out."

"Why would that freak me out?"

She shrugged one of her shoulders. "Maybe you thought I was passing through. Maybe you see this—*us*—as temporary."

Not a chance. He'd thought she was on the same page as him. Maybe not. Maybe she needed him to say it.

"There's not a single thing that's temporary about us, Quinn. I see you. I see everything about you. And it sucks me in and makes me want more. I don't see that ever changing."

He heard her quick intake of breath, then the pounding of her heart.

She was surprised. Whether she was surprised by his honesty or surprised by how he felt, he wasn't sure. He'd say it again and again if she needed him to. Because he meant every word.

"I don't see us as temporary either."

Wyatt lifted her onto his lap. Even though she'd been right beside him, he wanted her closer.

"Good. Because if you left, I would follow."

She leaned against his chest, her head resting over his heart. "I'm not going anywhere. But if I do, follow me, break down my door and talk some sense into me."

"Was already planning on it."

CHAPTER 20

Quinn pulled up in front of The Duck Motel. It was Friday, and she had just delivered items to three different addresses. This was her last stop before she was done for the day.

From the corner of her eye, she caught sight of a gray sedan pulling in across the lot. She didn't need to look up to know who it was.

Oliver. He'd been trailing her to each address, not even attempting to remain hidden.

Quinn didn't mind. Particularly after the gas-in-the-bakery episode. Clearly, Wyatt felt better if she was watched, so watched she would be.

Peering up at the motel, her first thought was that it looked neglected. Old. Basically, the place needed some serious TLC.

Lifting the box of apple pies, Quinn climbed out of the car. Mrs. Potter used a delivery service, but the usual delivery man had called in sick. Quinn didn't mind getting the gig. Mostly because *she* had been the one to bake the pies. Just like she'd been the one to make the fresh donuts that had sold out by midday.

And in her opinion, both tasted amazing. She knew because she'd had a generous serving of both.

If Quinn wasn't careful, she'd be gaining some weight here in Marble Falls. In fact, she probably already had.

As she made her way across the lot, Quinn decided she didn't care one bit if she gained weight, and she doubted Wyatt would mind either.

He seemed happy that *she* was happy, both baking and remaining in Marble Falls.

Quinn had no idea how Mason would react. He was due to return tomorrow. She couldn't wait. They had a lot of talking to do.

Glancing around, Quinn scanned the door numbers. The building was two stories, and half the rooms were on one side, while the other half faced the forested area around the back. She was looking for room twenty-two but couldn't spot it anywhere. It must be one of the back rooms.

As she headed around the building, footsteps sounded behind her. Turning her head, she saw Oliver a few feet away.

She offered a smile, but it wasn't returned. Oliver had a hard look on his face. Like he was watching. Waiting for trouble.

She was glad he was here. The place gave her the creeps. There were only a handful of accommodations in Marble Falls. This one had to be the worst.

Scanning the doors at the back of the building, she noticed twenty-two was at the end of the first floor.

At least there were no stairs. Even though she was only holding one box, with her luck, she would trip on her own feet and roll down. She was sure Oliver would catch her. But it was the potential embarrassment that would hurt the most.

When she stopped in front of the door, Quinn lifted her hand to knock, only to pause when Oliver's hand went to her shoulder.

"There's someone in the woods." He spoke quietly but quickly.

"I heard them moving. They're fast. It's one of my kind. Go back to the car."

Quinn looked to the spot Oliver was watching. She didn't see or hear anyone.

"He's almost here. Go, Quinn."

Jolting at the urgency in Oliver's voice, Quinn turned and began a fast walk back to the car. She shot a look over her shoulder just before turning the corner to see Oliver still watching the same spot.

Quickening her steps, she scanned the parking lot as she walked.

What the heck was someone doing in the bushes? Were they waiting for her? Was the whole delivery a setup to get to her?

A shiver coursed down Quinn's spine at the thought.

Once at her car, she placed the box on the roof while pulling the keys from her pocket. It took her longer than it should have and she dropped the keys in the process.

Damn nerves.

Once the door was open, Quinn quickly slid behind the wheel. She was about to lock the car when the passenger door suddenly opened.

A small gasp escaped her lips at the sight of Darren beside her. *What on Earth?*

The man was almost unrecognizable. Dark circles shadowed his eyes, and his normally perfect clothes were dirty and wrinkled. His hair, which was always slicked back, was a ruffled mess.

The guy looked as far from his normal self as possible. And when she breathed in, she immediately smelled the pungent odor of whiskey. It made her want to gag.

Grasping the door handle, she was stopped by Darren's hand on her wrist.

"You're not going anywhere." His grip was tight and painful.

"What are you doing here, Darren? Why aren't you in New York?"

"Why aren't I in New York?" He didn't even sound like himself, his voice hoarse and desperate. "Because you can't do what you're fucking told!"

She tried to yank her arm from his hold, but his fingers were like a manacle around her wrist. "What are you talking about?"

"Don't play dumb with me. You know what I wanted from you. One thing. One lousy damn thing! And you couldn't do it." He shook his head. "You know, they wanted me to kill you the moment you started researching the story. Stupid me, I thought I could just fire you. But they were right—you need to die."

Ice slid through her veins.

"I tried to make it look like an accident," Darren continued. "The bakery was supposed to explode. Your death would have been quick and easy. That was my mistake. Now I know I need to man up and do it with my bare hands."

Her heart began to pound in her chest. "It's done. I've dropped the story. I even deleted the little I'd written."

He laughed. The sound made her stomach turn. "And you want me to just believe you? After I went so far as to fire you and you *still* didn't drop the story? I don't think so."

"So what's the plan? You sent your genetically altered soldier after me? Was he supposed to attack the moment I stepped up to the door?"

Darren's body visibly tightened. "What are you talking about?"

"The genetically altered guy in the bushes! I'm assuming he's with you."

Real fear entered Darren's eyes as he cast his gaze outside the car. "No. I'm alone. I'm doing what they asked. I'm shutting you up. They shouldn't be here!"

"They told you to shut me up? Darren, how did you even become involved in this?"

If possible, his fingers tightened further. Pain roared up her arm. "That's none of your damn business! I'm doing what I need to do to survive. They've got me by the balls."

Darren reached for something behind him.

Crap. He was going to pull out a knife. Or a gun. Whatever it was, she was sure she wouldn't like it.

Moving on instinct, Quinn grabbed the key, wrapped her fist around the base and, with all the force she could muster, punched it into Darren's thigh.

The man yelped in pain. When he let her go and grabbed his leg, she took advantage of his distraction. Yanking the door open, she threw herself out of the car and ran back toward the building.

Please, oh, please, someone be at the desk. Preferably someone with a weapon.

Quinn was halfway across the lot when she was hit full force from behind.

Slamming to the ground hard, Quinn cried out in pain as her cheek scraped against the pavement. She tried to push up, but Darren's body was like a giant weight holding her down.

Before she could attempt to buck him off, Darren fisted a handful of her hair, lifting her head, then slammed it back to the pavement.

Pain ricocheted through her skull. For a moment, she ceased fighting, her brain foggy.

She was vaguely aware of being rolled onto her back, but her limbs felt too heavy to move.

Large hands went to her neck.

"I didn't want to kill you, Quinn. I tried to fire you. You wouldn't let it go! And if I have to choose between your life and mine, I choose mine."

Darren's fingers tightened around her throat, cutting off her air. Quinn grabbed at his large hands, desperate to make him stop.

Panic surged through her as dark spots entered her vision.

She was on the verge of losing consciousness. And if she did that, she was dead.

Mason had taught her self-defense. She needed to focus. Remember.

She couldn't break his hold. She needed to attack the attacker. Attack his weak point.

The last scraps of energy were quickly leaving her body, along with her breath. This was her only chance.

Forcing her arms up, she put her thumbs to his eyes and dug in with as much strength as she could muster.

Darren yelped in pain before releasing her neck. His hands immediately went to her wrists.

Quinn coughed and spluttered as she sucked in as many breaths as she could.

"You bitch!"

She didn't see it coming until it was too late. Darren punched her in the eye. The hit was fast and hard.

Through the fog of pain, she could just make out his arm reeling back, about to punch her again.

No. She couldn't let him. She'd lose consciousness for sure this time.

As his fist came down, she moved her head to the side just in time. There was a loud *crack* as his fist slammed into the pavement.

Darren grabbed his wrist and rolled to the side. The man was now howling in pain.

Pushing to her feet, Quinn stumbled forward. Her legs were unsteady and her head pounded. She focused on putting one foot in front of the other.

She'd almost made it to the door of the reception office when footsteps sounded behind her.

When a hand grabbed her shoulder, she let out a scream and spun.

It wasn't Darren. It was a man wearing a uniform. A police

officer. More police stood behind him. One of those men was currently arresting Darren.

She was safe. Not as safe as if Wyatt were here. But safe for now.

CHAPTER 21

$\mathcal{W}$yatt took aim and fired.

Target practice was something he and his team did regularly. It was part of their training, which didn't stop just because they had altered DNA.

That was the only reason he wasn't watching Quinn right now; he'd missed their last practice.

"Worried you're going to lose your touch with all that time you're spending with Quinn?"

He turned to look at Luca. The two of them were shooting in the forest behind his house. As per usual, they'd set up targets on trees in the form of human silhouettes.

So far, Wyatt had hit his target every time.

"Don't tell me you're losing faith in my shot?"

Wyatt took aim at the next target. The bullet landed right in the forehead.

"I wouldn't say I'm losing faith...I *would* say that a little distraction can throw some men off their game."

Some men, maybe. Not Wyatt. Quinn wasn't a distraction for him. She was a motivator for him to be at his best. He planned to stay at his best for a very long time. At the very least, until every person he cared about was safe.

"I won't be missing my target. Particularly, not while Project Arma is still operating."

Luca stepped forward and lifted his own pistol. He shot at three different silhouettes, each at varying distances. Every bullet landed in the center of the forehead. He lowered his weapon and turned back to Wyatt. "Hylar lost his main base. His drugs were seized. Most of his soldier were arrested or dead and his scientists were taken in. Other than a few men and doctors who weren't there the day we attacked, he must have very little."

Yet, he'd sent men to rob pharmaceutical companies and attack Maya. That told Wyatt he still had more resources than he should.

"I keep expecting him to come for us. We've taken so much from him."

Luca shook his head. "He won't kill us. His ego alone would stop him, what with him thinking he created us and all. He wants us to come back to him. He just doesn't know how to make it happen yet."

Unfortunately, Wyatt had to agree with his friend. Not long ago, Project Arma had invented a drug call Toved. Hylar had probably hoped it was the solution. Asher and Eden had both been injected with the stuff, just as Sage's brother had. All it had done was make the recipients black out with rage.

If Hylar wanted a loyal army—men who would follow orders —Toved wasn't the answer.

"Let's just hope we find him before he achieves anything like that."

Wyatt took aim again, this time hitting the silhouette in the heart.

Luca leaned his shoulder against a tree. "By now, he probably knows we took the drugs from Portland. All he had to do was question one of the five scientists who were in that room."

It was true. Hylar probably would have known without the witnesses, though. Who else would be able to stop his soldiers?

"The security's now been upgraded on everyone's family members, hasn't it?"

Wyatt aimed his gun at the last silhouette. This time shooting it twice, once in the heart and once in the head. "Upgraded security to alert us if their homes are breached. GPS devices have been inserted into everyone's phones."

It wasn't ideal. Far from it. For now, at least, it would have to be enough. Until Wyatt came up with another layer of protection for them.

Luca nodded. "With the exception of Sage and her brother, he hasn't come after our families yet. Let's hope he doesn't start now."

The man would want the Portland drugs back sooner rather than later. Wyatt just wasn't sure how he planned to obtain them.

Holstering their weapons, they both began heading back to the house. "Let's also hope Eagle hasn't practiced *his* shots lately."

Wyatt laughed. It was a nervous sound. "You think he'll kill me?"

"Probably depends on what your intentions are with his sister."

His intentions were to spend every spare moment he had with the woman. To be with her for as long as she'd have him and hope like hell it was forever.

"I'm in it for the long haul."

Luca clamped a hand on his shoulder. "I know you are. That look you get when you talk about her reminds me of myself when I think about Evie. You've fallen for Quinn. So maybe Eagle will spare you."

Or maybe he'd murder Wyatt with his bare hands. Who knew?

Just as they stepped out of the woods, Wyatt's phone rang from his pocket.

His brows drew together when he noticed it was Oliver. He was watching Quinn—and the only reason Wyatt could think the guy would be calling was if something was wrong.

"Ax, what is it?"

Shuttering breaths sounded down the line before any words were spoken.

"Wyatt, it's me."

He stilled at the sound of Quinn's voice. She didn't sound right. "Are you okay?"

"Can you come get me? I'm at The Duck Motel. I have Mason's car, and I'm with Oliver and the police, but...I need you. Darren was here."

Wyatt forced calm into his body.

Luca had insisted on driving Wyatt to the motel. His friend then planned to drive Mason's car home.

It was smart, because Wyatt was so mad he could barely think straight.

Darren had put his hands on Quinn. Hurt her. Wyatt was itching to track the man down and hurt *him*. But he needed to check on Quinn first. Once he saw her in person, heard exactly what had happened from her mouth, then he could act.

Though she'd said the police were there, so Darren had probably been arrested. Which was good. Less chance for Wyatt to go after him and snap the man's neck.

"She's safe, Jobs. Focus on that."

"How did he get close enough to touch her? Ax was supposed to be watching her, dammit! We put precautions in place. She should have been safe."

What the hell had happened?

"We'll find out. You and I both know he must have a damn good reason why he wasn't there to protect her."

After what felt like far too long, Luca stopped the car in front of the motel. Wyatt was out before he'd pulled the brake. He scanned the area, immediately stopping on Quinn.

She was sitting on the back of an ambulance while Oliver stood by her side. She held an icepack to the right side of her face. Angry red marks covered her neck and one eye was starting to turn black.

The rage inside him increased.

Without pausing, Wyatt walked straight up to her, ignoring Oliver. If he paid his friend any attention, he might hurt the man.

Bending down, he looked Quinn in the eye. "Are you okay?"

She nodded, but there was nothing that looked "okay" about her. She looked scared. Tired. Hurt. As far from her normal self as possible.

Wyatt wanted to kick his own ass for not being there to protect her.

He gently slid his fingers around her wrist and pulled her hand down. The moment he saw her cheek, his body stiffened. More purple bruising marred her face and the skin was broken. Wyatt didn't need to be told what happened. The asshole had shoved her face into the pavement. Punched her in the eye. And by the look of her neck, he'd choked her.

Wyatt took a moment to fight down his rage. "I'm sorry I wasn't here."

For a moment, she appeared confused. "This isn't your fault, Wyatt. You can't always be there to protect me. If you hadn't asked Oliver to watch me, I'd probably be dead."

Wyatt finally looked up at his friend. The man looked like guilt was weighing on him. He nodded once to confirm what she'd said.

So, something else had happened here. Something he couldn't talk about around police and medical staff.

Keeping one hand on Quinn, Wyatt looked at the officer standing by the ambulance. "Can I take her home?"

When the young man confirmed she was okay to leave, Wyatt lifted Quinn.

"Can I have your keys, sunshine?"

Quinn didn't ask him why. Just reached into her pocket and handed them over.

Passing them to Luca, Wyatt headed to his car. On his way, he caught sight of Oliver walking toward Mason's car with Luca. Probably discussing the sequence of events.

Wyatt planned to get a rundown from Oliver, but first he needed to get Quinn home.

Once they were in the car, he placed one hand on the wheel and one on her. He needed to be touching her. To remind himself that she was here, beside him. Safe.

Neither of them spoke for the ten-minute drive. Every time he glanced her way, she was watching the road.

His grip tightened on her hand.

After they'd arrived back at the apartment building, he walked around the car and lifted her out of the passenger seat.

"Wyatt, I can walk."

"I know. I want to carry you." It would probably be a while before he felt comfortable *not* carrying her everywhere.

He expected a fight. He didn't get one.

Once they were standing inside Quinn's apartment, he lowered her to the floor and did a quick sweep of the rooms.

Nothing. Good. He didn't need any more surprises tonight.

It wasn't until Quinn had changed into comfortable clothes and was tucked under a blanket beside him on the couch that Wyatt's heart really stopped racing.

"Tell me what happened."

He watched as her chest rose and fell a couple of times before she spoke. "The Duck Motel was my last delivery. The name on the delivery was 'Stephen,' so it never even occurred to me that it was Darren. Oliver was right behind me as I walked across the lot. I was just about to knock on the door when he stopped me.

Told me to go back to the car because there was someone in the woods. Someone like you. Like him. They were moving fast."

Wyatt bit back a curse.

"Oliver obviously thought the man in the woods was the only threat. I'm not sure if he found him. He never said."

When Quinn paused, Wyatt pressed another kiss to her head. "What happened next?"

"I got into my car, but before I could lock the doors, Darren appeared in the passenger seat. He grabbed me so I couldn't get out. Told me the gas leak was his doing. That he needed to kill me because I was researching the story. That it was his life or mine."

Quinn breathed out a shaky breath while a muscle ticked in Wyatt's jaw.

"I managed to get out of the car. He chased me, grabbed me…I was able to get away though, and that's when the police showed up."

Wyatt was sure that was the very condensed version of the story.

"I didn't get any information on Arma, sorry."

He squeezed her hand. "Please don't say sorry. You fought the asshole. You survived. You did exactly what you were supposed to do, Quinn. Your life is the priority."

It was up to Wyatt and his team now to find out exactly why Darren was sent to kill Quinn. Why Arma didn't just do the job themselves. The fact that they hadn't didn't make an ounce of sense.

She turned her head into his chest. "Thank you."

"For what?" As far as Wyatt was concerned, he'd done nothing. And it was tearing him apart.

"For coming when I called. For wrapping your arms around me when I needed your touch. For listening."

Those weren't things she had to thank him for. "I'm here for whatever you need, whenever you need. Anytime, Quinn."

She snuggled further into him. "I like you."

A small smile touched his lips. He more than liked her. He loved the woman. But now wasn't the time to tell her that. He wanted to say those words when she hadn't just been through hell.

"I like you, too."

They sat like that for a while, Wyatt holding her. Not wanting to let go. It wasn't until her breaths evened out, indicating she was asleep, that he finally stood and carried her to bed.

Placing her under the sheets, he watched her chest rise and fall, unbelievably grateful that the woman he loved had been strong enough to protect herself today.

CHAPTER 22

Quinn had no idea where that banging was coming from, but she needed it to stop. She'd gotten a couple of hours' sleep, if that. Most of the night had been spent tossing and turning.

She needed to play catch-up. And that banging was doing nothing for her.

After listening to a solid thirty seconds of it, she let out a groan and rolled onto her back.

It wasn't going to stop.

Reaching across the bed, she felt for Wyatt. The only thing her hand touched was cold sheets.

Great. She had no choice. She had to get up.

The banging sounded again.

"Okay, okay, I'm coming."

But very unwillingly.

Climbing out of bed, Quinn grabbed a dressing gown on the way to the door. When she passed the dresser, she caught a glimpse of her reflection in the mirror. Her feet stopped.

Holy Hannah, she looked like hell.

Angry bruises covered her neck. It was so distinct she could just about see where Darren had placed each of his fingers. As her gaze slid up to her face, she grimaced. More bruising on her eyes, but also down her cheek combined with grazes and cuts. The cheek Darren had slammed into the ground.

Quinn shut her eyes for a moment. She attempted to push down the fear and panic that were trying to crawl their way up her throat.

You're okay, Quinn. You fought him off. He's can't get you now.

Just because the brain knew information to be true, didn't mean the mind accepted it.

Straightening her shoulders, she moved to the door and looked through the peephole. Her breath caught.

Mason.

Throwing open the door, she leapt into her brother's arms.

Like usual, he caught her easily. His waiting arms ready for her. There had never been a time in her life when her brother hadn't caught her.

A silent moment passed where Quinn just wanted to hold, and be held by, the man who had always been there for her.

Even though they hadn't seen each other in over a year, he felt familiar. She almost had to remind herself that they'd both been through a lot in that time. Both of them were different.

It was kind of like she'd blinked, and they'd both lived ten lives in one.

"I missed you, Q."

Tightening her arms, she dug her head into his shoulder. "I missed you more, big brother."

Giant bucket loads of missing had happened.

When he finally pulled away, his gaze shot straight to the injuries covering her face and neck. A dark rage she'd rarely seen on her brother came over his face.

"If that asshole was here, I'd kill him for doing that to you."

Quinn knew he meant what he said. Just as she was sure Wyatt had meant it when he'd said something very similar.

Stepping back, she let Mason in and shut the door behind him.

"He's with the police," she said, dropping onto the couch. "He can't hurt me."

Something passed over his face as he took a seat beside her. The expression was so fleeting, most wouldn't have picked up on it. "What is it?"

He ran a hand through his hair. Almost like he was deciding whether to tell her or not.

Heck no. "Don't even think about it."

Mason frowned. "What?"

"Not telling me whatever it is you're thinking about. If it involves me, I'd like to know."

"Quinn, yesterday—"

"Was a lot. I know. I know exactly what happened. I was there. I'm not damaged beyond repair. I can handle whatever it is. Tell me."

His jaw clenched. "Darren's dead."

Her mouth opened at his words. Whatever she'd thought the information was going to be, it wasn't that.

Immediately, her mind went to Tanya. God, her friend just lost her husband. Even if the guy was an asshole, he was still hers.

"When?"

"The police went to his cell this morning and found him dead."

"Dead how?"

Her brother closed his eyes. "Q—"

"*How*, Mason?"

"Strangulation. With the bed sheets."

She studied the rigid planes of her brother's face. "Let me guess. It's being labeled as a suicide when really it isn't."

"There were no police around and the video surveillance cut out when it happened."

"Cut out" meaning, whoever killed him made sure no one saw it happen.

"Why would they kill him?"

"Most likely because he got arrested," Mason said, not hesitating in the slightest now. "The people connected to him, the people who told him to keep you quiet, don't want a trail leading back to them."

It was her fault. Tanya had lost her husband because of Quinn. Because Quinn kept looking into the story. Because she let Darren know she wasn't going to let it go.

Mason leaned forward. "Don't. I can tell what you're thinking. It's not your fault. You didn't let the case drop because you knew something bigger was going on. You wanted to save more innocent people from dying. Darren didn't care about that. He cared about saving himself. And then the moment he did something to get himself arrested, he signed his own death certificate."

Everything Mason said was true. But it didn't change the fact that Tanya was innocent in the whole thing, and yet she'd lost the man she loved. Regardless of how Quinn felt about Darren, Tanya loved him.

"What about the guy Oliver went after? The guy behind the motel."

Mason's lips pressed together before he spoke. "He never caught the guy. Darren told you he didn't know about him, so it's possible he was there to kill your ex-boss. Or, he might just have been tailing him to ensure he achieved what he was supposed to."

Which was killing her. God, it was all so awful. It may have been the very guy Oliver chased who killed Darren.

Mason reached out and placed his hand on her leg. "I'm sorry this has touched you."

And by "this," he meant Project Arma. Suddenly, she was reminded of the fact that Project Arma was exactly what she wanted to talk to her brother about.

"Why didn't you tell me?"

He didn't seem surprised by her question. If anything, he was probably expecting it. "Because knowing anything about the project is dangerous. The last thing I wanted to do was put your life in danger."

"If my life *was* in danger, you would want to know."

"Damn straight I would. But that's different."

She shook her head. "It isn't. I might not have the muscle or the combat training that you have, but I want to know what's going on in your life. Good or bad. Safe or downright dangerous. There are other ways I can help, even if it's just being there for you." She placed her hand on top of Mason's. "You're the only family I have left. I love you. Next time something astronomical happens in your life—actually, scratch that, the next time something on *any* scale happens in your life, tell me. Even if I'm at a super self-absorbed point in my life and I act like I have no time for you...I'm going to make sure that, from now on, family is priority."

Which is something she should have done a long time ago.

One side of his mouth lifted. "I won't ever put your life in danger if I can help it. But I'll try to tell you more. And the same goes for you." He tapped her leg. "The next time you find yourself fired on suspicious grounds, and stuck in the middle of a dangerous investigation, you tell me."

She rolled her eyes. "The 'stuck in the middle of a dangerous investigation' part has happened more times than I can count."

Hell, just about every story she'd written had put her in some sort of danger.

Mason growled.

"You might be happy to know that I don't plan to write anymore. Or at least, not for now. I might change my mind down the track."

Mason pulled back. The look of shock on his face almost made her laugh. "I find that hard to believe."

"I know. Twenty-five-year-old Quinn would be shocked. In

fact, if you'd told me a year ago I'd be living in a small town, baking cakes and dating a local, I'd think you were crazy."

A certified lunatic.

"I'm going to leave the topic of you baking for the moment—although I do have serious concerns for anyone eating something made by you—and let's focus on that 'dating a local' part."

Quinn tilted her head to the side. "I know you know, Mason." His expression didn't change. Not one bit. "That's why Wyatt wasn't here when I woke up, isn't it? He was out there, explaining it to you. Probably in the hall so he could stay close."

"I know what *he* told me." Yep. She was right. "I want to hear it from you. Then I'll decide if I need to break the man's nose."

Yeah, right. There was no way Mason would stop at breaking Wyatt's nose if she told him the guy wasn't treating her like he should.

Luckily, Wyatt was one big package of perfect.

"I really like him." Actually, she was pretty sure she loved him, but she wanted Wyatt to be the first to hear it. "He's funny, smart, has a great ass."

She added the last bit for her brother's benefit.

Mason shrugged. "He *does* have a great ass."

Quinn threw her head back and laughed. God, she'd missed him.

"Honestly, Mase, he's become the center of my world. It sounds corny, but I feel like he's the guy I've been waiting for."

Mason's eyes scanned Quinn's face. No doubt looking for any signs of deceit. He wouldn't find it. Soon, a slow smile stretched across his lips. "You're happy. I love that. It's all I've ever wanted for you. And if you like him, then I'm damn glad you found each other. He's a good man. I couldn't think of anyone better suited to you."

Mason probably had no idea how much his support meant to her. "So his nose is safe?"

"For now. But I'll be watching the guy like a hawk in case he ever steps out of line."

Quinn was pretty confident that wasn't going to happen. She had a feeling Mason knew it too.

"How are *you* doing, Mason? With Project Arma and everything."

Mason had always been very loyal to the system. He was loyal to his government and diligent in doing the right thing for his country. Being betrayed would have seriously rocked his belief system.

"I'm not going to lie, it's been hard. Especially because my commander—Hylar, the man who set everything in motion—is still out there. Running the damn project. Having my team by my side has made it easier. The real game changer is Sage. When she's around, the anger dims. All I see is her."

Oh gosh. That was beautiful. If anyone was deserving of peace, it was Mason. "Tell me about her."

"You'll love her. She's smart as hell and has a heart like no one else. I can't wait for you to meet her."

Neither could Quinn. Any woman who could put that look on her brother's face was family. "When *will* I meet her?"

He lifted a shoulder. "Whenever you want. But no third degree. None of your journalist interrogation stuff."

Quinn leaned back, feigning offense. "Me? Interrogate someone?"

Mason raised a brow.

"I won't. Only because I love you and you love her. Now, tell me about your trip to Lockhart."

Mason began talking about Sage and her brother, Jason. Quinn listened to every word, unable to draw her eyes away. He told her about Sage and Jason's past. About the drama that had unfurled and almost caused Mason to lose her.

It was like something you'd hear in one of those Hollywood action movies.

Before Quinn knew it, her brother had been talking for close to an hour.

"Are you sure you're okay?" Mason asked, when they both finally stood and headed to the door. "After yesterday?"

Quinn stopped and folded her arms. "A little bruised and battered—both physically and emotionally. But I think I'll be okay."

Mason scanned her face. He looked every bit the deadly soldier in that moment. But then, there was rarely a time he didn't.

"Before you go, I do have a question. How did you know I was safe all these years? Couldn't Project Arma have used me to get to you?"

Mason's face hardened. "When we first got out, we all visited our families. Spent some time with them."

Quinn remembered that. And it made her feel guilty for not seeing the pain he was in. For being too consumed with her own life. "I remember."

"Do you remember how I put high-security locks on your door and windows? I also put an alarm in."

"You didn't put a camera up, did you?"

"No. But I hired security companies to send someone to check on you regularly."

If Mason had told her that before she knew about Project Arma, she probably would have been mad. She probably also would have thought the man was crazy.

Now she knew how dangerous the organization was.

"Thank you. For looking out for me."

He nodded. "Always."

Mason was turning when Quinn put a hand on his shoulder. "It was you who saved me yesterday, you know."

Her brother stopped, his brows pulling together. "How?"

"All that self-defense you forced me to practice years ago. It saved me."

Reaching out, he squeezed her shoulder. "Thank God for that."

Yep. Thank God for family.

"Now get back to your woman so I can get back to baking."

Mason laughed. "It's going to take me a while to get used to that."

"Hey! Mrs. Potter says I'm a natural."

"Q, I know you can achieve anything you put your mind to." A serious look came over Mason's face. "When I'm not around, make sure you stick close to Wyatt. Darren may be dead, but the people behind Arma aren't. It would be better to err on the side of caution for a while."

Quinn agreed. Darren was a small fish compared to genetically altered criminals roaming the streets. No way did she want to get mixed up in that.

"Fortunately, staying close to Wyatt is my preference."

Leaning down, Mason pressed a kiss to the top of her head. "Stay safe, sis. I'll call you."

Watching her brother head down the hall, Quinn felt overwhelming gratitude. Gratitude that her brother was back, that she had Wyatt, and that she was safe.

CHAPTER 23

*W*yatt pushed his body to run faster.

The wind brushed against his face, his feet pounded the pavement. God, he loved running. Always had. It made him feel alive.

He needed to make more time for it. If for nothing other than his mental health.

He used to be able to wear his body out. Run until his lungs burned and legs threatened to cave beneath him. That was just about impossible now. His body no longer had an off switch. It never seemed to run out of steam.

One day, he would test whether his body had a limit. He would run faster. Harder. Farther. Find out just how far he could push himself. Surely, at some point, his body would need to stop.

He used to run every day, even if it was just for half an hour. Lately he'd been distracted. Today, he needed to get out. Get the images of Quinn's battered face out of his head.

There was a running track that could be accessed from behind Marble Protection. It led to a local park. That's where Wyatt was running today.

The park was always busy. People from all walks of life went there, from families to men in suits. All out and about, living their normal lives.

Being around people made Wyatt feel normal. A feeling that was often out of reach. Especially when he spent such huge chunks of his days searching for Hylar.

A week had passed since Quinn had been attacked. Since Darren had been killed. Hylar hadn't shown his face. No one from Project Arma had. Wyatt almost *wanted* them to attack, just so he had a location for the guy.

As Wyatt drew closer to Marble Protection, he saw Mason stepping outside. The other man stilled by the door, his arms crossed over his chest as he waited.

Coming to a stop in front of his friend, Wyatt tried to read Mason's body language. It was impossible.

"Hey. You waiting for me?"

Mason nodded. "I wanted to talk about Quinn."

Wyatt ran his hands through his hair, not surprised that after an hour of running, he hadn't cracked a sweat. "Sure. What's up?"

The blank mask fell from Mason's face, and frustration took its place. For a moment, Wyatt wondered if he'd changed his mind about being okay with him dating his sister. If that's what he was about to say, Wyatt had no idea how he would respond.

"A week has passed since the Darren situation. I know today is Quinn's first day back at the bakery. I just wanted to check that we're sure she's protected."

"We can never be completely sure there are no threats. You know that." He wished he *did* have a way to ensure her safety. Apart from keeping her by his side twenty-four seven, which had basically been the case for the last week, he didn't think that was possible forever. "She took a week off work, she hung out here, nothing happened. She wanted to go back. I don't like it any more than you do, but we can't force her to do anything she doesn't want to do."

Wyatt had already tried.

Mason shook his head. "It kills me that Ax didn't catch the guy behind the motel. We're assuming it was the person who killed Darren, but he might have been after Quinn too."

Wyatt pushed down the fury at the fact he couldn't question Darren or the man from behind the motel.

Mason scrubbed his hands over his face. "I just worry."

Wyatt understood worry. It had become a constant companion. Stepping forward, he placed a hand on his friend's shoulder. "I do too. Every minute of every day that Hylar is alive, that his organization is running, I'm worried. And I hate that Quinn got hurt. That I wasn't able to locate Darren earlier. Quinn wouldn't have had to fight for her life if I had."

The guilt would probably never fade.

Mason frowned. "The guy paid for his room at the motel with cash and used a fake name. It would have been impossible for anyone to know it was him."

True. Didn't stop his brain from telling him otherwise.

"I just wish we knew all the facts though," Mason continued. "Like why the hell would Hylar send a man like Darren, when his men are so much more powerful and efficient?"

Wyatt would love the answer to that question. Unfortunately, all he could do was hypothesize. "It's likely Darren was sent to Marble Falls because of his ability to get close to Quinn without suspicion. Also, Hylar knows we pose a threat to his men. He was hit hard by the raids, by all the men he lost. He may not have wanted to risk sending them here." Wyatt lifted a shoulder. "That doesn't tell us how Darren became involved with Arma, though."

"Soon. We'll get our answers. And our redemption."

Hell yes, they would.

"In the meantime, someone will be constantly watching Quinn. Not in their car from the street. In the bakery. Eyes on her. Always. There won't be a moment she's unprotected."

Mason chuckled. "She's gonna hate that…I love it."

"I know. I think she understands the importance of it. But I'm still gonna tell her it was your idea."

"Go ahead. She'd believe it. My sister knows I'm an over-bearing big brother."

Wyatt had heard that many times from Quinn, but always with affection. The woman secretly loved her brother's protective nature. He hoped she felt the same way about Wyatt's. It wasn't something that would be changing.

The humor dropped from Mason's face. "I still hate that the asshole hurt her."

Wyatt's body tensed at the memory. Her bruises were fading, but they would be etched in his mind for a very long time. "I'm damn glad you taught her how to protect herself."

"Yep. Basic self-defense. Something everyone should have knowledge in. Especially women. I've been teaching Sage, too. It makes me nervous as hell that she knew nothing before."

"Maybe we should run some free 'come and try' classes for the community?"

"Great idea." Mason looked like he was going to turn around when he stopped. "She seems happy. So do you. In case I haven't said it yet, I'm going to say it now—you're a good man. And I'm glad you found each other."

That sure beat the broken nose Wyatt had been expecting from his friend.

"Thank you, brother. I plan to stay with her for as long as she'll have me and make her happy every single one of those days."

"Not a decision you'll regret." Mason gave Wyatt a nod before heading back inside.

Wyatt had no doubt it was a decision he'd never regret. Only last weekend, Luca had proposed to Evie, and she'd said yes. Wyatt knew it was too early for him to do the same, but he had a feeling it wouldn't be too far in the future.

The feel of his phone vibrating in his pocket caught his attention. When Wyatt pulled it out, he couldn't help but smile at Quinn's text message.

She missed him. Which was exactly how Wyatt felt every moment he was separated from her. Guess she didn't hate the bodyguard situation too much.

When he glanced at the time, he noticed there was only an hour left of her shift. An hour until he got to pull her into his arms and hold her for as long as he wanted.

Well, not quite as long as he wanted. In that case, he'd never let her go.

~

"So how did you get stuck with babysitting duties?"

Kye glanced at Quinn as they neared the entrance of Marble Protection. He was just as big as the other men.

He had dark eyes. So dark, they were just about black. It went perfectly with his black hair. Plus, the man always looked serious. He had a small scar above his right eyebrow that did nothing to detract from his features. If anything, it added an element of danger.

The guy was good-looking. But then, so were all the men. Woman probably swooned over the lot of them.

None of them made her heart race like Wyatt, though.

"The man asked, I said yes. It's pretty standard amongst our team."

"And by 'the man,' you mean...?"

One corner of Kye's mouth pulled up. "I think that's something for you to find out."

Dammit. She'd thought he would confirm her guess. "I'm almost ninety percent certain it was Wyatt who decided you were necessary. Only because Mason's got a girlfriend to focus on now."

"Whereas Wyatt has you."

Correct. She studied the man's face, but still he gave nothing away.

Quinn released a sigh. "It doesn't actually matter who it was. I'm lucky I have people who care about me. It just peeves me that he didn't tell me."

"Peeves you?"

"Yeah. Annoys me. Pisses me off. Makes anger rise in my belly."

Kye chuckled. "Would you have argued with him?"

"Not so much argued, more negotiated."

She wouldn't have been able to help it. She felt sorry for the guys, having to sit at a table all day.

When she walked into the bakery this morning, Asher had been sitting at a table beside the window. He'd continued to sit there for three hours.

Yes, he'd had a laptop and seemed to be doing work, but she still felt guilty. The man had a baby. Surely he'd rather be with family than watching her.

Then, to Quinn's surprise, Kye had walked in.

Previously, the men had been watching from their cars. Apparently, that wasn't the case anymore.

They had to be bored. Or at least tired of sitting.

"Ah, so he probably knew you were capable of talking him into giving you more space. That's a compliment, considering the training he's had."

She lifted a shoulder. "Well, I grew up with Mason. I had to learn how to be a good negotiator. The man's stubborn and over-protective."

She'd secretly loved it. Not that those words would ever leave her mouth.

When they reached the entrance of Marble Protection, Kye held the door open for her. "I'm the same with my sisters. They didn't get much breathing space growing up."

Quinn stepped inside. "How many sisters do you have?"

"Two. So I like to think I understand women."

They both stopped at the front counter. "No one understands women. Not even women."

"You're probably right."

Quinn was definitely right. Women were complex creatures; she had yet to work out how she'd come to most of her own life decisions.

Glancing around the big space near the front desk, she searched for Wyatt. Luca and Eden were running a self-defense class, but there was no sign of her man.

"He's probably in the office," Kye said, walking around the desk.

"Thanks for watching me today. It was a hoot."

He laughed again. "Watching a beautiful woman is always a hoot." He gave her a wink before turning around.

God, why hadn't all these men been locked down yet? Looks and a good personality should have meant they went off the market years ago.

Heading to the office, Quinn spared Luca and Eden a glance. They were demonstrating a particular self-defense move. It was one Mason had taught her years ago. They made it look easy. Quinn probably looked like a baby giraffe while doing it.

Stepping into the office, she spotted Wyatt leaning back in his seat, looking straight at her.

"Do I need to go have a word with Cage?" Even though his face was hard, his voice was light.

Quinn moved forward and sat sideways on his lap, loving the feel of his arm sliding around her waist.

"You don't think I'm beautiful?" she joked.

"I think you're the most beautiful woman on the planet. I just don't know how I feel about other men telling you that."

She wrapped an arm around her neck. "Would it make you feel better to know that it means the most coming from you?"

He lowered his head so that his lips were stalled just above hers. "Yes."

Then he was kissing her. Melting her to the spot. Her free hand immediately went to his chest, sliding across the hard ridges. The man was all muscle.

Just as she started to deepen the kiss, a ringing phone sounded. Her phone.

Damn technology.

Reluctantly, Quinn pulled her lips from his and took her cell from her pocket. When she looked at the screen, she was almost tempted to let it go to voicemail. Which surely made her a horrible person. Because it was Tanya.

Tanya, who had just lost her husband and needed friends to talk to.

She'd spoken to the woman numerous times over the last week. As far as her friend knew, Darren had been arrested after attacking a woman. But she hadn't been told that woman was Quinn.

And Quinn didn't plan to share that information.

Taking a quick breath, she put the phone to her ear. "Hi, Tan. How are you doing today?"

"Okay. Well, as okay as I can be."

The woman was grieving the loss of her husband. She wasn't okay. Which was expected. "Do you have family with you?"

"My mom's here. It's almost annoying, though. She just hovers. I get a new cup of tea every hour."

At least she wasn't alone. "I'm glad she's taking good care of you."

There was a sniffle through the line. "I just wanted to call to double check you're coming to the funeral tomorrow. I mentioned that it was on, but you haven't said when your flight gets in."

Crap. She'd been avoiding this.

Hanging her head, she immediately felt Wyatt's soothing

circular strokes on her back. It helped. But guilt still ate at her inside.

"I'm really sorry, Tan, but I can't make it."

She nervously bit her lip, waiting for her friend's response.

"What? You can't be serious. You're not coming? I don't understand! Why not?"

Because your husband tried to kill me. Because I still have bruises and marks on my body, done by his hand.

"I was in a car accident. A small one." She scrunched her eyes shut, hating that she was lying to her. "I'm okay, but the doctor recommended I don't fly at the moment. I'm so sorry."

There was a short pause. "You were in an accident? When?"

Oh, God. She was going to be smited or something for lying to a grieving woman.

"A few days ago. I didn't want to say anything because you're going through so much. I promise, though, as soon as I'm better, I'm going to fly over and spend quality time with you."

As long as the danger was gone and the guilt hadn't eaten her alive.

"Oh...okay. I'm sad you won't be here. But I hope you're okay."

Yep. The guilt was going to be the end of her.

"Remember, I'm only a phone call away. Even if you don't want to talk. I'll just sit on the line with you. Okay?"

"All right. Thanks, Quinny. Talk soon."

There was clear disappointment in her friend's voice before she hung up.

Placing her phone on her lap, Quinn shook her head. "Ugh. I hate myself."

Wyatt pressed a kiss to her cheek. "Don't say that. You would have been uncomfortable attending a funeral for a man who tried to kill you. Tanya would have felt your energy. It's better this way."

Wyatt was right. Didn't change the fact that she felt terrible.

Curling her body into his, she let his warmth soothe her guilt. "What did I do to deserve you?"

"I should be asking you that question."

CHAPTER 24

*W*yatt knocked on Quinn's door, excitement stirring in his gut.

It was ridiculous. He'd only just seen the woman. Hell, bar the time they were working, he'd been spending every minute with her.

It didn't seem to matter. He didn't think he'd ever tire of seeing Quinn.

Of course, seeing the woman wasn't the only reason he was excited.

It also had something to do with the fact that once they were home from Luca and Evie's engagement party, Wyatt planned to tell Quinn he loved her.

That was likely why a distinctly nervous feeling accompanied the excitement.

He'd never told any other partner that he loved them. But this felt right. The woman had captured his heart, and he needed to say the words out loud.

Footsteps sounded from inside the apartment just before the door was pulled open. Wyatt's heart stopped, then sped up at the sight of her. For a moment, he had to remind himself to breathe.

The woman was gorgeous.

Quinn wore a figure-hugging black dress that went to her knees. There was a slit up the side, which showed a generous amount of thigh. Wyatt itched to reach out and run his hand up her leg.

When his eyes rose, he noticed the thin straps and low-cut design of the bodice. That, in combination with her hair being pulled up, gave him an ample display of her creamy skin.

It took a hell of a lot of self-restraint not to push the woman inside the apartment and peel the dress right off.

When his gaze reached her face, he stared into the same deep blue eyes that haunted his dreams.

One side of Quinn's mouth lifted. "Like what you see?"

No. He was destroyed by what he saw. The woman in front of him was a goddess. *His* goddess.

Stepping forward, Wyatt pulled Quinn into his arms. She was soft and pliant and smelled like a damn flower store.

His mouth lowered to hers, and Quinn sank into him, her fingers running through his hair. A quiet moan sounded from her throat.

Christ, the woman was the only person on Earth able to ignite such a fire within him. A part of him wanted to blow off the entire evening and get lost in her. If Luca wasn't family, he would do just that.

Reluctantly, Wyatt pulled his head away.

A soft whimper escaped her lips. "No. You can't kiss me like that only to pull away. That's torture."

She was right, it *was* torture. For him as well as her.

"I want to ravage you, but that will take a long time. You deserve hours, not the mere minutes we have. Tonight."

"Hm. Okay. But I expect lots and lots of ravaging."

That was something Wyatt could happily promise.

Turning, Quinn grabbed her bag from the kitchen counter

before stepping outside. His arm snaked around her waist as they headed to his car.

"Are you excited to celebrate their engagement?" she asked, glancing up at him. "From what I hear, it's been a long time coming."

"It has. Too long. I'm excited that they're finally taking the plunge. Those two are great together. Rocket wanted to wait until Hylar was caught, but who knows when that will happen? It could be years. We can't put our lives on hold forever."

At least now their old commander was at a disadvantage with all that he'd lost. That was something.

The drive to Luca's was quick. Wyatt spent the entire time trying to keep his eyes on the road. It was an effort when the woman beside him was so damn alluring.

As they stepped inside Luca's home, Wyatt and Quinn spent the first half hour moving around the room and greeting everyone.

Moments like this, when they were all together celebrating, just reminded Wyatt how lucky he was. These people were his family. Not everything in his life may be perfect, but these guys gave him a lot to be thankful for.

Growing up as an only child, Wyatt had never had that sibling relationship that so many others experienced. The moment he was given his SEAL team, he'd finally learned what that connection felt like.

They'd been through a lot together. The intensity of their shared experiences created a bond that was all but unbreakable.

"Jobs! You look like you need another drink."

Wyatt smiled at Kye's booming voice. He lifted the beer he was holding. "Got one." Where Kye had clearly had a few to drink already, Wyatt was still on his first.

"No rule that says you can't have two..."

Wyatt chuckled. He wouldn't be getting through his first. He needed a clear head. "I'm good, thanks. Just happy to celebrate the engagement of two of our closest friends."

Kye nodded. "I feel like there'll be plenty more on the way."

That was true. By the way things were going, each man would be married off in no time.

Luca came to stand with them. "The more engagements, the better. Everyone should marry the woman they love."

Wyatt smiled at Luca. "Couldn't agree more, brother. Congratulations again. You pulled this party together quickly."

Hell, the couple had only been engaged a little more than a week.

He shrugged. "The sooner we have an engagement party, the sooner I get to marry her."

Damn straight. "That's awesome. I'm happy for you."

Luca dipped his head. "Appreciate it. Sometimes I feel like I need to pinch myself because I can't believe I found her. Or that my feelings are reciprocated."

Kye scoffed. "With a face like that, how could she not love you?"

Wyatt nodded sagely. "Cage is right. That face is a winner."

One side of Luca's mouth lifted. "I guess the face helps."

Wyatt glanced across the room to Quinn at the same time Luca looked over at Evie.

Kye groaned out loud. "Look at you guys. Can't go a minute without searching for your women. I think I'll remain single. Maintain my sanity."

If Wyatt had to choose between his sanity and Quinn, he'd be choosing her. Every time. "I've got bad news for you. When the time comes, you won't have a choice." Wyatt kept his eyes on Quinn as he spoke. "One day, someone will walk into your life and nothing will be the same again."

Luca nodded. "And there won't be a single part of you that will regret it."

"Nope." Wyatt looked at his friend to see him shaking his

head. "Not gonna happen. I'm like a mountain lion. There's no taming me."

Kye had no idea. Wyatt had little doubt that the day would come when he would find out.

"Bodie will probably be next," Luca said. "I think the man wants what we have. Someone by his side."

Wyatt agreed. "That guy will make a woman very happy."

Kye swung his arm around Wyatt's shoulders. "You would know. You're the smart one in the group."

"That's the only reason he's allowed near my sister," Mason commented as he joined them.

Kye pulled back, removing his arm. "I'm smart. You saying I can date your sister?"

"You ever touch her, I'll kill you."

"I'll give you a hand," Wyatt added.

"You just said you don't want to date," Luca said. "Besides, the woman's obsessed with Jobs. You wouldn't stand a chance."

Kye feigned offense.

As if she heard them talking about her, Quinn turned her head to look at them. Her eyes stopped on Wyatt, and a slow smile curved her lips.

He smiled back. He couldn't *not*.

"No sign of anyone lurking around, searching for those drugs we took?" Mason asked.

And just like that, Wyatt was sucked back to reality. "Not yet. And if they were, they wouldn't find them. We've hidden them somewhere they won't be found."

The team had tossed up whether to hide or destroy the stuff. They'd gone with hide...for now. Something was stopping them. Call it gut instinct.

Mason lowered his voice. "If he does come looking, we'll be ready."

Wyatt nodded. They weren't just a team, together they made an army.

Kye threw his arms up. "Okay. Enough shop talk. This is Rocket's engagement party. We need to drink, drink, then drink some more!"

∼

"Wow, your life in New York sounds so exciting!"

Quinn smiled at Shylah's comment. She wasn't sure if "exciting" was the best word. It was busy. There was rarely a dull moment.

"And you're going to give it all up and stay in Marble Falls?" Lexie asked.

The only thing she was giving up was chasing a job she no longer had much desire to do. But she knew what the women were saying. That her life may be less interesting, working in the bakery of a small town. It really wasn't.

"I've been researching and writing about other people's lives for years. I think it's about time I started living my own."

Both women seemed to melt at Quinn's words.

Quinn's ringing phone pulled her attention. She looked down to see it was Tanya.

Nibbling on her bottom lip, she eyed the back door. She should take it. Darren's funeral was yesterday, and she hadn't spoken to her friend since the day before that.

Excusing herself from the group, Quinn stepped out the back. "Hey."

"Quinn. Hi. Sorry to call so late, I just wanted a friendly voice to speak to."

Quinn took a seat on the top of the steps that led out to the yard. Tanya sounded tired and worn out. "Of course. Call anytime. How did the funeral go yesterday?"

She almost didn't want to know, but she felt she had to ask.

"It was impossibly hard. I had to say goodbye to the only man I've ever loved."

Quinn knew all about saying goodbye to loved ones. Losing her mother, then her father in such a short time frame had been soul wrenching.

Tanya sighed. "And there were all these people there who barely knew him, acting like they cared. I *hated* it."

Even though Tanya wouldn't be able to see, Quinn nodded. "I remember feeling the same at my parents' funerals. I tried to remind myself that they were entitled to be there. That everyone suffers grief in their own way, even if the person barely touched their lives."

There was a moment of silence. "You always know what to say. That's why I needed you there."

A part of her wished she had attended. Just for her friend. But a larger part of her knew that not attending was the right decision. "I'm sorry."

What else could she say? She didn't want to repeat why she hadn't made it. The lie. She'd felt wretched enough the first time.

"I know. Maybe I can visit sometime soon? You're still in Marble Falls, right?"

Gosh, Quinn didn't know if she'd be able to look her friend in the eye, knowing she'd played a part in her husband's death. "I *am* in Marble Falls. You're welcome to visit, Tan."

"I could use a good friend right now," Tanya sighed. "Anyway…just wanted to hear your voice. I should go now. Thanks for chatting, Quinn. I'll call again soon."

"Anytime."

Hanging up, Quinn dropped her head into her hands and groaned. She knew what happened to Darren wasn't her fault. God, the man had tried to kill her, for heaven's sake.

So why was the guilt so all-consuming whenever she spoke to Tanya?

Quinn already knew the answer to that. Because her friend was hurting. And if Quinn hadn't pushed so hard to uncover the truth about the story, then Tanya may still have her husband.

"You okay?"

Turning her head, Quinn caught sight of Sage stepping outside.

"Oh, you know, just having a battle between my head and my heart. It's a normal occurrence in the Quinn Ross world."

"Who's winning?"

Good question. "My heart. But that's no surprise, I've never been one to use my head that much." Sage laughed as Quinn patted the spot beside her. "Come sit with me. Take my mind off my problems."

Sage dropped onto the step beside Quinn. The other woman was gorgeous with her soft blond hair and sky-blue eyes. Not only was she beautiful, but from the little Quinn had spoken to her this evening, Sage seemed both smart and genuinely nice.

It was easy to see why her brother was so infatuated with her.

"I hope it's not Wyatt you're stressing over?"

Quinn almost laughed. "No. That man is the only thing I am a hundred percent certain about."

He was her clarity in a world of confusion.

A knowing smile came over Sage's face. "I know that feeling."

Quinn nudged the other woman with her shoulder. "I love that you love my brother. And that he loves you. He deserves to be happy."

Sage shook her head. "I still can't believe that he loves me back. I keep waking up, expecting it to be a dream or for the guy to change his mind."

Nope. That wouldn't be happening. "When my brother decides on something, he doesn't go back. And trust me, he's decided on you."

Sage's cheeks tinged with pink. "That means a lot coming from you."

Quinn laughed out loud. A real belly laugh. "You mean coming from his crazy little sister who makes questionable life decisions?"

"He never used the word crazy. He did use determined. Strong. Driven."

"Ah, the positive spin to 'bossy' and 'doesn't listen.'"

Sage chuckled. "I'm really glad you're in town and we can get to know each other. I hope that we can become friends."

"You're dating my brother, so in my eyes, we're more than friends. We're family. I'm so looking forward to spending time with you."

Quinn wasn't just saying that. She wanted to know every little thing about her brother's new love. About the woman who had captured his heart.

"It's funny how life works out," Quinn continued. "You can never predict it. Look at me. I'm a coffee-making, cake-baking, small-town-living gal. It's nuts."

Sage chuckled. "I know what you mean. No matter how much we plan our future, it all goes out the window when life actually happens. We can't predict what will happen tomorrow, let alone next week."

"So I should cancel the trip to Europe."

Sage shrugged. "Maybe keep it, just for now."

Both women laughed. Yep. They were going to be good friends in no time.

Just then, the back door opened, and they turned their heads to see Mason. "Ladies, Luca's about to speak. Then I hear there might be cake."

Quinn knew there was going to be cake. She had *made* the cake. Under the guidance of Mrs. Potter, of course.

Standing, Quinn followed Sage back inside. As the door closed behind her, there was a beep on her phone. Opening the email, she noticed it was from an unknown address.

Then she read the contents.

Maya. Telling Quinn she was alive and safe.

Quinn felt a wave of relief. She hadn't heard from Maya in over two weeks and had feared the worst.

Of course, there was a chance that the email wasn't from her at all. And even if it was, Maya hadn't included an address.

Wyatt was a wizard with technology though. It was likely he'd be able to work with this to find her. At least, Quinn hoped that was the case.

CHAPTER 25

"*I* could sleep for twelve hours straight."

And she wouldn't regret a single hour.

She glanced up at Wyatt's chuckle. His big warm hand was wrapped around hers as they made their way up the apartment stairs.

After speeches and cake, Quinn had shown Wyatt the email from Maya. When he'd said he might be able to track the location of where the email was sent from, she'd been beyond relieved.

Hopefully, then, he could send one of the guys to make sure she was safe.

Everyone had remained at the party for another couple hours before people had begun to disperse. The cake had been a hit. Quinn loved the rave reviews. What she'd loved the most, though, was the look on her brother's face when she'd told him she'd made it.

"It's only eleven thirty."

Quinn shrugged. "Guess I'm a nanna now. Nanna Quinn. Has a ring to it, don't you think?"

"Goes with the baking, I guess."

"You're right! All I need is a walking stick and some grand-kids. Hmm, might be a bit hard without kids though."

Wyatt lifted a shoulder. "I'm sure we can find some somewhere."

Quinn giggled. She loved that he just went along with her.

She looked up at Wyatt as they reached their floor. "You never told me whether you liked the cake?"

"It was the best cake I've ever tasted."

Heck yeah, it was. Mrs. Potter was sharing all her baking secrets, and Quinn was absorbing them like a sponge.

She beamed up at him as they stopped outside his apartment. "This is why I need you in my life."

"To tell you how amazing you and your baking are?"

"Amongst other things."

Many, many other things.

Wyatt unlocked the door to his apartment. Quinn waited for him to take the first step inside, but he didn't. Instead, he stepped back.

For a moment, she wondered whether he was listening for an intruder. Or maybe anticipating danger. Although, he didn't appear tense. The complete opposite, actually.

"Aren't you going to go in first? Sweep the place or whatever you normally do?"

"I'd be able to hear if someone was in there. It's safe." He touched his hand to her back. "Ladies first."

Ah…okay. Strange, but she'd go with it.

Taking a step inside, she switched on the light—and her breath caught in her throat.

Lilies. Hundreds of them. Scattered around the room like confetti. They were everywhere. Pink lilies, yellow lilies. The room was a rainbow of colors.

Wyatt's breath brushed across her neck as he whispered from right behind her, "I noticed that you look at the lilies a lot on your walk to work. I assumed they were your favorite."

They were. Always had been. Since she was little, she'd loved them. Whenever she passed one, she needed to stop. Smell it. Take in its beauty.

The fact that Wyatt had noticed was amazing to her.

Quinn opened her mouth to speak, but she was lost for words.

"Did you know that each color has a meaning?" Wyatt's breath was again warm on her neck. She heard the soft closing of the door.

"I didn't."

"Well, let me tell you what I've learned. Yellow lilies represent happiness. Which is something I think we'll have plenty of together. Orange means energy. Energy is something you have in spades. It draws me to you. Purple is for admiration, which is quite fitting, because I admire the hell out of you. Your fire. Your determination."

Wyatt moved to stand beside her. She immediately turned to face him, wrapping her arms around his shoulders while his swept around her waist. She wanted no space between them.

"What about the pink lilies?"

There were far more pink lilies in the room than any other color.

"Ah. The pink lilies…They represent love." Quinn's heart sped up a notch. "There'll definitely be plenty of that in our lives. Because I love you, Quinn Ross. Every little thing about you."

Wyatt loved her. Like…actually *loved* her.

Warmth filtered into Quinn's soul. Those words brought her so much peace. She'd loved him for a while, and now she knew that those feelings were reciprocated.

"I love you too, Wyatt. Big truckloads of love."

Wyatt dipped his head, nuzzling a spot behind her ear. "Truckloads of love is good. You have no idea how amazing it is to hear those words from your lips."

A shiver coursed down her spine. "I can say them as many times as you want. I love you, Wyatt Gray."

His mouth pressed to her neck before trailing up her jaw. Then his lips touched hers. The outside world faded. All that existed was her and Wyatt. Her world.

"I could kiss you forever and it would never be enough." His words were muffled in between kisses. Lifting her, Wyatt pressed Quinn against the wall. Caging her with his body.

The feeling of him surrounding her was ecstasy. But what existed between them wasn't just physical. Her whole heart and soul belonged to the man who held her.

Wyatt's lips trailed down her throat. His hand slid across her shoulder, pushing her dress strap down. When her breast was exposed, he cupped her.

A whimper escaped her throat, her fingers sinking into his shoulders.

The man's touch did things to her body that she didn't know were possible.

When he pinched her pebbled nipple, her entire body jolted. Electricity shot from her breast to her core. He flicked his thumb over the sensitive peak.

She tightened her legs around his waist, pressing herself closer.

The air moved around her as he walked them to the bedroom. The feel of the soft mattress touched her back.

Quinn opened her eyes to find Wyatt hovering over her. His eyes fixed on hers. Something passed between them. Something intense and real and raw.

No words were spoken. They didn't need to be. Both Quinn and Wyatt felt it. The deep connection.

His mouth lowered to her cheek. Then her neck. He trailed soft kisses down her body, peeling her dress away at the same time.

When her chest was bare, Wyatt was quick to take one nipple into his mouth.

Heat spiraled through her oversensitive body. She arched her back, hungry for more. Wyatt tugged and sucked. Every touch driving Quinn wild.

His hand crept up the slit of her dress. Taking hold of her underwear, he slid them down her legs. His hand wasn't gone long. It quickly returned to her, this time covering the apex between her thighs.

Her breath caught.

At first his fingers stroked. Long, slow strokes that made her sex vibrate with need. Then he began to apply more pressure, moving in circular motions. Touching and teasing her clit.

Gravelly pleas left her mouth. Her voice didn't sound like her own. "Now, Wyatt. Please." Desire spread through her body like wildfire. Rapid and unstoppable.

"Patience, sunshine."

The material of her dress got pushed down farther. Soon, she lay naked. Her eyes followed Wyatt as he stood.

He undressed slowly. Revealing his hard, muscular body bit by bit. Quinn couldn't take her gaze from him.

When all his clothes were removed, Wyatt lowered himself between her thighs, trailing kisses up her legs. She held her breath as he neared her core. Then his lips closed around her clit.

Her sharp intake of breath was followed by a strangled cry. She threw her head to the side, her hips jolting. Wyatt held her firm.

He knew exactly what to do to drive her wild. Every touch caused a new ripple of pleasure to race through her. His tongue lapped her sensitive bundle. Over and over until she was ready to beg.

"Wyatt. Please! Come to me."

WYATT REACHED into the bedside drawer and quickly rolled a condom over himself. Then he was back with Quinn.

With the softest touch, he moved some hair from her cheek. "You're mine."

She nodded. "Yours. Forever."

Forever. That's exactly how Wyatt saw it.

Slowly, he sank into Quinn, loving the array of emotions that splayed across her face. Passion. Heat. Untamed need.

God, she was beautiful. There would never be a day when he tired of looking at her. Not if he lived a hundred years. "I love you."

Her eyes softened. She ran her hand from his shoulder to his heart. "I love you, too."

Lowering his head, Wyatt tasted her. She was so sweet. An intoxicating mix of strawberry and honey. Then he began to move his hips.

A gruff moan tore from him. It took every ounce of willpower he possessed to go slow. His body urged him to move faster, but he wanted to savor her. To draw it out. Because being inside her was like a drug.

As he thrust, a rosy pink entered her cheeks. Her breasts bounced with each movement. Lowering his hand, he flicked her pebbled nipple, enjoying the soft moan that escaped her throat.

So damn responsive.

Soon, she began lifting her hips. Meeting him thrust for thrust.

"I'm not fragile, Wyatt," she gasped. "Fuck me."

His control snapped. Blood pounded in his ears as he pushed deeper. Faster.

The pressure built inside him. Like a storm he was unable to tame. Every thrust brought them back together. Back to his heart.

"I want all of you, Quinn."

Every little flaw and strength.

"You have me."

Her eyes began to shutter, but Wyatt lifted his hand to stroke her cheek. "Look at me, sweetheart. I want to see you come apart."

Lowering his hand, he stroked her clit. Immediately, her walls tightened around him. Then her entire body shuddered as she cried out his name.

His name sounded so good on her lips in the throes of passion.

Wyatt couldn't draw his gaze from her. She was wild and free. It was fucking beautiful.

Her walls pulsed around him as he continued to thrust. Wanting every little bit of her. Then his muscles tightened before an orgasm so intense and powerful took over his whole body.

His breaths came out hard and fast. Quinn took everything from him. She shattered him.

Holding himself above her, he worked to control his breathing. His heart galloped. She was the only woman to ever raise it. The only one to touch his heart at all.

Their bodies were tangled as he dropped his temple to touch hers. "How did I find you?"

"Something tells me we were always going to find each other."

He raised his head to look at her. He liked that thought. That they were meant to be. That their lives were always going to intertwine.

CHAPTER 26

Quinn stepped inside her apartment. She felt light. Happy. Like the final piece of her life had just slotted into place.

Wyatt loved her. His words and actions last night had been the stuff that dreams were made of. The stuff she thought only existed in movies.

Shaking her head, she moved to her bedroom to change. She'd already had a shower. Not that she and Wyatt had done much in the form of washing. Heat bloomed in her cheeks at the thought.

God, the man was making her blush, and he wasn't even here.

Pulling the dress from the previous night over her head, she replaced it with blue jeans and a gray T-shirt. While Quinn was due at the bakery within the hour, Wyatt had just left for Marble Protection. Before leaving, he'd let her know that Kye was around. Watching. Making sure she was safe.

Jeez, the guilt she felt at these men losing chunks of their days to babysit her never ceased.

Kye would probably take one look at her and wonder why a smile the size of New York was on her face. Not that she cared.

Everything in her life felt *right*. For the first time in a long time, possibly ever, she wasn't moving at a hundred miles an hour. She wasn't researching the world's deep, dark, and ugly. She wasn't working all hours of the day. She was just *living*. And in doing that, she'd found everything she'd been missing.

This was a life she never knew she wanted. Now that she had it, she would be holding on tight.

Pulling her hair up into a ponytail, Quinn was about to brush her teeth when a knock on the door sounded.

She frowned. Who would be knocking at her door at eight in the morning? Bar Wyatt or Mason, she couldn't think of anyone.

Possibly Wyatt coming back to give her more of those delicious kisses?

Boy, wouldn't that be nice.

Her abdomen heated at the thought. Chances were slim to none. But a girl could dream.

Moving to the door, she looked through the peephole. Her jaw dropped open in surprise. She almost thought she was hallucinating until she yanked open the door.

"Tanya!"

The woman stood in front of her, hands ringing together.

Tanya's gaze darted down the hall, then back at Quinn. She looked nervous. Almost like she was waiting for someone to pop out and attack.

"Hi, Quinn. Can we talk?"

Concern wrinkled Quinn's forehead. "Of course, come in."

As the other woman stepped inside her apartment, Quinn caught sight of Kye by the stairs. She whispered that all was okay. Tanya wouldn't hear, but she was sure Kye could. She had no doubt the man would still remain in the hall and listen for trouble, just in case.

Closing the door, Quinn took a seat at the table, gesturing to the chair opposite. "When did you get to Marble Falls?"

"My flight landed an hour ago. I came straight here. Darren had given me your address before...well, before. Anyway, I'm sorry I didn't call. It was a last-minute decision. I just jumped on the plane and left." She scanned the living area. "Is anyone else home?"

"It's just us. What's wrong, Tanya?"

Something was wrong. Something that had put tangible fear and panic in the other woman's eyes. Just the fact that she'd flown from New York to Marble Falls without so much as a call indicated something was up.

"I'm being watched." Tanya said the words quickly, then took a deep breath before continuing. "I mean, I *feel* like I'm being watched. Every minute of every day, I feel eyes on me. I don't even think I'm safe in my own home." Dark circles shadowed Tanya's eyes and her skin was pale.

Quinn's heart went out to her. "When did this start?"

"The moment Darren left New York. But this last week, it's been worse. No matter where I am, I hear footsteps behind me, but when I turn, no one's there. And when I arrived home the other day, my back door was unlocked. Quinn, I *always* lock every door and window."

Quinn believed her. She knew how safety-conscious Tanya was.

A million thoughts raced through Quinn's mind. On one hand, it made sense that it would be Project Arma. Perhaps they were trying to figure out what Tanya knew...and whether she knew too much. Maybe her connection to Darren made her a liability.

On the other hand, from everything Wyatt had told her, Project Arma were professionals. They wouldn't let Tanya catch on to what they were doing.

Plus, if they *were* worried, wouldn't it be easiest just to kill her?

Either way, sitting here wouldn't help them figure it out. She needed to get Tanya to Wyatt. At the very least, he would be able to talk to her and make a decision about what to do next.

Quinn reached across and touched her friend's hand. "I know people who can help you. They own a security business here in town. I don't have much time before I need to start work, but I can take you there first."

Quinn expected to see relief but, if anything, the fear on Tanya's face increased. "Please, don't leave me! I don't want to be alone with people I don't know! I've been so scared, Quinn. I need a familiar face."

Indecision tore at her. Tanya was a friend. Not only had she just lost her husband, she'd also flown all the way from New York for help.

At the same time, she didn't want to let Mrs. Potter down.

She gave her friend's hand a squeeze. "I'll call my boss and see if there's any way I can miss my shift today."

Grabbing her phone from the kitchen counter, Quinn called the bakery.

"Mrs. Potter's Bakehouse," Mrs. Potter answered with a chirpy voice.

"Mrs. Potter, it's Quinn. I'm so sorry to ask this when my shift begins in less than an hour, but is there any chance you can do without me today? I've had a friend fly in from New York last minute. She has an emergency and needs my help."

She couldn't help but cringe as she asked. She'd never in her life canceled on a boss so last minute. It went against every hard-working bone in her body.

"Dear, that's fine. I don't anticipate it being busy. Go, help your friend."

Quinn let out a sigh of relief. She still felt guilty, but so grateful for Mrs. Potter's understanding. "You are so wonderful. Thank you. This won't happen again. I promise."

"I'm sure it won't. I hope your friend is okay."

So did Quinn. Once she hung up, she smiled at Tanya. "I can stay with you at Marble Protection."

This time, Tanya *did* look relieved. "Oh, thank you!"

Popping her phone into her back pocket, Quinn grabbed her keys, and they headed down to the car.

"I can drive if you don't mind directing me. I got a rental car from the airport."

"Oh, um, sure." Quinn wasn't the biggest fan of driving, but she found it slightly strange that the other woman wanted to drive when she didn't know the area.

Tanya had parked across the street. Before they reached her car, she saw Kye sitting in his. He'd probably sped down the stairs to beat them.

Quinn placed her hand on Tanya's arm as she slowed beside Kye's car.

"Morning, Kye! This is my friend Tanya. She needs your team's help, so we're heading to Marble Protection now."

He nodded, his eyes shooting from Tanya to Quinn. "I'll trail you."

She never doubted it.

Moving to Tanya's car, they'd just climbed in when Tanya touched her arm. "Is it okay if we make a quick stop at the pharmacy? I've run out of my anxiety meds."

Quinn's brows rose in surprise. She knew her friend suffered from anxiety, but had never heard Tanya mention anything about needing medication for it. "Of course."

"I'll let your friend know."

Quinn was about to tell Tanya she could just text him, but Tanya was already out the door.

While she waited, a message came through from Wyatt. She smiled when she saw the three heart emojis.

Christ, she loved the man.

She was about to respond when Tanya climbed back into the car. Rather than start the engine, Tanya first removed something from her arm. Something that appeared to have been sitting beneath her sleeve.

Before she could get a good look at it, Tanya was shoving it below the seat. When her friend didn't offer any sort of explanation, Quinn frowned. "What was that?"

Tanya remained silent as she started the engine and began to drive. Quinn waited, but the silence only lengthened.

"Tanya, is everything okay?"

"Of course."

She didn't look Quinn's way. Just kept her eyes on the road.

Strange.

Glancing behind her, Quinn searched for Kye, but the road was empty. No one was trailing them.

"Where's Kye?"

"Oh, he said he'd go straight to Marble Protection."

The hairs on the back of Quinn's neck stood up.

Something wasn't right. If Wyatt had asked Kye to stick close to her, there was no way the other man would have left her unprotected.

Turning her head, Quinn studied Tanya's body language, immediately noticing how stiffly she sat behind the wheel. "You never mentioned anything about being scared in any text message or phone chat," she said casually.

Tanya lifted a shoulder. "I guess I left some things out."

There was a flatness to Tanya's tone that had unease slithering up her spine. "Take this right to get to the pharmacy."

Tanya didn't take the right. She just kept driving straight.

Quinn's unease intensified. "Tanya, what's going on?"

"For example, I might have forgotten to mention my brother?" Tanya continued as if she hadn't heard Quinn's question. "Although, I guess it's not forgetting if it's intentional."

Quinn frowned, unsure where Tanya was going with this.

"He's my half-brother. Different dads, so different last names. He's also a bit older than me; we never grew up together. Super helpful guy, though. He's been supporting us financially for years. No to mention, he used his connections to help Darren advance in his career."

"Are you saying Darren didn't earn his position based on merit?"

Tanya scoffed. "No. Not even close. And I doubt he ever would have. Didn't you ever notice what a bumbling idiot he was? I mean, he couldn't even kill *you*, could he?"

Ice instantly shot through Quinn, followed by a blast of prickling heat. "You knew?"

The words from her lips were barely a whisper.

Tanya shot an irritated look across to her. "Of course I know. I'm the one who sent him here. He was supposed to shut you up! The moment you picked up the story, in fact. He thought firing you would be enough. The fool."

Shock rendered Quinn silent for a moment. Adrenaline pumping through her body.

"*You* told Darren to kill me?"

"Well...me and James. You probably know him better as Hylar."

At the mention of the familiar name, Quinn sucked in a quick breath. "Hylar as in—"

"Former commander of your boyfriend and brother? Architect of Project Arma? My half-brother? Yes. Him."

No. That wasn't possible. Surely, the world couldn't be so small that the woman beside her, the woman she'd considered a friend, was also related by blood to Wyatt and Mason's greatest enemy?

"Having Darren as the executive editor of *The New York Times* served two purposes: watching the news and watching *you*. Not sure why James was so fixated on you. Something about your brother." She turned onto the highway. "I do pull my weight, though. I'm the one who made sure the lab break-ins stayed out of the news. Alabama, Salina, and Portland...they each almost reached some type of news outlets. If I hadn't paid off a few people, the information would be out there already."

Quinn had suspected *someone* was paying them off. She just

hadn't expected it to be one of her closest friends. "So everything you said in my apartment was a lie?"

Tanya smirked. "Of course it was. To clear your day and get you in the car with me."

Everything...including telling Kye they were making a stop.

Crap—where was Kye?

"What did you do to Kye?"

"They gave me this band to wear on my forearm. A tranquilizer. That's why James needed me. To get you away from them." She lifted a shoulder. "It worked. Your friend trusted me enough to let me get close. All I had to do was touch his arm and the tranquilizer fired. Now you don't have anyone protecting you."

Quinn sucked in a pained breath. "You shot him?"

Tanya studied Quinn before looking back to the road. "Don't tell me you're surprised? Didn't you hear what I've been saying? James *supports* me. Ensures I live in comfort. Now that Darren's dead and I don't have his income, that makes me even more reliant on my brother. If he says you need to die—then you need to die."

Quinn hated the fear that was running through her blood. Not just fear. Uncertainty. Panic. Anger at herself for not seeing who Tanya truly was. She'd completely missed the fact that greed was the driving force in the woman's life.

With the hand closest to the door, Quinn slowly began to move the phone to her thigh. Maybe she could call Wyatt without Tanya realizing.

Quinn had barely moved her hand a couple inches before Tanya opened the center console and pulled out a gun. She pointed it directly at Quinn.

"You think I'm stupid? That I don't see what you're doing?"

Quinn stopped moving.

"Throw it out the window."

No. Wyatt would have no way to contact her.

"Don't mess with me, Quinn. James wants you alive for now,

but I'd have no hesitation in shooting you in the hand. You want that?"

Holy hell…Tanya was a psychopath.

Rolling down the window, Quinn reluctantly threw it out. Her chest felt heavy with the knowledge that she'd just lost the last connection she had with Wyatt.

"Good. I don't need any surprises from you. You'll go to James and my payments will continue. It's that simple."

She had to think of a way out of this, and fast.

"Tanya, can you trust him? Like, *really* trust him? I know he's your brother, but I've heard about the terrible things he and his men have done—"

"Shut up! You always thought you were so much smarter than me. You're not going to save yourself, so don't bother trying. I'm not going to let one stupid bitch come between me and my cushy life."

Blowing out a long breath, Quinn tried to slow her galloping heartbeat. It was hard with a gun trained right on her. She believed the other woman when she said she'd shoot. For the time being, at least, there was nothing she could do. She was stuck.

She wondered at what point Wyatt would work out she was gone. She doubted it would take long. She rarely went a few minutes without replying to his texts. That right there would be cause for concern.

When Tanya lowered the weapon, Quinn felt a moment of hope. But that hope died when the gun remained pointed in Quinn's direction from her lap. It would be very easy for Tanya to shoot at her if she were to move suddenly. Too easy.

All Quinn could do was sit and pray that Wyatt somehow figured out what was going on.

Eventually, Tanya pulled off the main road and began driving down a dirt lane. The farther she drove, the more panic built inside Quinn. "Please, Tanya. You don't need to do this."

Tanya scoffed. "Actually, I do. Handing you over is a small price to pay to maintain the life I've become accustomed to."

So basically, her friend was handing her over so she could keep buying expensive things. Who the hell was this woman? "Was our friendship ever real?"

Tanya shrugged. "I kind of liked you at the start. It wasn't until I saw how you flaunted yourself in front of Darren that I realized you couldn't be trusted. I couldn't believe my luck when James finally gave us the task to get rid of you."

Flaunted herself in front of Darren? That wasn't even close to being true. Not that she would be defending herself to the crazy lady beside her.

Quinn must have been blind their entire friendship to miss the signs. She'd always considered herself a good judge of character. Clearly not.

Finally, Tanya stopped the car in front of an old cabin. It looked like they were deep in the woods, which was not good for her chances of being found.

Tanya turned her attention to Quinn. There wasn't an ounce of compassion. The woman may as well have been a stranger. "Undo your seat belt and get out. Don't even think about trying any funny business. You'll regret it."

What the heck did Tanya think Quinn would do? Run into the woods only to get shot in the leg? No thanks.

Tanya stepped out first, and Quinn followed. They'd just stepped in front of the car when the door to the cabin opened.

A man stepped out. He appeared to be around their age. He was built just like Wyatt and the guys. Like a soldier.

"Where's James?"

The man didn't flinch at Tanya's question. "He couldn't make it."

While his face was devoid of emotion, his voice was steely hard. It made goose bumps rush over Quinn's skin.

"Well, I brought her. I followed all of James's instructions and made sure we weren't followed."

The man's gaze washed over Quinn, studying her face. She stood taller, refusing to let him know just how scared she was.

When he seemed to be satisfied, he nodded.

Then, before either woman could anticipate his next move, he pulled the gun from the holster on his waist and shot Tanya in the head.

CHAPTER 27

"*T*ell me, how many lilies did you actually order?" Oliver asked as they stepped outside Marble Protection.

Enough to make Quinn one happy woman. So, in Wyatt's opinion, just enough. "Hundreds."

Oliver shook his head. "Damn, you're such a romantic. Remind me to ask you for advice when I need to woo a woman."

Love did strange things to a man. It tied a person in knots and made them want to go to the ends of the Earth to please someone.

"When you meet the right person, you'll know what to do."

They headed to Mrs. Potter's Bakehouse. It wasn't far, but any distance between him and Quinn seemed too great. She hadn't responded to the text he'd sent her. He'd only sent it thirty minutes ago, but those responses were what kept him going while they were apart.

"I'm glad you found her, Jobs. I know Eagle doesn't have another sister, but do you think there's a cousin he could introduce me to?"

Wyatt chuckled. "That might be pushing the man's kindness."

"You're right. What about you? Got a hot cousin you haven't told me about?"

"The only cousin I have is married with kids." When Wyatt looked over at his friend, Oliver was nodding like he was actually considering the prospect. "*Happily* married," he pressed, feeling the need to emphasize the happily part.

"Yeah, yeah. No family members. Gotcha. Maybe Cage has someone."

Wyatt laughed as they pushed through the door to the bakehouse. Scanning the area, he was immediately disappointed he couldn't see Quinn.

Mrs. Potter moved from the work bench to the counter. "It's nice to see you boys so bright and early today. What can I do for you?"

Wyatt listened for Quinn's heartbeat. Her breathing. Anything. As far as Wyatt could tell, Mrs. Potter was alone. "Is Quinn running late?" It wasn't like her to be late for a shift.

A confused expression crossed the older woman's face. "She didn't tell you? A friend of hers had an emergency so she asked for the day off. She called maybe," Mrs. Potter scanned the clock on the wall, "forty minutes ago."

A friend? Quinn hadn't mentioned anything to him about helping a friend today. This morning, she had been all set to go to work. It was unusual that she wouldn't have let Wyatt know her plans had changed. At least a text message...

Pulling out his phone, Wyatt dialed Quinn's number.

At the same time, he saw Oliver calling someone. Kye, Wyatt assumed.

Dread began to pool in his gut when both calls went to voicemail.

Shoving the phone back in his pocket, Wyatt turned to Mrs. Potter. "How did she sound when she called?"

Her brows lifted. "Oh, um, she didn't sound too different than normal. Very apologetic. I could tell she felt bad for asking to have the day off."

That was good. No different than normal was good. Maybe Wyatt was panicking for no reason.

Oliver stepped closer. "If she has her phone, we can find her and Cage's location."

Yes. The team had put location trackers on all team and family member phones.

Wyatt smiled at the bakery owner, wanting to put her at ease. "Thank you for the information, Mrs. Potter. I'm sure there's no need to worry. She's probably at Marble waiting for us."

Mrs. Potter nodded.

On the outside, Wyatt forced himself to appear calm. To move at a normal pace as he exited the bakery. To keep himself from sprinting back to Marble Protection.

On the way, Oliver's hand clamped down on his shoulder. "I'm sure there's no need to worry."

The unease clawing its way up his throat said otherwise. It was unusual for her not to respond to his messages. To let his calls go unanswered. Not to mention the fact that she wasn't at work and he had no idea who this friend with an emergency was.

When they reached the business, Wyatt headed straight to the office. Oliver walked away, likely to find Mason.

Opening his laptop, Wyatt went to the tracking software.

He prayed that the sick feeling in his gut was wrong. That this was just a breakdown in communication.

The moment the location came up, he knew something was wrong.

The side of a highway. That's where her phone was. Where there was nothing but open road.

Wyatt cursed under his breath just as the door to the office opened. Mason walked in, trailed by Oliver, Eden, Bodie, and Luca.

"Did you find her?" Mason asked, heading straight for the laptop.

Wyatt stood back so his friend could see where the tracker was located.

Mason cursed as well. "She didn't say anything to you this morning about helping someone?" Mason's voice was thick with worry. It was a mirror of what Wyatt felt.

"When I left her, she was stepping inside her apartment to get ready for work. Kye was on guard in the hall." Wyatt leaned down and pulled up Kye's location. Any last shred of hope he may have been harboring quickly died. "Kye's location is reading from his car outside the apartment building."

Which had to mean she'd been taken.

How? Wyatt had no idea.

Oliver went to the supply closet. The one that was heavily locked and stored all of their weapons. "I'll go check on Kye."

He grabbed what he needed, then disappeared through the door.

Wyatt was about to grab his own weapons when the ringing of his phone stopped him. When he fished it out, he noticed it was an unknown number. "Who is this?"

A soft chuckle sounded. "Wyatt...hello, old friend."

Blood froze in Wyatt's veins at the sound of Carter's voice.

Carter was Hylar's right-hand man. The leader of the other former SEAL team that had also been part of Project Arma. The team that remained with Project Arma.

Wyatt had been searching for Carter as well, but always came up empty.

"Where is she?"

"What, no small talk first? Don't you want to know what I've been up to? Where I've been?"

Oh, he wanted to know exactly where the guy had been. "Tell me where the hell she is, right now."

Again he chuckled, like this was one big joke. Wyatt was running out of patience.

"Okay, okay. I'll get to it. I have a plan, and I need you to follow that plan. Or you might not like what happens."

"Stop wasting my time and tell me then."

"I need you to meet me at a location with the materials you took from the Portland lab. You can bring your team or not—I don't really care. But if you come without the supplies, she dies."

Wyatt's fist tightened around the phone. Rage was pouring through his body. "Where?"

"Patience. I'll text you the location. Whatever you do, don't take long discussing a plan with your team. The longer you take, the less happy your girlfriend will be."

The phone line went dead.

Wyatt had to physically stop himself from crushing the devise in his fist. A couple of seconds later, he was sent a location.

Moving to the storage cupboard, Wyatt began arming himself. The others did the same.

"What's the plan?" Luca asked.

Wyatt shoved a gun into his IWB holster, then another into his ankle holster. "There's not much we can do except what the guy said. I'm not losing Quinn."

"And I'm not losing my sister," Mason added.

It didn't take long for the men in the room to arm up. In that time, they messaged the women and asked them to head to Asher's house. He would remain with them.

The location Carter had sent was forty-five minutes away. Too damn far.

Moving out to the parking lot, they took two cars. The guys talked strategy around him. Wyatt participated in the conversation as much as he could. But fear and anger were clawing at his insides, so much so that he could barely think straight.

The asshole had Quinn. Had *touched* Quinn. Wyatt was only just containing his fury.

～

QUINN WATCHED as Carter hung up the phone. He seemed to get a lot of pleasure out of the conversation. It made her feel sick.

It wasn't just the conversation that made her nauseous. It was also the fact that Tanya had been shot dead right beside her. Blood splatter still covered Quinn's body.

It made her want to scrub her skin to within an inch of her life.

As soon as Tanya had dropped to the ground, Carter had dragged her into the old cabin and shoved her onto a sofa. She was pretty sure there were living things inside the furniture but there was no way she was moving an inch from where he'd placed her.

"Won't you get in trouble for killing Hylar's sister?"

Carter glanced over to Quinn as he shoved his cell in his pocket. "Honey, I follow orders. My orders were to kill her, so she's dead."

Hylar gave orders to kill his own sister? What kind of a sociopath was he? "Why would he want to kill her?"

Carter shrugged. "I don't ask because I don't care. If I had to hazard a guess, I'd say she was a loose end. Hylar's probably sick of supporting the woman. Plus, if she's gone, she can't be used against him. After all, family is a vulnerability."

Christ. How were all these people so damn cold-hearted?

"Ready to rock and roll?"

No. She was perfectly fine exactly where she was. "Where are we going?"

"Somewhere fabulous. There's water and trees and no one within a fifty-mile radius."

Yeah, Quinn was sure it was a real paradise.

Carter moved across the room.

"Wyatt will save me, you know."

Maybe if she said it out loud enough, her brain, which was clouded by a thick fog of panic, would start to believe it.

"Oh, I'm counting on it. Because it means he's played by my rules. While he saves you, I'll be so far gone they won't see so much as a print in the dirt."

Quinn frowned. "So, you're not going to kill me?"

She watched as he rummaged in a bag. His body blocked what was inside so she had no idea what he was doing.

"Not if I get what I want. Your future lies in their hands."

When he appeared to be done, Carter tossed the backpack onto his back and moved in front of her. She had to stop herself from moving away when he bent down, a mere inch separating their faces.

"So you see, I'm hoping you live. Because if you live, my boss gets what he wants."

In the next moment, Carter threw her body over his shoulder. The air was temporarily knocked out of her by the impact. There was also a pang of pain.

She struggled to catch her breath as he began moving outside. "Why did you call Wyatt an 'old friend'? Who are you?"

Carter laughed. "Because once upon a time, we were both SEALs. Supposedly fighting for the same cause."

"Supposedly?"

"Your boyfriend Wyatt is a Boy Scout. His whole team is. Whereas I never enlisted to help people. I enlisted because I like the feel of a gun in my hand. The power that surges through my body when someone else's life is at my mercy. You should see the desperation that shows on a man's face when he wants to live. It's pathetic."

Okay. If it hadn't been confirmed before, it was now. The guy was a homicidal maniac. "So you like scaring people."

"I like control. And power. That's what Hylar has given me and my team. Unrivaled power. He gave that to Wyatt's team, too, and the guys just threw it back in his face. They should have gotten down on their knees and thanked the man."

There wasn't a chance Wyatt, her brother, or any of those men would have "thanked" Hylar for what he did.

"Hold on, darlin'."

That was the only warning Quinn got before Carter sped up. He began moving so fast, everything passed in a blur.

Quinn gripped him. She doubted he would drop her. But then, she didn't really know *what* he'd do.

It felt like a good fifteen minutes, maybe more, before she was dumped on the ground.

There was a moment of relief that she no longer had a rock-hard shoulder pressed to her stomach. Then she heard the water. Rapidly moving water that was loud and angry.

Turning her head, she saw a river with powerful rapids behind her.

"What are we doing here?"

Carter pulled his shirt over his head. "You sure you want to know? I can tell you, but sometimes a surprise is easier."

No. She wasn't sure she wanted to know. But whether he told her or not, she was sure she would be finding out soon enough.

When Carter began removing his shoes and pants, her heart started to race. "Please tell me you aren't taking me into the water."

Carter's mouth pulled into a smile. The guy was enjoying her fear way too much. "You're a clever girl, aren't you. I am taking you into the water. There's no need to be scared, though. I told you you'd probably survive this."

It was the "probably" part that Quinn was concerned about.

"I don't understand what you hope to gain by doing this. If you sent them the address to the cabin, the guys will easily be able to track us here." Quinn's voice betrayed her shortness of breath. Her palms were sweaty.

Carter was now naked, bar a pair of underwear. "Oh, darlin', I won't be meeting them at the cabin *or* here. The location I sent is a twenty-minute drive north. They won't find you unless they play by my rules."

Standing, Carter lifted a gun that looked to be straight out of fiction—some kind of grappling gun, with a lethal-looking steel hook protruding from the end.

Was Arma in the business of developing weapons other than men and drugs?

Before she could ask, Carter turned toward the river and aimed the weapon at a huge boulder that sat in the middle of the water, then pulled the trigger. The hook attached to the rock. Connected to the hook was rope leading back to the gun. To Carter.

Shoving the gun in his bag, he returned the bag to his back. Carter took two steps toward Quinn. "You ready for a swim?"

Absolutely not. She was pretty sure it wasn't optional though.

Carter lifted Quinn into his arms, her chest pressed to his, and moved toward the untamed rapids. The hold was almost intimate, and Quinn wanted to lean away. The moment he stepped into the water, however, she wrapped her arms tightly around his neck and her legs around his waist.

A violent trembling began in her limbs. Her stomach was doing twists and turns. There was no part of her that wanted to continue into the water, even if she was being carried by a genetically altered super-soldier. "What if we don't make it across?"

"Then you'll probably die."

There was no remorse in the man's voice. Not even a hint of it.

Asshole.

She probably *would* die, too. The water looked like it would suck her in and steal the life from her body. Completely unforgiving.

Carter navigated his way through the river, using the rope to pull them across.

The journey was wet and dangerous. The water beat at her body. Unrelenting in its fury. It was impossible not to ingest mouthfuls when it hit her full force in the face.

She hated using Carter's body as a shield, but it was the only remnant of protection she had.

There were a few moments when Carter seemed to physically strain at the effort to get them across. Quinn just held him tighter, until her fingers ached from her grip on his neck.

When they finally made it to the rock, Carter pushed her up first before following. There was just enough room for both of them.

She watched in dread as he unstrapped the bag from his back and pulled something out. Something large. A vest, maybe?

Carter crouched in front of her.

Yep. It was a vest. But not a regular vest.

He shoved it over her head before she got a good look at it, then quickly secured the straps on the sides. The thing was heavy. Almost like it was weighed down with stones.

When the vest was firmly in place, he reached into the bag and pulled out a small device, which he swiftly pushed into Quinn's hand. He pressed her thumb to the top. His own thumb remained above hers, applying pressure.

"Now, Quinn, I need you to listen carefully. The item I've just placed on your chest is a bomb."

At the word "bomb," fear stabbed at her heart and stole her breath.

"There are a few ways for it to detonate. The first is if I press the button on this remote detonator right here." He took a remote out of his bag and waved it in front of her with his free hand before putting it back. "The second way is for time to run out on the timer. The third and final way for you to blow up is if you remove your thumb from the detonator in your hand. Nod if you understand what I just said."

It took about five seconds for his words to sink in. To grasp the fact that she was wearing a bomb on her chest. That there were three separate ways it could detonate. Three! And one was literally in the palm of her hand.

"Quinn?"

Was there humor in the asshole's voice?

Even though tears built in Quinn's eyes and fear pulsed through her veins, she couldn't help but feel the all-consuming anger that was bubbling to the surface. Anger that the man in front of her had put her in this situation. That he was *enjoying* her absolute terror.

"I heard you."

"Good. Now, because I'm going to make a promise to that boyfriend of yours that you'll live if he gives me what I want, and I'm a man of my word, I'm going to tell you something. Something important—green signifies life." He laughed. "Guess that's why I've never been a fan of the color. I'm more a gory death kind of guy."

Quinn barely registered his words. She was more focused on his thumb lifting from hers.

Suddenly, it was just her holding down the button. The button that could blow her up on the spot.

Closing her eyes for a moment, she felt the trickle of a tear slide down her cheek.

You're okay, Quinn. Everything will be okay. Just focus on maintaining the pressure.

When Quinn opened her eyes, she shot fire at the man in front of her. "They might not kill you today, but make no mistake, they *will* kill you. And when they do, I hope you regret every terrible thing you've ever done in your life."

One side of his mouth lifted. "I like you. If circumstances were different, I may have even kept you." Carter stood. "Unfortunately for you, they won't kill me. Eventually, they'll either join us or die. The good news for Boy Scout is that it will probably be his choice. Hylar loves the guy. He loves all of them, actually. No idea why."

Quinn didn't believe any of that for a second. Wyatt and his team would find a way to destroy Carter, Hylar, and everyone else helping them. She knew it with absolute certainty.

She watched as Carter detached the hook from the rock and shot it back toward the riverbank.

It took him less time to cross the river without her. He quickly dressed before disappearing into the woods.

The vest felt like a giant manacle tying Quinn to the spot. Every wave that crashed against the rock jolted her into sitting a bit straighter. She couldn't afford a lapse in attention. That's all it would take. One moment of distraction, and she would be gone.

Lifting her other hand, she placed it over her thumb.

Focus, Quinn.

Closing her eyes, she tried to push away the fear and uncertainty. Trick her mind into believing she was somewhere else. Somewhere safe.

She was with Wyatt. They were by the ocean. Sitting on the sand. Her big protector. The man she never asked for or expected, but now, never wanted to lose. The man who listened to her heartbeat every single day and knew that it beat for him.

CHAPTER 28

*E*very minute that passed fueled Wyatt's rage.

Where the hell was Carter?

The location he'd sent them to was an empty field about ten miles off the highway. The place was deserted. They'd been waiting at least fifteen minutes, and Carter and Quinn were nowhere to be seen.

Oliver and Kye had joined them ten minutes ago. Kye had been shot in the shoulder with a tranquilizer gun. The stuff was fast-acting but clearly had a short duration. Which meant he was now fine, just angry as hell about what had happened.

Tanya, Darren's wife, had shot him.

Tanya, who Quinn had been adamant was innocent in all this.

Well, that definitely wasn't the case.

The bag of stolen materials sat at Wyatt's feet. There wasn't a chance he was parting with the stuff until they knew Quinn was safe.

His frustration was just about to boil over when the sight of a car caught his attention. Wyatt watched closely as Carter parked a few feet away before stepping out.

The moment Wyatt realized Carter was alone, the fury he'd only just been containing rose to the surface.

Wyatt was in the other man's face before he'd stepped away from the car. "Where is she?"

Carter's expression remained neutral. "Wyatt, in case I wasn't clear on the phone, every decision you make pushes your girlfriend closer to living another day...or dying within the hour. Guess which way you're tipping her right now."

The anger was like a living, breathing species inside him. Even though it was the hardest damn thing he'd ever done, Wyatt stepped back from the man.

Carter straightened his shirt before looking back to Wyatt. A smile stretched across his lips. A smile that was nowhere close to reaching his eyes.

"Lovely day for a catch-up, isn't it?"

Mason stepped up beside Wyatt. "If you don't tell us where my sister is, we're going to tear you apart limb by limb."

He chuckled. The sound was soul-wrenching. "You won't. Not if you want her alive. You kill me, she dies. I guess you could always try to torture the information out of me, but we both know that, just like you, I've been trained to withstand it. By the time you have what you need, she'll be long gone. Don't believe me? Go ahead and try."

Wyatt forced his body to remain where it was. To not grab the guy by the throat and throw him against the vehicle.

"I assume by your silence, you understand." Carter turned his head and looked at the rest of the team. "We've got almost the whole gang here. That's great. Unfortunately, I'm under strict instructions from the commander not to kill any of you. Something about not being able to afford any more losses. Shame, really. I wouldn't classify the death of any of you as a loss."

Luca stepped forward. "Just tell us where she is, Carter."

"Patience, my friend. If I get what I need, I'll give you her location. And I really hope I do, because she wasn't in the best position when I left her."

Wyatt lunged forward, but Mason stopped him. Barely. "I'm going to destroy you, you asshole."

The smile slipped from Carter's lips. For the first time since stepping out of the car, the friendly facade fell and Wyatt got to see the real Carter.

"*I* should be the one destroying *you*." He took a step closer. "You decimated our army, killed just about every soldier we had. Every soldier I'd trained. You freed our prisoners. You imprisoned our lab technicians and medical staff. If the commander wasn't so set on keeping you alive, you'd be lying in a pool of your own blood right now."

Not a chance.

"So why does he want us alive?" Kye asked.

"Because he places inflated value on you. Because his ego is blinding him. He created you. He *owns* you. He doesn't want to destroy what he's created. He wants to control it. He just hasn't clicked onto the fact that you'll never fight his war. But soon, he'll come around." Carter's eyes swung to the bag behind Wyatt. "Today, all he wants are the drugs you took from him. The drugs that will be used to make more soldiers like us. To rebuild what you tore down. They're the last of their kind in the country. Time is of the essence. Hence their importance."

None of Wyatt's team moved a muscle.

"How do we know that if we give you this bag, you'll give us her location?" Mason asked.

"You don't." Carter almost looked happy about that. Wyatt took deep breaths, forcing his body to calm. "But even though I have very few positive qualities, one thing I *do* possess is loyalty to the commander. He told me to keep her alive unless you didn't follow my orders. And that's what I intend to do."

"Why would he let her live?" Oliver asked the question, and it damn near tore Wyatt in two.

"The same reason he ordered the hit on his sister. Because family—love—is a liability. Something that can be used against you, should the need arise. We want as much of that as possible."

Killed his sister? Wyatt didn't even know Hylar *had* a sister.

"Ticktock. Quinn has," Carter looked at his watch, "less than an hour. That's if she hasn't blown herself up already."

"You put a fucking bomb on her?" Wyatt was seething.

Oliver stepped forward. He pressed one hand to Wyatt's shoulder and used the other to shove the bag into Carter's chest. "Take it. Now, where is she?"

Carter opened the bag and inspected the contents before looking up. "In ten minutes, I'll be pulling over and checking the bag. If I find any trackers, or anything else that shouldn't be there, I blow her up. If, in the next twenty minutes, I realize someone is following me, I'll blow her up. You get what I'm saying?"

Oliver nodded. "We got it."

"Good. She's a twenty-minute drive away. I'll text you the exact location when I'm in my car." He opened the door and placed the bag inside. "Well, it's been fun, boys. Until next time."

He was just bending to slide into the car when Luca's question stopped him. "How did you know the materials were in our possession?"

He only paused for a moment before sliding the rest of the way into the car. "Maybe when you join us, you'll learn our secrets."

~

QUINN'S entire body shook violently. She wasn't sure if it was from the cold wind blowing on her wet body or fear. Probably both. It was all she could do to keep her thumb pressed to the button in her hand.

It wasn't just the button that was causing terror to paralyze her. It was also that damn timer.

Nine minutes. That's how long the countdown timer said she had until the thing blew up. Nine minutes until her life could be over.

She watched as another minute ticked down. A small whimper escaped her lips.

The timer had probably been the worst part of this whole thing. Watching time tick by was torture. Every minute that passed brought her a minute closer to her death.

Every so often, waves hit her back. Threatening to push her right off the rock.

God. What a nightmare.

If she died, she prayed that Wyatt was okay. That her brother was okay. That they didn't spend their lives punishing themselves over her death. The entire blame lie with that damn organization they were fighting. She really hoped they remembered that.

Wyatt and Mason deserved to be happy. Wyatt deserved to find someone who would love him as long and as hard as he deserved.

"Quinn!"

At the sound of her name, she jolted so badly her body lurched forward. She had to remove the hand on top of her thumb and grab onto the rock to keep from falling.

When she looked up, she saw not only Wyatt, but also her brother and most of the team.

Her heart sped up a notch. "Don't come any closer! I'm wearing a bomb. There's not much time left before it detonates."

Rather than listen to her, Wyatt kicked off his shoes and jumped straight into the water. She saw her brother studying the space on the rock, clearly trying to figure out whether he would fit.

He wouldn't. She and Carter had barely fit.

She watched as Wyatt navigated his way through the water. It in no way appeared easy, even for him. And he didn't have the rope that Carter had. Meaning, he was relying on brute strength to push himself across.

A few minutes later, Wyatt climbed onto the rock. He kneeled in front of her, his feet hanging off the edge.

Even though she wished he was away from her—even though it was dangerous as hell for him to be here—some of the terror that had been gnawing at her insides waned.

Glancing down at the vest, she noticed there were four minutes remaining. Not enough time for the two of them to get to the other side of the river and work on the bomb. Maybe enough time for Wyatt to leave. Go somewhere safe. Away from the explosive vest.

"Wyatt, you need to go! There's not enough time."

He studied the vest. "We need to get this thing off you."

"No! The devise I'm holding is connected to the vest, and I can't remove my thumb because it will explode."

Wyatt cursed under his breath and pulled a pair of scissors from his back pocket. "Carter said he put a bomb on you. I assumed it was a vest bomb. I researched as much as I could about them on the way here. I need to cut the wire that carries the current to the detonator."

As Wyatt continued to inspect Quinn's chest, her heart hurt for the man. If the vest exploded, he would die. He would lose his life trying to save her.

She saw an array of emotions cross his face. Focus. Frustration. Panic.

For the first time, he wasn't masking anything.

"Please, go back to the shore. There's still time. I don't want you to die, too."

"Quinn, stop it."

She swallowed. "I love you. So damn much. You taught me how to be happy. How to really live my life to its fullest potential.

You taught me more about love than I ever would have known. Please…"

Finally, Wyatt lifted his eyes and placed his hands on either side of her head. "Quinn, stop. No one is dying. I have three minutes to figure out which color wire carries the current. I'm going to do it."

Quinn felt raw with pain.

His attention went back to the vest, and she followed his gaze. He'd uncovered two wires. Green and black.

Suddenly, something jolted in her memory. Something Carter had said. Her mind had been so foggy with fear, she'd barely heard him. But it had been something important. Something about life. A color that signifies life…

Her brows pulled together as she tried to recall his words.

Think, Quinn! What did he say?

She sucked in a sharp breath as it hit her. Green. Green signifies life.

"Don't cut the green!"

"What?"

One minute. There was one minute left on the timer. "Carter said that green signifies life, and that's why he hates it."

Wyatt shook his head. "He might have been lying."

Quinn didn't think so. "No. He plays games. I know his type. I've written about his type. You play by his rules, you live. *You* played by his rules, and so did I. He's letting me live. Wyatt. Trust me."

Wyatt placed the scissors around the black wire.

He fixed his gaze on her eyes—then cut.

Silence. No big bang. No fire. No one was dead.

She glanced down to see that the timer was now blank.

Holy heck. Had they really done it? Were they really going to live?

Wyatt's hand covered hers. Gently, he placed his thumb beneath her thumb, and pushed it up.

Nothing happened.

Quinn's breath came out in a whoosh.

Oh God. It was over. The nightmare was over.

The relief was so overwhelming; she felt light-headed. She was barely aware of Wyatt removing the vest from her chest and pulling her into his arms.

As her body relaxed into his, she wanted to cry. Scream. *Something.*

But she felt faint and weak. She needed to hold it together. At least until they were somewhere safer. Not on a rock in the middle of a dangerous river.

Wyatt pulled back, but kept a firm hold on her shoulders. "I need you to hold on to me really tight. I'm going to need two arms to work my way across the water."

She could do that. She'd done that with Carter, even though touching him had made her feel ill.

The only problem was, now her arms felt like jelly.

Quinn pulled on every reserve of strength she had as she wrapped her arms and legs tightly around him. She pressed her head into his neck.

Wyatt stepped into the river. Her body was already numb from the cold, so she barely registered the icy water. They slowly began to wade through the river.

The water was moving fast. Faster than it had been the first time she'd crossed it. And, without the rope, Wyatt struggled a lot more than Carter had.

They'd been in the water for less than thirty seconds when Quinn heard another voice. It was faint over the deafening rapids.

Mason?

Turning her head, she saw Mason grabbing onto Wyatt. Behind her brother, she saw the rest of the guys had formed a chain from the embankment. They were all connected, each one pulling the next.

Even though there was so much manpower, the men were still straining to get everyone to the embankment.

When her body began to weaken, she gritted her teeth and held on tighter.

Just a couple more minutes, Quinn.

Along the way, she thought she might have heard Wyatt's soothing words, but the river around her was deafening.

Blocking out the water and noise, she focused on the heat that emanated from Wyatt's body. The thumping of his heart.

That's when she felt the water begin to recede. Looking up, she saw Mason and Eden pulling Wyatt and her from the water.

Then they were out. But Quinn didn't let go of Wyatt. She didn't think she would ever be letting go.

CHAPTER 29

Quinn folded another shirt into the dresser. Wyatt's dresser. Because she was officially moving into his apartment.

A week had passed since she'd had a bomb strapped to her chest. A week of recovering. Not just physically, but also mentally and emotionally.

She'd thought she was going to die. She'd been so certain that the bomb was going to kill her that when Wyatt had reached her, she'd wanted to push him right back off the rock to save him.

But she hadn't died. Neither had Wyatt. And not a day had passed since that she didn't feel heavy with gratitude for the fact. Although she'd had a couple of nightmares and flashbacks, she'd been doing relatively well.

Wyatt deserved a lot of the credit for that. He was like a god sent from the heavens just for her. They'd spent almost every waking moment together. There wasn't a chance for her to feel scared because she always felt so damn protected.

The thing she probably struggled with the most was knowing that Carter got exactly what he wanted. That their organization would be one step closer to rebuilding what the guys had shut down.

She hated that. Although Wyatt didn't admit it, she knew he had to be hating it, too. Any time she attempted to raise the topic, Wyatt brushed it off like it was no big deal. Like his old commander having the materials to create more super-soldiers was a non-issue. Wyatt would just say that he'd get the guy eventually.

Quinn had every faith that he would.

Shaking her head, she went back to the bed. Everything was now unpacked, bar one box. A box that had remained unopened since moving to Marble Falls. It was filled with her old work materials—reporter's notebooks, articles she'd written...even some old external hard drives.

Basically, stuff she no longer needed. Stuff she should have thrown out weeks ago.

Grabbing the scissors from the top of the dresser, Quinn slid the sharp edge through the tape. She got halfway across when the scissors slipped and sliced the hand that was holding the box.

Crap.

Wincing in pain, Quinn grabbed her hand and raced to the bathroom.

As cool water ran over the cut, she let out just about every curse word in her vocabulary...which was a lot.

When warm hands touched her waist, her eyes shot up to see Wyatt standing directly behind her.

A slow smile stretched across her lips. "This feels a bit familiar."

Quinn turned around. At the same time, Wyatt reached for the hanging hand towel. He wrapped it around her hand, applying pressure to the wound.

It was only a couple months ago when Quinn and Wyatt had been in this exact position. Her with a sliced hand, him acting as her medic. Only now she stood in *his* bathroom, not hers.

"Is this where you tell me the open door wasn't an invitation?"

Quinn chuckled, remembering those exact words coming out her mouth. It was crazy how quickly things changed. How fast a new face became a familiar one.

Now she made it a habit to leave the door wide open, hoping and praying the man would take the hint to come inside.

"That only applies to strangers, and that's not you anymore."

Wyatt's gaze heated. "Good. Because a door that's been bolted shut probably wouldn't keep me out."

Thank God for that.

Rising to her tiptoes, Quinn wet her lips. "Promise?"

Leaning down, Wyatt paused when his lips were almost touching hers. "Promise." Then he was kissing her.

A long, sensual kiss that had every part of her body coming to life.

A small moan escaped her lips but was swallowed by the kiss. She melted into him. Loving the feeling of him surrounding her. Touching her. Stirring a fire in her that she never wanted to dim.

Too soon they separated, but neither let go of the other.

Wyatt indicated toward the hall with his head. "Come on, let's fix this cut before I lose all control."

Hmm. The thought of an out-of-control Wyatt didn't sound too bad at all.

Almost like he read her thoughts, Wyatt shook his head. "You are trouble. Come on."

Giggling, she followed him into the living room. "Is it my fault you're so sexy?"

Quinn took a seat on the couch while Wyatt grabbed the first-aid kit. "Not your fault at all."

This time it was Quinn shaking her head.

Wyatt took a seat beside her. He growled softly as he inspected her hand. "Next time you want a box opened, you call me. You can't be trusted around them."

As much as Quinn wanted to disagree with that statement,

she clearly couldn't. "Sad but true." She didn't see herself as a careless person, so she didn't know what the heck her problem was when it came to opening boxes. "Maybe I was just missing you and knew slicing my skin open would make you come back to me."

Wyatt didn't crack so much as a smile at her joke. "Say the word and I'm exactly where you are. No injuries required."

Quinn's heart swelled. "This is why I love you."

"You love me because I ban you from opening boxes?"

"Because you care about me enough *to* ban me from opening boxes."

"I'll never understand women." He shook his head but smiled at the same time. "Why do you have a sealed box? We moved most things over without boxes."

"It's work stuff. Just the usual papers I couldn't part with. Articles saved to external hard drives. I should just put the whole thing in the trash."

Quinn wasn't a "keep things just in case" kind of person, so there was no need to save any of it. The only reason she still had the box was because she'd assumed she would need it again.

"What if *The New York Times* wants you back?"

Quinn hesitated at the question. The very fitting question, considering the call she'd had today.

Wyatt looked up from what he was doing, his brows pulling together. "They already called, didn't they?"

Christ, the man was perceptive.

"There's a new executive editor. He called. Today, actually. While I was on break at work. He offered me my old job back. Said he'd read some of my stories and had no idea why Darren fired me."

Had that call come through a few short weeks ago, she would have been jumping out of her skin for joy.

Wyatt finished bandaging her hand and fixed his gaze on Quinn. "Do you want to go back?" His face was devoid of all emotion. He made it impossible for Quinn to tell what he was thinking.

Not that it mattered. It wouldn't change what Quinn wanted to do.

"Not even a little bit."

He studied her face, almost like he was looking for any signs of dishonesty. He wouldn't find any.

"I actually got a better offer," Quinn continued, already feeling the bubble of excitement at what she was about to tell him. "Mrs. Potter asked me to buy into the bakehouse. Become part owner."

Wyatt tilted his head, a slow smile stretching across his face. "Is that so?"

"Yep. I told her I wasn't in the financial position to do that right now but asked her to give me a year. A year to save and to learn all the ins and outs of the business. Learn the rest of her secret recipes." Quinn shrugged. "She said yes."

Wyatt scooped Quinn up onto his lap. "And this is what you want? To be part owner of a bakery and live in Marble Falls? To live with me? Small towns can be quiet, you know. Boring compared to New York."

Quinn threw her head back and laughed out loud. "There is nothing boring or quiet about Marble Falls. But, even if it was just a normal small town, it wouldn't matter. Because it's not the drama that's keeping me here."

"Really?"

"Mm-hmm. It has more to do with this guy. This guy who just waltzed into my apartment not that long ago. Let me kiss him… kissed me back." Raising a hand, she pressed it to his cheek. "He's basically taken over my whole heart. Made me the happiest I've ever been in my life."

There was a twinkle in Wyatt's eye. "Would this guy have a name?"

Wetting her lips, Quinn leaned closer. "I think I can do one better."

Then, just like she had that day they'd first met, Quinn pressed her lips to Wyatt's. Only this time, there was no first-kiss flutters or slow exploration.

This time, it was a kiss that stole her breath and consumed her heart. A kiss so passionate and real that she didn't know if she'd ever be able to stop. Because the man who held her was as important as the air she breathed. Her greatest love and wildest adventure.

~

WYATT WAITED until Quinn's breaths evened out before sliding from beneath the sheets. Moving to the living room, he made sure each step was as silent as the last.

He didn't want to wake her. Even though it had been a week since she'd been taken, the experience was traumatic. Sleep was important for her healing and recovery.

Taking a seat on the couch, Wyatt powered up his laptop and connected to the group chat. He was the last one to join. Staring back at him were his seven team members, as well as the eight members of Jason's team.

"Sorry I'm late."

"You're right on time, Jobs," Luca said. "Red was just telling us about his mission."

Wyatt looked to Bodie. "You made progress, Red?"

Evie was able to track the physical location Maya's email had been sent from. Bodie was tasked with the job of finding her and keeping her safe.

Bodie ran a hand through his hair. "I spotted Maya a few days ago and have been watching from a distance since. She seems to have settled here in Keystone, Colorado. Got a job working at the local bar. Tomorrow I'm going to go in and meet her."

"Do you need backup?" Eden asked.

Bodie shook his head. "I'm going to get a feel for the situation.

From what I've seen, she's skittish. If she's in trouble because of Project Arma, my goal is to protect her. Make her feel safe."

Wyatt nodded. He hated that so many lives had been harmed or destroyed because of that damn program. He also knew that Quinn felt a lot of guilt for not doing more to help Maya. If Bodie was able to help her in any way, everyone would be grateful.

"Sounds like a good plan, Red," Mason said. "Jobs, you got any news for us?"

Wyatt leaned back. This was the main reason for the chat. "All family members have full-time protection. Evie and I hired the best security companies from around the country. All of whom remain armed at all times."

It had been a big job for him and Evie to set that up, but worth it to add an extra layer of protection for loved ones.

"They know to remain hidden, so no family members should be alerted to what's going on," Wyatt added.

All fifteen men nodded.

"Is anyone worried about their family?" Wyatt asked.

"We know you've done your research and hired the best, Jobs," Asher said.

He had. It didn't mean their family members were assured safety, but it was a hell of a lot better than no one watching them.

"I still can't believe Hylar had his own sister killed," Oliver muttered. "We knew the man was an asshole, but that's a whole new level of cold hearted."

The team was silent for a moment.

Wyatt was still in shock. *Everyone* was. Hylar had been their commander for years. But obviously, they'd never truly known the real him.

Everything he did, just confirmed that he wasn't redeemable.

"He's proved yet again that there are no lines he won't cross."

Logan was right. The man needed to be stopped.

They'd found the cabin where Tanya had been shot, but

there'd been no sign of her body. There had also been no evidence that Carter had ever been there.

"Have you told Quinn about the switching of materials?" It was Mason who asked.

"No. I wanted her to spend this last week resting, rather than worrying about Hylar coming after us in retribution. I'll tell her tomorrow." The woman was damn strong, and she'd been doing better than he expected.

"At what point do you think Carter and Hylar will realize we switched out the materials?" Kye asked.

It was Jason, Sage's brother, who answered that question. "Only an experienced lab technician who's worked with the materials before would be able to tell the difference between what we gave them and the real thing. I made sure the substitutes were chemicals of a similar look and smell. Carter would have been trained on what they looked and smelled like, but the difference is too subtle for someone who lacks experience in the field."

Jason had studied Pharmaceutical Science at MIT. The team trusted that he knew what he was talking about, so no one questioned whether he was capable of making such a switch.

Luca shook his head. "This might be the final straw that forces Hylar to hunt us down. He'll want the materials. Hell, he might also want revenge for swapping the drugs out, for the demolition of their main facility in Valley Spring..."

"Not to mention we've killed five more of his men, including two members of Carter's team—Troy and Alistair," Oliver added.

"And you freed *our* team," Logan said.

There was a heavy pause before Eden spoke. "This could be it. The moment we've been waiting for."

Wyatt was counting on it.

CHAPTER 30

*B*odie stood in front of Inwood Bar in Keystone. From what he'd seen, the place was busy most days and evenings. But not tonight. Tonight, he estimated there were maybe half a dozen customers inside.

That was good. Fewer customers would give him a better chance of speaking to Maya.

Bodie had been watching the bar for a few days now. Ever since Maya had stepped foot inside the place and been hired as a waitress.

Tonight, it was finally time to go in and meet her.

Pushing through the door, Bodie immediately scanned the large room. Seven customers were scattered around the open space. Two waitresses. Maya was down at one end of the bar while a woman who looked to be in her fifties worked the other.

Bodie moved to Maya's end and took a seat a few feet away. She didn't look up. Her entire concentration seemed to be on the two glasses she was filling with beer.

The worried look on her face wasn't a surprise to Bodie. Since he'd been watching her, he'd learned the woman wore a constant mask of worry and fear. She also couldn't walk down a street without a half dozen glances over her shoulder.

Which told Bodie one thing. She was paranoid.

Not that he needed to see the fear on her face or the backward glances to know that. A person doesn't just up and disappear unless they're running from something. And that something was clearly Project Arma. After all, she had witnessed a crime committed by the organization.

Bodie watched from his peripheral vision as she carried the beers to a booth at the back of the room.

She stood at average height—maybe five-seven—and had long brown hair and sad hazel eyes. Her experience working in a bar was clearly limited. Not only had she needed to empty and refill one of the glasses three times, but she also walked slowly across the room. Overly cautious as to avoid spilling the drinks.

"You watching my new waitress?"

Bodie looked up to see the other waitress in front of him.

Damn. He'd been so distracted with Maya, he hadn't even noticed her coming. The fact the woman had noticed him watching Maya—from his peripheral vision—made it even worse.

"Just waiting for a drink."

She leaned a hip on the bar. "Right. I'll pretend I believe you... for the moment. What will it be?"

"I'll have a Bud Light." Not that he intended to drink much of it when he had a job to complete.

The lady grabbed a bottle from the fridge and removed the lid. "She's new."

Bodie kept a neutral expression on his face, not wanting to give anything away. "Good to know."

"Terrible waitress," she continued, planting the beer in front of Bodie. "But the girl needs help. So, I'm trying to be that help."

Clearly, this woman was one of those people who told everybody everyone else's business. It almost made him annoyed for Maya.

"How do you know she needs help?"

She crossed her arms over her chest. "I know that look on her face. Used to see it in the mirror every day until I pieced my life back together. You're scared every minute of every day because you expect the person you're running from to find you."

Bodie's muscles tensed. He suspected she was talking about a man—likely an ex. It made Bodie see red. He'd been raised to believe it was a man's job to protect his woman. Any man who abused that trust, who used their strength against the person they were supposed to protect, were the lowest scum on Earth.

"I'm sorry to hear that."

She nodded. "Appreciate it. My demon's gone. Hers clearly isn't."

"Has she told you any of this?"

The woman laughed. "No. And I haven't asked. If someone had asked me about it when I was in the thick of trouble, even if they were in a position to help me, I probably would have run from them before they'd finished their sentence. Fear does funny things to people."

That's exactly what Bodie was afraid of. That the woman would attempt to run. She wouldn't be able to. Not now that he'd found her. But he needed to put her at ease first. He wanted to help her, not scare her further.

"Why are you telling me this?"

She lifted a shoulder. "You have a look in your eye."

"A look?"

Before she could respond, a loud crash sounded behind him.

The woman looked over his shoulder. "Oh, dang it."

When Bodie turned his head, it was to see Maya standing with an empty tray, her face red with embarrassment. She immediately dropped to the floor and began collecting shattered glass.

Bodie didn't hesitate. Pushing away from the bar, he headed

toward Maya. Along the way, he heard snickering and laughter from the men at the table she'd just served.

Not one of them stood to help. Assholes.

Dropping to his haunches beside Maya, Bodie began moving shards of glass to the tray. "You okay?"

Maya's gaze shot up. There was fear and apprehension on her face. Also surprise. Surprise that he'd offer to help?

He took a moment to study her features. Even though her eyes were hazel, there were also golden flecks. Her lips were full and pink. Her skin so creamy, his hand itched to reach out and touch her.

Holy hell, the woman was stunning.

"I'm okay. You don't need to help me."

One side of his mouth lifted. "I know. I want to."

Her mouth opened, like she was about to argue, but she didn't. A few seconds passed before she nodded. "Thank you."

It annoyed Bodie that she seemed surprised by his offer to help. Like she wasn't used to kindness.

"They say you're not really a bartender until you've broken a dozen glasses. You're only a couple away," Bodie joked.

He wasn't actually sure if that was a saying. But it sounded about right.

Maya gave a tight smile. The strain on her face was clouding just about every other emotion. "I already broke some this morning. Gosh, I've only been working here a week and I've broken a heck of a lot more than twelve." Maya shook her head as she moved more glass onto the tray. "Trish will fire me for sure..."

She'd started to ramble. He had a feeling the words were more her internal thoughts than conversation.

"Is that Trish at the bar?" Bodie nodded to indicate the woman he'd just been speaking to. She was now laughing with an elderly customer.

"Yeah. That's Trish."

Nope. There wasn't a chance that Maya was fired. "She doesn't look bothered. I think you'll be okay."

When Bodie reached for the last piece of glass, his hand brushed across hers. Her skin was as soft as it looked, and the touch sent a shot of electricity through his system.

He was almost certain she felt it too, because she immediately pulled her hand back. Touching the very spot he'd touched.

Christ, what the hell was going on?

"I'm Bodie Ryan, by the way."

"I'm Maya Ha—" She shook her head. "Johnson. Maya Johnson."

She'd almost slipped up and told him her real last name —Harper.

It was good she'd kept her first name the same. Smart. It would be too easy for her to accidentally ignore another name. Particularly working in a busy bar.

"It's nice to meet you, Maya Johnson."

He was tempted to hold out his hand. Mostly because he wanted to touch her again. But the woman was already retreating into herself. Pulling away from him physically and mentally.

They both stood at the same time, Maya immediately taking a step back.

"Well, thank you, Bodie. I really appreciate your help."

Bodie smiled. "It was nice to meet you, Maya."

And it really was. He watched her walk away, still feeling that same pull toward the woman.

He didn't know what was going on with his body, just that being around her, touching her, had heat unfurling in his gut.

Bodie had a feeling he was going to enjoy getting to know Maya Harper. This might be his favorite mission yet.

Read Bodie today!

ALSO BY NYSSA KATHRYN

JOIN my newsletter and be the first to find out about sales and new releases!

ABOUT THE AUTHOR

Nyssa Kathryn is a romantic suspense author. She lives in South Australia with her daughter and hubby and takes every chance she can to be plotting and writing. Always an avid reader of romance novels, she considers alpha males and happily-ever-afters to be her jam.

Don't forget to follow Nyssa and never miss another release.

Facebook | Instagram | Amazon | Goodreads

CPSIA information can be obtained
at www.ICGtesting.com
Printed in the USA
BVHW030344300421
606131BV00006B/434

9 780648 946243